WHERE HAPPINESS BEGINS

An EVERMORE novel

N.S. PERKINS

Copyright © 2024 by N.S. Perkins

All rights reserved.

No part of this publication may be reproduced, distributed, or transmitted in any form or by any means, including photocopying, recording, or other electronic or mechanical methods, without the prior written permission of the publisher, except as permitted by U.S. copyright law.

The story, all names, characters, and incidents portrayed in this production are fictitious. No identification with actual persons (living or deceased), places, buildings, and products is intended or should be inferred.

Book Cover design by Murphy Rae

Edited by Emily Lawrence

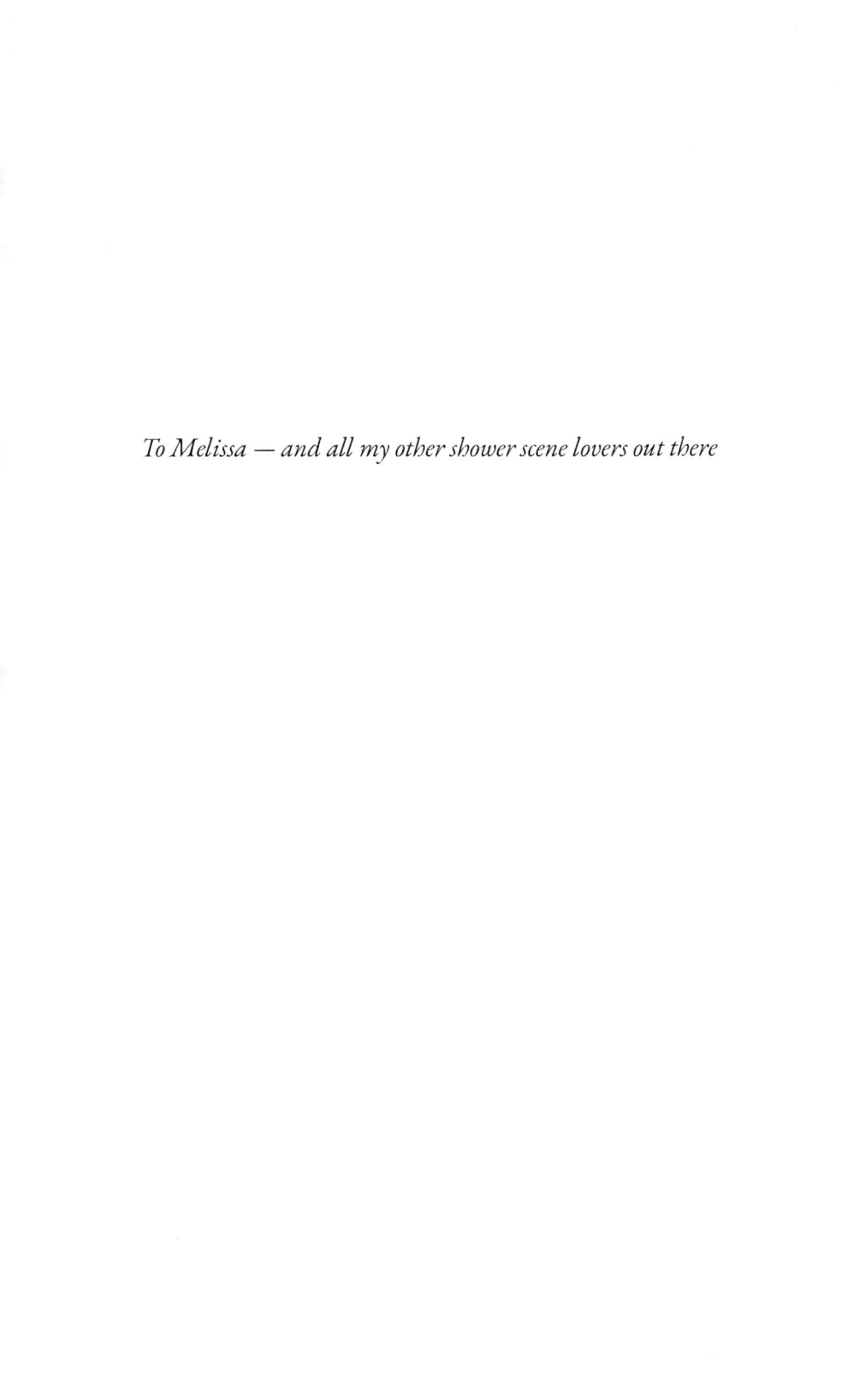

To Melissa — and all my other shower scene lovers out there

Chapter 1

I should've prepared myself.

It's not like I haven't expected this moment to happen at some point. I just didn't think it would come quite this fast. And while I'm usually a firm believer that there's nothing that can't be helped with good music and a short, cathartic crying session, with the email I just received, not even a bucketful of tears while listening to Lana Del Rey would cut it.

Around the bar, people are standing with drinks in their hands or sitting at the few tables scattered around the space as low '90s alternative music plays from the built-in speakers. Wednesday nights aren't usually this busy except tonight we have live music coming in. While the performers who play here are normally local, lesser-known artists, we still get swarmed on show nights, which means I can't have a breakdown right now.

Get a grip, Lil.

With a roll of my shoulders, I force myself to put my phone away and get back to work. It's not like I could forget what I just read anyway.

There's a half-hour or so before the start of the show, so the line at the bar is still small enough that my colleague Leah has got it under control. I pick up a rag and wipe the mess I made when pouring my previous drinks before new customers arrive.

The Sparrow is not a rusty hole in the wall, but it isn't particularly chic either. The space is one large room that echoes when it's half-empty like it is now, but that creates insane acoustics when bands come to play. The interspersed round tables are made of rough wood slats and decorated with rustic candles, the overhead lights are dimmed, and thick black velvet covers the walls and windows, making it impossible to know whether it's noon or midnight. When I walk in here, it's as if time stops until I exit at the end of my shift. Not being able to see the sunlight while working might not have been my first choice, but when I was offered this job, I didn't have the luxury of being picky. By the time I was able to start working, at twenty-two years old and with no prior experience, it was either that or starving.

Once the bar is clean, I glance around once more to make sure no new customer needs to be served. Everyone has already spread out across the room, only one man sitting at the actual bar.

Of course the second I'm back to having nothing to do, I try but fail to keep my mind from running back to the image that will probably haunt my nights from now on. The email that popped into my phone just as I walked into my shift pulls at my attention like a lighthouse in the dark, unavoidable.

The inheritance account has been emptied out.

I'd been warned about it over the past two years. Mrs. Ibrahim, my accountant, had suggested on multiple occasions to invest the money instead of letting it sit in my account, but that option was never realistic. Not when I had medical bills, both past and present, that required imminent payment. Spending the money wasn't a dumb youth decision. It was life or death.

That account had been my saving grace after losing my dad two and a half years ago. Before, we'd relied almost exclusively on the health insurance we were granted through his job, but when he died unexpectedly, I got stuck with mounting bills and no way of affording them, and it's not like I could've stopped dialysis. As hard as I tried, I couldn't find a job that offered benefits either. Thankfully, Dad had thought of getting life insurance, which allowed me to pay for my treatments and for the kidney transplant I eventually got.

Except now, I've used it all and I'm stuck with nothing. Nada.

My hand freezes over the counter, shaking. I'm going to be sick.

No matter how hard I try to find solutions and rationalize things, I can't come up with a single good answer. Even if I asked to double the hours I do at the bar and did all the collabs I got offered on my social media accounts, I wouldn't be able to afford all the drugs I still take on a daily basis.

My head spins as my heart rate picks up, images of pill dispensers and stacked-up bills hitting me from all sides. With my eyes shut tight, I lean against the bar and force a breath through my nose.

You're alive. You're as healthy as you ever could've hoped for. You'll find a way.

The soothing words don't work like they usually do. In fact, I only get more and more lost in my panic. I need to stop this. Lips pinched, I turn and do something I've never done.

I pour myself a shot.

I barely look at the bottle I grab before filling the tiny glass I picked from under the bar. Might be ironic for a bartender to be an almost alcohol virgin, but when you're used to living with failing kidneys—and now with a single, precious one—you don't go around messing things up by drinking.

However, today calls for desperate measures.

The amber liquid in the glass calls to me, and before I can remind myself what a stupid mistake this could be, I bring the drink to my lips and swallow.

Then proceed to choke on it.

I remember trying a sip of Tequila on my twenty-first birthday with my best friend Finn and it not tasting so bad, but this is *horrible*. Why would anyone voluntarily drink something that tastes like those disgusting Valentine's Day cinnamon hearts?

I try to inhale through the burn in my throat, but all it does is make me cough even more, tears rising to my eyes.

"What the fuck?"

I hadn't realized I was standing this close to the man sitting at the bar until his voice makes me jump.

Still choking on the burning liquid, I force myself to look up and match a face to the deep voice that just made me want to go hide under a rock forever.

And what a face it is.

Plump lips turned into a scowl, thick brows overlining a set of light brown eyes—or are they green?—sharp cheekbones, and a sculpted jaw covered in a perfect five o'clock shadow. A jaw that is currently clenched as the man stares at me, cheeks speckled with liquid.

Liquid I probably coughed out right onto him.

"Oh my God, I'm so sorry," I exclaim, jumping to grab the rag, and lean over the bar, not pausing long enough to realize that wiping the face of the man I just spat on might be making things worse.

"Please don't." The man pulls back from my cleaning assault with a look that tells me he probably thinks I'm crazy, wiping his cheek on his shoulder instead. Thankfully, he's wearing a black T-shirt, so it doesn't leave any traces.

"I-I'm so..." I sputter, disposing of my shot glass as if it could magically erase what just happened. I don't even have words for the level of embarrassment overwhelming me right now. And then I realize he's looking down in disgust at his glass of bubbly liquid, which I probably also spat in. "My God, let me get you a new drink." *Somebody sedate me.* I go to grab the glass, but he stops me by putting his large hand on it.

"It's fine." He doesn't even bother looking at me as he says it.

"Please, I—"

"I said it's fine." This time, he does look up, and the annoyance in that scowling, perfect face makes me want to disappear. "Maybe just skip the fireball next time."

Maybe skip drinking, period.

I force myself not to focus on how he probably knows what I drank because of how it smelled on his skin and instead look to my left, where new groups of customers are walking in and heading toward the bar, just in time for the show that should be starting any minute now.

Quickly, I look back at the victim of my poor choices, who's now scrolling through his phone, completely ignoring me. A part of me tells me I should probably stay and apologize once again—after all, him making a formal complaint to Jayson, my boss, and putting my job in jeopardy would be the cherry on top of today—but there's also a line forming at the bar, and leaving customers hanging wouldn't be much better. Leah is already busy with orders, but she won't have enough hands for everyone.

"Okay, well, sorry again," I say in a low voice, and when he only grunts his response, I try not to take it personally.

I force my attention away from him, then try to shake this funk off. I still have to survive tonight, and sulking will only make it worse.

When a couple walks over to me, I put on a smile and get back to work.

The tips I make here are certainly a big part of why I'm keeping this job instead of looking for new postings, but the real highlight of it is the music.

There's nothing like a live set to make you forget your problems, at least for a while. The way the loud music feels, like it's resonating inside your chest, the bated energy of the crowd when an artist has them wrapped around their finger, is something I could never get enough of.

Tonight, I had doubts I'd be able to enjoy it, my head lost elsewhere, but that was before I'd heard them.

I'm cheering as loud as the crowd, forgetting for a while that I'm at work. When the four-man band set up earlier, they did not seem particularly charismatic or different from the musicians we usually host, but from the first note, they caught everyone's attention in a way I've never seen since I started working here.

They are way too good for this place.

I've never heard of Crash & Burn before, but they're going to be big.

Once the lights turn on, the room is still dim but clear enough that people can walk away from the stage. The bar gets swarmed again, and I spend the next thirty minutes serving people left and right. I have no clue what time it is or when I'll be leaving, but I don't care. I'll take the distraction of work. I don't want to think about how I'll feel when I go to bed, alone with my thoughts and ready to spiral.

Once I've served the last drink to a group that's been hanging around the bar for a while, I head toward a customer who's waving at me, standing with a group of guys. I don't have my glasses and forgot to put my lenses in today, but when I get close enough,

I recognize the singer of the band, surrounded by the rest of his team. I smile and rush to them.

"What can I get for you?"

The guy—who looks to be in his late twenties and who probably would've held everyone's attention even if he hadn't sung, with deep brown skin, close-cropped hair, and a piercing stare—orders five beers.

Once I've poured them all and placed the glasses in front of them, I say, "Your show was really great tonight. The best we've had in a while."

"Appreciate it," the singer says, once again giving me a panty-dropping smile. He passes the beers around, and only when he shifts do I spot a fifth person in their small group.

The cold guy from earlier.

I avoid looking at him and try my best not to replay the scene of me spitting on him in my head. With blond hair and fair skin, even just thinking of an embarrassing memory can turn me red as a lobster.

"Are you from the area?" I ask the singer.

"Damn right we are," the one I recognize as the drummer says, jumping so he's sitting on the bar. I should probably tell him not to do that, but after the hour-long relief they've given me tonight, he can do whatever the heck he wants. Jayson's not here tonight anyway, and Leah's not the type to snitch. "Been wanting to play this place for a while. Pretty fucking cool."

"We're gonna have much better venues in the next months," the guitarist, a guy with long red hair and a thick beard, says.

"Going on tour soon," the singer explains. "Tonight was kind of a practice run."

"Well, I don't think you really needed it," I answer. The bar is slowly emptying out, with only a few customers spread out across the room, so I can take the time to lean against the counter and rest my aching feet.

"Nice of you to say, but we certainly feel like we do."

"Do you have any music out? I'd love to listen to it."

The guys proceed to tell me all about their first studio album, which was released only a week ago. Behind them, the stoneface from earlier keeps silent, hand in his pocket as he sips from a water bottle.

"Hey, don't I know you from somewhere?" the singer asks. "I feel like we've met before."

I shake my head, brows furrowed. "I don't think so, no." I'd remember a face like his, but more importantly, a *voice* like his. The guy can sing. Plus, I had to do online school for most of my high school, so I didn't meet anyone there.

"She does look familiar," the redhead says.

They both stare at me with narrowed eyes and cocked heads until the guitarist snaps his fingers and says, "Oh, I know! You're that chick my girl keeps watching on YouTube."

"Yeah, that's it!" the singer says, leaning back on his stool. "I've seen you on my feed a few times."

If I was able to avoid reddening before, this time, it's game over.

It's pretty rare I get recognized in public. Even with a few hundred thousand followers combined from all my platforms, it's only happened a handful of times, and while I'm usually happy to chat with girls who've been following me since I started documenting my health troubles, having five sets of eyes watching me makes me want to disappear for the second time today.

The laughter that comes out of my throat is more than awkward. "Um, yeah, that's possible."

It's not like I'm embarrassed about my channels. In the beginning, it started as a form of therapy for me. I posted my first YouTube video after I received my diagnosis of end-stage kidney disease after years of struggling with a failing renal function, mostly as a way to vent. I didn't have many friends and I didn't want to burden my dad with it. I knew he was worried enough on his own; he didn't need to have the task of comforting me on top of it.

I didn't expect people to start following me, but sure enough, with every video I posted, I grew my audience little by little, eventually transitioning my content to more day-in-the-life capsules, sometimes talking about my health and the process of going through dialysis and then an organ transplant, and other times talking about normal stuff like my skincare routine.

"I'm Ethan," the singer says. "This is Emmett, our guitarist. That's Joe, our bassist—"

"And I'm Bong," the drummer interrupts, extending his hand in my direction.

I don't bother asking where that name came from and shake his hand as I say, "Good to meet you all."

"Oh, and that's our guy Carter," Ethan says as he points at my number one fan.

As if being called out, *Carter* lifts his head and his gaze immediately finds mine. I'm not sure why a stare from him feels like being struck by lightning, but I don't like it.

"It's really great what you do," the redhead—Emmett—says, thankfully bringing my attention away from him. "I have to say, some of your videos made me emotional as shit."

"Em's our big crybaby," Bong says as he claps his friend on the back.

"Fuck off. I'm serious, man."

"He's right," Ethan notes, leaning forward on the countertop. "You have great platforms."

"Thank you, seriously," I say, only slightly wanting to combust. It's one thing talking about every single detail of my life with strangers when we're separated by a screen, but this is a whole other game.

"Hey, you think we could ask you for a favor?" the singer asks.

"Sure," I say, tone wary.

"Think you could share our album on a story or something? Maybe say something good about tonight's show? We could use the publicity."

I wouldn't usually agree to it if I didn't enjoy their work, but after the show they gave, I have no trouble saying, "Sure thing. Actually, you know what?" I grab my phone out of my back pocket and turn so I can take a selfie with them in the background.

Funny how you can guess the dynamic of a group based on the way they place themselves in a picture. Ethan, smack dab in the middle, his arms wrapped around his friends, Emmett with a shy grin, shoulders hunched, Bong with his fingers in a rock and roll sign, Joe with a straight face in the back, looking like he'd rather be doing anything but this, and Carter outright gone from the camera's view.

One hand thrown in the air, I take the picture, and once everyone approves of it, I write a message encouraging people to go listen to their debut album, tag them in the story, and post it.

"There," I say. "All done."

"You're the best," Bong says, taking my hand and placing a kiss with a loud smack on the back of it. I burst out laughing.

"What a gift. Thank you," I tell him. From the corner of my eye, I spot a figure waving me down from the other end of the bar, probably wanting to close their tab. "Well, duty calls, but it was truly great meeting you all. Best of luck with the album and the tour."

"Thanks," the guys say in unison, with Joe staying silent in the back. "Same to you."

I give them one last smile before leaving.

Once I'm done with my other client, I throw a glance behind my shoulder, and while I still can't see well from afar, I'd swear I feel a pair of murky green eyes on me.

Chapter 2

My mood is much better today.

I gave myself until the end of last night to sulk over my situation, but by the time I went to bed, I was pretty much done. There are so many things actually worth spending my time worrying about, and money is not one of them.

Taylor Swift's *Lover* album is blaring through my speaker as I knead the dough I've been working on for the past thirty minutes. I'd never call myself a great baker, but it helps put my thoughts in order. I remember being seven years old and breaking into hysterical crying over math homework, and my dad pulling me to the kitchen and draping an apron over my chest before telling me to get the mixing bowls and the flour. He made the best cookies in the entire world, and while I could follow his recipes to a T and never get it quite like he did, I still love the sentiment. Plus, I'll be going to my accountant's office later today, and I like to think that my cookies will make her more lenient on me. I know she's technically only responsible for *handling* my finances and not for deciding the actual amount that's in the accounts, but being delusional from time to time has never done me any wrong.

I'm belting out to my favorite song on the album, strands of hair falling out of my bun and into my face, when the music suddenly stops and a robotic voice alerts me of an incoming call. I go over to my phone, then smile when I see the name on the screen. Hands full of flour and dough, I press *answer* with my elbow, then lean down to grab the phone between my shoulder and ear.

"Nan, hi!"

"Sweetheart, you were taking too long to call," she says in that raw, deep voice of hers that gives away all the cigarettes she smoked in her life.

I laugh. "We spoke two days ago."

"Exactly. Beginning to think you'd forgotten about me."

"You're such a drama queen." She's also one of my favorite people on this planet.

My grandmother tsks. "I might've wanted to hear your voice, but I also wanted to talk to you about something."

"Sure," I say, already having a feeling where this will inevitably lead to.

"There's this man who plays darts with me, Gary. Very nice guy. Anyway, he has a grandson—"

I pull the phone away so I can groan in peace.

"I know you probably just made an ugly face, but hear me out."

"How many times do I need to tell you I don't need my nana to find me someone?"

"Since you still don't have a man, I'd say you do need me."

"Did we just go back to the 1950s?"

"Hush and listen to me."

That woman will be the death of me. She proceeds to tell me about how this guy is handsome and charming and would make a great match with me. I partially tune her out as I spread my dough on the counter and flatten it.

When I realize she's stopped speaking, I say, "Thanks. I'll consider it."

"You're a terrible liar, just like your daddy."

I roll my eyes. "Really, Nan," I say instead of trying to lie once more. "I'm good for now."

Ever since my ex dumped me two years ago, she hasn't stopped trying to find a man for me, sending me unwanted propositions left and right. I'm sure the men she mentions don't even know she does it. The second she finds someone who's more or less my age, she throws them my way.

She's trying for nothing. The way I felt when I was with Greg is something I never want to experience again.

Nana sighs dramatically, her kitchen fan humming in the back. "I'm just worried about you. You don't live enough, darling."

My cookie cutter stalls mid-air. "I do live." My voice sounds defensive even to my ears.

"When I was your age, I'd go dancing, and partying with friends, and meeting handsome strangers. That's what being twenty-four is about."

I'm sure she's exaggerating some of it—if I remember correctly, she was already married at that age—but even so, I hate to admit she has a point. I'd promised myself when I was younger that once

I had my kidney transplant, I'd start doing all the things I'd always pushed away, and yet I haven't even begun to scratch the surface.

But a man sure as heck won't solve that.

"I'm still not interested in your blind date at the senior center, but thanks for the thought."

She chuckles. "One day, you'll say yes."

Sure.

"Otherwise, what else is new?" she asks.

I don't even consider telling her about yesterday's email. That woman has suffered through so much in her life, from the rheumatoid arthritis that causes her daily pain, to the death of her husband when they were in their sixties, and then to the loss of her son two years ago. The last thing she needs is to hear about my own worries.

"Not much. You?"

It's as if she was waiting for the question. The second I finish, she goes on to tell me all the new Bellevue Center gossip, and while I try to stay focused, my gaze drifts to the stack of medical bills I opened this morning, still lying on the kitchen counter. I might have decided to stop worrying about my debts, but that doesn't mean I can forget about them entirely.

I'll never ask Nana for money, that's for sure. She's offered to help me before, but the truth is, she needs her savings to pay for her residence. I look around at the kitchen and the living room past it. If push comes to shove, I'll just have to sell the place.

I inherited the house when I lost my dad. It's not much, a simple seventies bungalow with a carport outside and linoleum floors in the kitchen, but it's the place I love most in this world. I've known for a while I should consider getting rid of it. I don't need all this space when it's just me here, and in the grand Boston area, it could cover my bills for a few more years, at least until I find a job with health insurance.

But this is the place where I grew up. The backdrop of some of my happiest memories, from soft Christmas mornings with bright light filtering in to hot chocolate shared around the kitchen island while talking about our days. It's the last place I saw my dad in. Selling it would feel like letting go of the only tangible piece of him in my life, and I don't think I can stomach that. Not another loss.

"Sweetheart? Are you okay?"

I realize she's probably said something and I was too lost in thoughts to realize it.

"Yeah, sorry, was just focusing on my cookies." A little white lie never hurt anyone.

"All right. Oh, wait, I've got Linette on the other line. Can I call you back?"

"Of course. Don't worry about it."

"Okay, talk to you later. Love you."

"I love you," I say before hanging up. I might not have been able to avoid the matchmaking today, but at least I dodged the topic of finances.

Once I've finished spreading the cookies onto the pan, I put the pan in the oven, then grab my phone. I'll post a picture of the finished result once they're out, maybe with a little story time of my phone call with Nana, who's well loved by my followers.

I scroll through my notifications and messages, and only once I'm halfway through my inbox do I recognize a name I've only just learned.

@crashandburn wants to send you a message

I accept the conversation, expecting a text, but it's a voice memo. I hesitate only for a second before pressing play.

"Hey, Lilianne! Sorry, I realized we didn't ask you for your name yesterday, but I saw it on your page. Oh, it's Ethan, by the way."

Even if he hadn't said his name, I'd have recognized his perky voice already.

"I just wanted to say how amazing it's been since you posted your story yesterday. We've gotten eight thousand new listeners and, like, a shit ton of new followers in less than twelve hours. That's insane. The guys can't believe it." In the back, a door slams, followed by the ignition of an engine. "I can't thank you enough. And I know that'd be asking a lot, but we'd love it if you were down to attend another show or two." He chuckles. "We were even messing around in the group chat this morning saying you should definitely come on tour with us. We wouldn't say no to that kind of promo. Anyway, that was just us shooting the shit, but if ever you're down to listen to more music, hit me up. 'Kay, bye."

When the message ends, I realize I'm smiling from ear to ear. It's so good to learn that my platform can do great things. It might seem silly to people that I post photos and videos about my daily, boring life, but I've received so many messages throughout the years saying that someone had been inspired by my story or that they were encouraged to keep going through their dialysis after scrolling through my channel, and that's even more precious than all the sponsoring money I could get.

For an infinitesimal moment, I allow myself the luxury of picturing what he's just suggested. Joining these people on tour, hopping from one hotel room to the next or maybe even road-tripping across the country in the back of a hippie van. I have no clue how big or small their tour will be, but I have no doubt it'd be the experience of a lifetime. One I couldn't even have dreamed of years ago, when I spent more time in the hospital than I did at school.

However, that's all it is: a wild dream. People don't simply drop everything to go follow a band full of strangers to help promote them. Especially not people who need to be finding a good job with health benefits in the next few months. I looked through local—and not-so-local—job postings this morning, and just as was the case a few years back, I couldn't find one I was qualified to do that had the benefits I need. I never had the chance to figure out what I wanted to do with my life or go to college, and now that I look at what's available to me, I regret not getting a degree the second my health got stable, even though it would have been nearly impossible with my financial situation.

I begin typing.

> Hey Ethan (and everyone!)

> I'm so happy my story has increased your following. You guys are awesome and deserve all the recognition! Sadly won't be able to leave Boston, but let me know when-

> ever you come back to the area and I'll be in the front row cheering for you. :)

I press send, then spend the rest of my day trying to forget about how, with a single message, I proved Nana right.

Chapter 3

Not a lot can rile me up.

I don't waste precious time getting angry. If I'm not happy with something, I simply walk away or distract myself from it. I don't get into fights or keep in touch with people who make me miserable. I try to find the good in most situations.

But one thing that never fails to make my blood boil is my boss finding a way to make me uncomfortable every time we work together.

Jayson isn't always here—the only reason why I haven't quit yet, debt be damned—but when he is, there's no way I'll spend the night without him talking my ears off or being touchy-feely, even when I send him all the signals in the world that I'm not interested. He doesn't care that it's inappropriate to clasp his employees' hips or pull on their ponytails like a third grader. If he can do it, he will.

"So what are you doing this weekend?" he asks as I prepare lemon wedges for the night ahead, probably trying to sound nonchalant, but he's done this enough times to fool me.

"Not much," I answer without looking in his direction. I don't want to give him even an inkling of information about my private life. Then, because my father raised me right and I don't have it in me to be rude, I make the mistake of asking, "You?"

"Oh, funny you ask," he says, putting down the tub of grenadine he was filling. "I'm hosting a little something at my place, just a few people, but I think you'd fit right in."

Damn it.

"That's nice of you, but I, uh..." I've never been good at coming up with lies on the spot, and as he stares at me expectantly and I can't come up with any good excuse, I wish I'd practiced that skill earlier in life. "I'm going to be busy cleaning my, uh...my garage."

The second the words are out of my mouth, I realize how stupid they sound—who schedules a garage cleaning?—but it's too late to step back now, so I just smile and play dumb, something he always seems to like.

"Oh, nice! I have some free time tomorrow if you need help with it?"

And risk being stuck in a room alone with him? I'll pass.

"That's kind of you, but I'll be fine."

"Are you sure?" He takes a step in my direction, now close enough that I can smell his sour breath from the cheese string he ate earlier, and he clearly doesn't notice or care about the stiffness in my body because he decides to let his rough hand drop onto my forearm.

"Very sure," I force out. When I see he's not moving and is probably only going to continue trying to find ways to intricate himself into my life, I add, "You know what? I just remembered I need to deep clean the cabinets." Then I pull back and speed-walk away from him.

You need the money, I say to myself on repeat. *You can't go stomping on his foot with your heeled boots.*

I feel Jayson's eyes on me as I walk to the shelves holding the different types of glasses behind the bar, so to keep up with my pretense, I pull glasses out one by one. I used the exact same excuse a week ago, so I know those shelves are pristine, but I'll take any excuse I can to escape.

I'm almost done scrubbing the first shelf when my phone buzzes in a pattern I recognize right away. I created it almost three years ago, when I was still with my ex and I wanted an easy way to figure out when he was the one who'd texted me. I'd gotten used to jumping on my phone the second it buzzed, hoping it was finally a message from him, and when Finn, my best friend, made me realize how pathetic that was, I made the special vibration for his contact alone.

Even now, so long after our breakup, I feel the inevitable stutter of my heartbeat, not out of excitement to hear from him, but as a guttural, instinctual reaction. I feel like a dog who's been trained with a Pavlovian method, and I hate the way he still has that hold over me. Hate that I tolerated crumbs from him, enough that the feeling of a text from him can still trigger a visceral reaction in me.

I don't want to look at whatever he's written to me this time, but I know if I don't do it now, I'll only prolong the inevitable.

Resting two wine glasses on the countertop, I pull out my phone from my jeans' back pocket.

> Greg: Hey! Long time no speak. Was wondering if you still had that contact over at Optique, that glasses company? I'd be down for a collab with them.

The balls on that guy. I refrain myself from eye rolling, not wanting to give him the satisfaction of even having a reaction. Instead, I delete the text and put my phone back where it was, resolute to forget I even saw Greg's name today.

When we met at an influencer's event four years ago, I thought he was the most magnetic, larger-than-life person I'd ever met. It didn't matter that I eventually realized his smiles were fake and his interest in people was only so he could climb the ranks and become the next big thing. I couldn't get enough of him, and even when we got together, I still felt like that twenty-year-old who would do anything to impress that man. It didn't matter that when he realized how sick I was, he decided he wanted out and only stayed out of pity. I couldn't see it.

I know better now.

I return to my unnecessary work, but the second I grab the glasses I'd just put down, I'm interrupted again, this time by a voice coming from behind that sends shivers down my spine with a single word.

"Fireball."

I freeze, giving myself a second to react internally before turning around. I wish I didn't recognize the man who just spoke, but after having lived through a thorough humiliation in front of him a week ago, I don't think I could even if I tried.

When the shock has worn off and I'm convinced I can look normal, save for the heat in my face at hearing the stupid nickname he's given me, I spin on my heels and smile brightly, the perfect actress.

"Hi. What can I get you?"

"Nothing," he says, no hint of a smile on his face.

I tilt my head as I take him in. He's once again wearing a tight-fitting, long-sleeved black T-shirt, showcasing sculpted shoulders and arms. Dark tattoos peek out from his sleeves, stopping at his wrists, his long fingers untouched by ink. His hair is ruffled as if he got out of bed this morning and only dragged his fingers through it, but somehow, it only makes him look hotter instead of messy like it would look on me.

"Oh-kayyy..." I say, taking a slow step backward.

"I need to talk to you," he explains, his face giving nothing away.

"Me?" I ask, looking behind me as if someone else suddenly appeared there.

His brows twitch inwardly. "Yeah. You."

I repeat a slow, "Okay," probably sounding a little slow, but I honestly don't understand.

Not wasting a second, he jumps right in. "You spoke with Ethan last week about a possible deal?" He says it as a question, but really, he's telling this to me.

"A deal?"

"Yeah. Doing some promo for them?"

I chuckle, knotting my hands in front of me. Somehow, he has a way of making me feel like I'm the one intruding on his space instead of the opposite. "That wasn't serious."

"Why wouldn't it be?" he asks as if he genuinely has no idea why anyone would ever joke around.

"I don't know, maybe because I only met them once?"

"So?" He leans forward, arms crossing over the bar. "We've seen your impact on our—their—streaming numbers from one post. Having you on our team would be game-changing."

As flattering as this is, he's also wrong. I'm not a music influencer. I post about my often-boring life and make videos testing makeup and giving reading updates. One story doesn't mean anything. We could just have been lucky.

"What's it to you anyway?" I ask, trying to give myself time to put my thoughts in order. Who even is he? He wasn't up there on the stage from what I know. "Are you their manager?"

"I'm their producer."

"Why would a producer be involved in a band's promo?"

"Let me worry about my reasons."

I don't know what's gotten into all these men today, but I've had more than enough. His answer doesn't change anything to me—I'm not even considering his offer—and yet the way he just spoke to me like I *have* to listen to him rubbed me the wrong way. I give him an overly-cheery smile and say, "Then allow me to walk away."

He only speaks when I turn around and get back to my cleaning, but not before he lets out a deep, loud sigh.

"Visibility for them is visibility for my work. The industry's saturated, and if I wanna stand out, I need their album to do well." While he answers, I slowly turn back around so I catch his bored blink as he adds, "Good enough for you?"

I hum.

"So?" he asks, having the nerve to sound impatient.

"So I still don't know exactly what you're asking of me." In truth, I do have an idea, but I like to see him work for it.

I'm sure he sees it with the look he throws me, but he still says, "You could become some kind of spokesperson for Crash & Burn. Share clips of shows and music, things like that. Get the public to know them personally so they want to look their music up."

Just like it did when Ethan initially mentioned it, flashes of following the band on their shows flood my head. Always listening to music, feeling that spike of adrenaline all the time... No matter what the marketing job actually entailed, it would sure be a hell of an experience.

However, I still don't have the luxury of quitting my nicely paying job to follow a group of people around, as fun as it sounds.

From the corner of my eye, I spot Jayson taking a few steps in my direction, probably noticing I'm just chatting and not working, so I turn around and resume my cleaning job. With my back to the guy—I think Carter was his name—I say, "It's a great offer, and I'm flattered that the band thought of me for it, but I don't think the logistics would work."

"Why's that? You'd get paid, obviously."

I turn around too fast, probably giving away my overeagerness. "What kind of payment are we talking about?"

My delusional bubble bursts the moment he mentions an approximate number. Even if they agreed to go higher than that number, it'd probably still be less than what I make here with tips. Plus, I'm hopeful that once I've been here for a few years, Jayson will add me to the health insurance policy he and a few of the higher-ups get. I don't think it's much, but it'd probably be enough to get me by.

"I'm sorry." I don't have it in me to give him attitude anymore. "Honestly, I wish I could say yes, but financially, it just wouldn't work."

His poker face doesn't move an inch. "What do you want, then? Name your price."

I shake my head, then snicker. "Honestly? Unless one of you has health insurance and is willing to marry me, then I don't think there's any way this can work."

For the first time tonight, I get a reaction out of him: a sharp huff out of his nose.

"But again, thanks for thinking of me."

As I turn around, he says, "Wait, you were actually serious?"

"No. Well, not about marriage anyway." I'm desperate, but I'm not *that* desperate.

I pull two glasses back onto the first shelf before he says, "Name something else. Anything."

He's really not making this easy, is he?

With a sigh, I turn around and lean against the bar, my face now close enough that I can see just how long his dark lashes are. In a tone low enough that Jayson won't hear, I say, "Look, I'll be honest with you. I have a crap ton of medical bills to pay, and unless you can get me insurance or a lot more money than I'm making here, then I can't leave." I give him a sad smile even though his face is still painfully blank. "I'm sorry."

He drags a hand through the dark strands of his hair, just like I imagine he has all day. "The guys are self-employed. They don't have insurance."

"I assumed." I lift a shoulder. "But you guys will be fine. There are plenty of influencers out there."

"But we know your platform works with their sound."

He has a point. Sure, the success they saw after my story could've been a fluke, but there's also a possibility my audience simply works for them. Being an influencer is a strange thing, one that can never be fully understood. Another blogger similar to me could have shared the same post and it wouldn't have led to the same results, just like sometimes, my own collaborations fail, all for reasons out of my understanding.

"I'm sorry," I repeat for the millionth time. "I really do wish I could help you."

His jaw tightens, and he waits for a long moment before nodding once and getting up.

Watching him walk away feels like staring at a golden fantasy, one I might have explored in another life, almost within reach but too far not to slip through my fingers.

It's almost 3:00 a.m. by the time everyone has left the bar and I get to turn off the lights and lock the doors behind me. My shoulders are tight and the one thing I want more than a hot shower is to drop onto my bed and sleep for three days straight.

Once I've tested the doors to make sure they're truly locked, I bring the trash bags to the dumpster, and when I turn toward my car, I jump out of my skin, noticing someone there. I clutch my chest, blood thumping in my ears as I take in the man there.

Carter.

He's leaning against the hood of a vintage Mustang, his arms crossed over his chest, one ankle thrown over the other. Even only illuminated by the single lamppost of the parking lot, he looks like a sinful dream.

I open my mouth to complain about how much he scared me and ask what he's doing here when he says, "*I have insurance.*"

My lips part.

"If that's what it takes, then I'll do it." He blinks, the only movement in his perfectly still body. "I'll marry you."

Chapter 4

"This is insane."

"You're the one who suggested it."

"But I wasn't serious." At least I think I wasn't.

I let my forehead drop onto the greasy melamine table. I'm too tired for this. After spitting my drink in his face and proposing a sham of a marriage, it's too late for me to be acting proper in front of Carter.

When he dropped his bomb in the bar's parking lot, I think he realized I was too shocked to be able to hold a conversation right then and there, so he suggested we drive to a nearby twenty-four-hour diner to "hammer out the details."

As if the details are the important part here.

I can't believe I'm even considering this. It's insane. Dangerous. So freaking stupid. And yet, I still followed him here.

"There are so many reasons why this is a bad idea." I lift my head and rub my eyes with my palms. Around us, the fifties-themed diner is empty, save for the two of us and Maggie, our waitress, who looks to be in her seventies and who's set up behind the counter to read a magazine after she brought us each a cup of coffee.

"So?"

"So?" I say loud enough that Maggie looks up. I send her an apologetic smile. Meanwhile, Carter looks cool as a cucumber, his long legs stretched out under the table and resting against my own bench of the booth, forcing me to sit with my legs crisscrossed. "So we're not talking about a day at Disneyland here. It's a *marriage*."

His only reaction is a lift of his brow and a repeat of the most annoying, "So?"

"So it's illegal, first off." Not the actual marriage part, but the part where we do it as a scam. It'd be considered insurance fraud, and I'm pretty sure that can send us to prison if we get caught, or at least earn us a fine that'd be the nail in the coffin of my poor finances. It's not like I could ask him to pay for my insurance out of his pocket either—that'd be unaffordable with my condition. It's either through his job or nothing.

He opens his mouth, and I lift a finger. "And please, for the love of all that is good, don't say 'So?'"

His lips pinch back together.

"I am not a criminal," I say, probably more to myself than to him.

That earns me another one of those single nose huffs I realize are probably his version of a laugh.

"What?" I ask.

He does a show of looking me up and down, from the scrunchie I used to tie my hair in a messy knot when getting out of my car to the pink puffer jacket I still have draped across my shoulders. "Somehow, I could've guessed that."

I grit my teeth. He's only agreed with me, and yet he found a way to do so in the most annoying manner possible. There's no winning with him, I'm starting to see.

"What I mean is, I don't normally do stuff like this. I'm not a good liar." The most illegal thing I ever did was steal a Ring Pop from a drugstore as a kid, and I'd felt so bad I went and put it back five minutes later.

"There's nothing normal about this. I don't go around marrying people either." He shrugs as he crosses his arms. "Plus, it's not like you're robbing a bank. You just live in a fucked place where you can't be healthy for free."

I guess he makes a good point with that.

On another note, I say, "If we meet someone and want to get married later on, we'll need to tell them we were married before." Not a bad thing, per se, but our lie will follow us for the rest of our lives. This is more than a temporary thing.

"No risk of that happening," he says, head cocked, eyes right on me. It's hard being under his stare, like he's even bigger than he actually is and I'm utterly exposed.

"It won't be some private thing. If this is to be believable, you'll need to meet my family and friends and vice versa. Do you really want me to tag along to your family dinners?" I ask. That part, to me, is not a problem. If Mr. Ray Of Sunshine here gives any indication, his parents might not be the type of people I usually hang out with, but I love meeting new people and I'd die to eat home-cooked meals with a full table around me every once in a while. However, he might not feel the same way.

"I don't have those, so problem solved."

"Have an answer for everything, don't you?"

He lifts a careless shoulder.

I trudge on. "We don't know each other." Or more like, I don't know him and he could be a serial killer for all I know.

"So? It's not like it would be a real marriage."

I swallow against the sudden dryness in my throat. I think out of all the reasons I've just named, this is the one thing that makes me the most hesitant. For as long as I can remember, I've always dreamed of marrying someone I loved. Even during my harder days during dialysis, when I'd get bouts of sadness at the thought that this was not what life was supposed to be like, I'd comfort myself by thinking of the life I might one day have, waking up with a man who loved me and maybe a few kids around. I didn't mind that it was cliché. I wanted it so much I ached for it. A life surrounded by love.

And now here I am, living my future life, but instead of marrying for love, I'm thinking of marrying someone who could not care less about me, me as a business transaction.

It kind of makes sense, though. I'm not the same naïve little girl I was when I lived that Barbie doll dream. I know that loving someone means being at the mercy of their own feelings toward you. I know how it feels to crave someone's attention and never feeling like what you are is enough. I know what it's like to be with a man who pities you instead of loving you.

Even though I still have a pinch of disappointment at the thought of not having a love marriage, deep down, I'm not sure I even believe in such a thing anymore, at least for me.

"*If* we are to consider this, we need to set some ground rules."

He nods once, all business-like.

"First, we can't get caught, ever. I'm not getting a criminal record anytime soon."

At that, I'd swear his face blanches, or maybe it's just the lighting in the bright diner.

"We'd need to keep our arrangement a secret," I continue.

"The band already knows we're not together," Carter deadpans.

"Right. I guess they can know, then, but you need to make sure they keep quiet about it. And we don't tell anyone else."

"Fine by me."

"All right." I tick another point on my fingers. "Then we need to set up an end date. Like…" How long is long enough to be believable and to give me enough time to profit from his insurance? "In two years, we get a divorce."

"All right," he says.

Look at us, agreeing on things. My shoulders loosen as we continue going through the terms, from prenups—not a problem for either of us—to my responsibilities as the band's promo worker. I'd have to mention publicly how I'm married to the band's producer to explain why I'm spending so much time with them, and then post at least three times per week to feature them and their music. Not too bad. I might end up losing followers who usually expect a different type of content from me, but it should mostly be okay if I continue to intersperse my own posts in between subtle promo.

"Great. Anything else?" Carter says, circles shadowing the underside of his eyes. I probably have the same, if not worse. Outside, the sky is starting to pale, the stars long gone and slowly getting replaced by hints of daylight. I need to go find my bed, and soon.

Maybe fatigue is the only reason I'm even thinking of going through with this insane plan. Maybe I'll wake up later today and realize how dumb I was. I almost wish I would.

But when I look at the pros of this, I can't pretend it's not a great deal. Short of robbing a bank, I don't know how else I'd be able to keep on going. Just two years. That'd give me respite for my medical bills and allow me to take on fewer shifts at The Sparrow. I could use that time to figure out how to get a job with insurance so that by the time we divorce, I'd be fine. A buffer of sorts.

"Yes," I say. If I want to actually consider this, I need a clear plan in my head that includes all possible questions that would arise. "We need to figure out where we'd live."

"What do you mean?"

"If we wanted our marriage to be credible, we'd need to live together," I say.

His jaw tightens as if he hadn't ever considered that possibility before. Or as if the thought of living with me disgusts him.

To be fair, I'm not that keen about living with a total stranger who's stoic and rude most of the time, but at this point, I don't have the luxury of shopping around for a better fake husband.

"I have a house," I say. "You could have the basement if you wanted." There's a second bedroom on the main floor, but I think us having our own spaces would be for the best. I don't know the man, after all. I don't think we're at the level of sharing a bathroom in our relationship yet.

He rubs his lips with his thumb as he studies the table for a moment. "I guess that works."

"Okay." I might not be writing down a contract—I don't want any more incriminating proof than there already is—but I fully plan on typing all of our conversation down on my phone once I get home so neither one of us can forget our agreements. I tick through all the things we discussed in my head, and the longer I go on, the less sense this deal makes to me.

I lay my hands on the table. "Are you sure you really want to do this?" Out of the two of us, I'm clearly the one benefitting the most from the situation. He's putting himself at risk of going to jail for committing a felony, and for what? Publicity for a band that's not even his? "It doesn't make sense." I might be shooting myself in the foot by arguing this with him, but I don't want to go into this unless there's at least a semblance of fairness.

Carter shifts in his booth. "If this goes according to plan, the band's success might put me on the map and launch my career. That's more than enough for me."

"Your career's that important to you?"

His gaze flits to mine. "It's the only thing I have."

I want to refute, ask him about his family, his friends, his pastimes. He must have more than a job, and yet there's something in his stony expression that tells me he truly believes this.

I nod just as our waitress comes by to pick up our empty cups of coffee.

"Thank you, Maggie," I say, while Carter makes an inaudible sound—I'm not a hundred percent sure that man is able to speak in more than two sentences at a time.

"Of course, honey," she says, then throws me a knowing grin, all the while glancing at Carter. I have to agree that by looks alone, she must think I'm lucky as heck to be on a date with a man like him. She might find him a tad less charming if she had a conversation with him, though.

I turn back to Carter when I remember something we definitely need to discuss.

"Oh, and one last thing."

He simply looks at me, totally done.

"If we want to make this believable, we also need to look faithful, so if you decide to see someone else, can you please be...discreet?"

Even if I can't see myself, I know I must be red as a beet. I can't believe this is what my life has come to. Asking my future husband to be subtle when he cheats on me.

It's not a real husband. I just have to keep reminding myself of that.

I know myself. I fall fast, and I can easily imagine scenarios where someone is interested in me when deep down, they couldn't care less. If I want this arrangement to work, I need to be careful.

"And of course," I add, "I'll do the same."

"Not a problem."

"Good," I say.

A bell rings at the front of the diner, followed by two men in work boots and dirty jeans walking in. The morning is truly here.

In front of me, Carter stretches his back, sucking me in with those eyes that remind me of a morning in early fall, when the leaves have just started to change color and are in that murky zone between a darker green and reddish-brown.

"It's a deal, then?"

This is insane. Absolutely insane. If I do this, it'd be so out of pocket for me. I've never done anything this reckless. But has being careful brought me where I wanted?

Live life to the fullest. If I want even a chance at it, this is the way to go.

With a deep inhale, I extend my hand, and only once he clasps it with his, warm and firm, do I say, "It's a deal."

Chapter 5

I can't believe I'm actually doing this.

My legs are shaking as I hide from the rain under the front porch of the Montpelier courthouse, coat wrapped tight around me. It might have been more than a week since we officially agreed to the marriage, but now that the day is here, I can't help but feel like I'm making the biggest mistake of my life. I keep thinking about what my father would say if he could see me, and somehow, I can't figure out what his reaction would be. On the one hand, he was always the one to tell me that life was an adventure and you simply had to make the best with what you had. On the other hand, he might be ashamed at the thought of his only daughter marrying and moving in with a man she met less than two weeks before. Even so, I wish he were here. I can't believe I'm getting married and my dad—the one person who's been with me through it all—isn't here to walk me down the aisle, as fake as this thing is.

Just as I feel that telltale tightening in my throat that precedes tears, I spot a figure walking my way, hands buried in the pockets of his trousers. I blink up and cough once, hoping I can sound normal by the time I have to speak to him.

"Hey," Carter says as he reaches me under the porch.

"Hey. Ready to get hitched?"

He doesn't answer, his tight line of a mouth turning into a frown. "What's wrong?"

"Nothing."

"We're getting married in twenty minutes. I think it's too late to bullshit me."

My expression twists into the sad smile I was initially wearing. "I just wish my father were here. That's all."

There. Now he can't fault me for being a liar.

His frown doesn't go anywhere. "We can call him and wait if you want."

Somehow, that's the last thing I expected to hear from him, and that small gentleness is enough to make me feel slightly better about today.

"He's not that kind of absent," I say, my voice catching on the last word. "But thanks anyway."

He seems to get it because he doesn't insist, only nodding once.

Well, this day got strangely emotional. I inhale, then let my shoulders drop as I release the air. "Still not backing out?"

"I don't know how many times you're going to ask me this."

I roll my eyes. "This one's the last, I promise." After that, it'll be too late.

"I'm good," he grunts. "You?"

"I'm good." Now that my head's clearer, I take the time to study him. He's wearing a white dress shirt tucked into clean slacks, and his polished shoes look brand new. I won't lie, I love that he made an effort. Even if this isn't a real marriage, I couldn't imagine wearing casual clothes at the courthouse. Since we were on a very short deadline—getting a wedding permit and a courthouse appointment in Vermont could be done fast—I didn't have time to go shop for a new outfit, but I still picked out a cream summer dress that is covered in pastel daffodils and that reaches all the way to my calves, paired with cream heels. I also wanted to do something cute with my hair, settling on curling it and tucking half of it up.

As I'm studying him, he's definitely studying me, and while I don't know how he feels about what he sees, I won't bring myself to care. He doesn't have to find me pretty or even okay. He just has to sign his name on the legal papers and share my life for two years.

Neither one of us moves for a couple of moments as if we're both waiting for some sign to get going. I wonder if he's also feeling like his body is being pulled in both directions, like he wants to do this as much as he wants to run away and never look back. Or maybe that's just me.

"Well, then." I extend a hand in the direction of the door, and he walks to it, holds it open for me, then follows me in.

The inside of the courthouse is pretty empty considering it's a Tuesday afternoon, and we take a seat where the clerk tells us, the dated, itchy chairs facing a set of doors I think will lead us to the room where we'll get married.

A painful silent minute passes before I exclaim, "We forgot to bring a witness." Even if I'd wanted to, I don't know who I would've asked. I haven't told any of my friends what I'm doing, and I certainly wouldn't have told Nana. I probably wouldn't have been able to go through with it if I'd had to listen to her or Finn tell me all the reasons why I'm dumb to be doing this. Although right now, I'd give anything to have them with me.

"Pretty sure they can give us one."

"Right."

I wait another second before saying, "Did we need to bring a passport or something?"

"Relax, Fireball. We did what was asked of us. We're good."

I know he's right. Still, I don't like his casualness as if this is a walk in the park for him. I don't think I've ever been this nervous—not even before going in for my transplant. Then, I knew I was doing what was best for me. Now, I'm not so sure.

The grandfather clock standing three feet away from us ticks loudly, each sound making my legs bounce faster.

My movements stop when a warm hand lands on my knee, not clutching, only holding it in place. I might be annoyed if it didn't feel so reassuring.

"You're making *me* nervous," Carter says.

"Finally time you join the club," I say with a fake smile.

"For Carter?"

We both turn toward the clerk standing between the now-open set of doors, a file held between her hands. Her dark hair is falling down in braids around the shoulders of her suit jacket.

"We're ready for you," she says.

So this is it.

I'm not sure I'd find the strength to get up if I didn't have Carter's hand on me, squeezing my knee once before he gets up

Carter's turn to do so. The moment he begins talking, my focus lands on him and remains there.

"I, Andrew Carter," he repeats after Belinda, jaw tight, "take you..." His chest puffs with a breath. "Take you, Lilianne DiLorenzo, to be my lawfully wedded wife." Even though I'm burning up, the way he speaks the words makes goose bumps appear on my arms. Thankfully, he doesn't seem to notice as he promises to love and cherish me, to have and to hold me in sickness and in health, and to do so until death do us part.

I've never felt more like a fraud.

Belinda proceeds to make us sign the legal papers, and I try to keep my mind blank as I write my name on the line. Carter does the same next to me, and when his arm brushes mine, it makes my breath hitch. I'm too on edge.

"Great. You may now exchange your rings."

My eyes round as I stare at Carter. Oh God. How did I forget the rings?

The second he lets go of my hands, I feel a loss of warmth, and for some reason, I want it back. I'm not sure why holding on to him makes me feel better, but it does. I need him to center me in all this craziness.

And when I notice the plain gold band he pulls out of his front pocket, I die a little inside.

"I completely forgot—" I start.

"It's fine," he says, not even looking at Belinda but only at me as he grabs my left hand and slides the delicate ring onto my fourth finger. I don't know how he did it, but it's the perfect fit, and as simple as it is, it looks beautiful.

I pretend not to notice the weird look Belinda is giving me, probably wondering what kind of a wife I'll be, and once the moment passes and she sees that I truly don't have one for him, she clears her throat and straightens. "By the power vested in me by the state of Vermont, I now pronounce you husband and wife. Andrew, you may now kiss your bride."

Another thing I hadn't really thought about before now. Getting married involves a kiss. Of course it does. I've been so busy all week, spending my days working and my nights dreaming of getting caught by the feds, that I didn't pay any attention to the ceremony part of things, hence the lack of a ring.

It's not like I have a choice to kiss him, though. Avoiding it would be the most obvious way to show we're not actually together. Plus, it's just a kiss. It doesn't mean anything.

Slowly, I lift my eyes and let them trail up Carter's body, from his wide chest to his long neck and clean-shaven jaw—how did I not notice he was this tall before?—and finally land on his eyes. I try to find some sort of emotion or tell about what he's thinking right this moment but find nothing but emptiness. Whatever he's feeling about having to kiss me, he's not letting it show.

The moment is becoming too long, and just as I go to climb on my tiptoes and kiss the corner of his mouth, he leans forward and softly clasps my cheeks between his rough hands before landing his lips on mine.

I gasp at the initial contact, both surprised and electrified. As chaste as this kiss is, the feel of his lips on mine, soft and yet firm, in control, feels like a bucketful of adrenaline being spilled down my veins. I know I should pull back, but for some reason, I keep it going for a breath longer.

He pulls away first, bringing with him his scent of bergamot and musk, his throat bobbing on a swallow as he looks away. Meanwhile, my gaze remains on him. The kiss was nothing wild, but I still feel a blush covering my entire neck and face.

Clapping from Belinda brings me back to earth, making me realize we've officialized this.

Whatever happens, it's done. Andrew Carter and I are in this together.

For better or for worse.

Chapter 6
Carter

Three and a half years ago

If you asked me to pick between stabbing myself in the eye with a drumstick or being here, I'm not sure which choice I'd land on.

I almost want to laugh as I look around at the circle made of chairs set up in the middle of the community center multipurpose room and at the people chatting in the back with cheap coffee in paper cups and stale cookies in their hands. How fucking stereotypical of them. It's exactly what you'd picture an AA meeting to be in some shitty indie movie.

The more people walk into the room, the more out of place I feel. It's a strange mix of folks, a blend of looks, genders, ages, and styles, but it still feels like the last place I should be in. They look like they want to be here, or at least like they need to be.

I don't. Listening to a bunch of strangers share details about their boring lives won't make me better. It won't tame the craving inside my chest for that last bottle of gin I couldn't find the strength to get rid of, calling my name from under my kitchen sink like a siren. It won't make my life less pathetic than it is. It won't make my brother want to talk to me again or help my destroyed career. The only thing it will do is land me out of jail, and that's what truly got me out of bed and into this rancid-smelling room tonight.

The judge was lenient on me, as my lawyer said. Six months of Alcoholics Anonymous meetings was the best I could've hoped for with a DUI charge.

I clench my teeth and stand as far away from the group as possible, hoping to blend in with the wall. I'm not even scared of recognizing someone. I don't know anyone on the East Coast, and at this point, if my face turns up on the Internet, exposing me as a drunk as a way of explaining why Fickle broke up, then so be it. It's not like it will ever matter.

"All right, people, gather 'round."

Immediately, people walk over to the chair circle, where a white man in his late forties or early fifties is already sitting, welcoming people around him. Everyone looks genuinely happy to see him but also to see each other.

I'm now alone at the end of the room, my feet like cement blocks, and just as I think this would be the perfect opportunity to scurry away, Leader Guy turns my way, like he knew I was hiding there. "Come on. There's plenty of space." The Ned Flanders lookalike even sprinkles in a smile.

Fuck me.

Not having another choice, I join the group, keeping my head down so I don't have the misfortune of making eye contact with anyone. Even when Leader Guy—who introduces himself as Frank—starts talking, I tune everything off. I'm pretty sure he invites us to speak because next, people join into the conversation one after the next. I just hope this isn't part of the deal. Sitting here is one thing, but ask me to share my feelings with these strangers who happen to have the same vice as I do and I'll drive myself to jail.

I zone in and out as one by one, people talking about their week, about what triggered them, what pushed them to want to relapse, and the only thing it does is remind me just how much I'd give for a drink right now. Just one sip, that first one that makes you feel like all your worries are about to go away, even if only for one night. My mind drifts to those times I'd let myself drown in liquor and forget everything. I wouldn't think about the void that was my life or the sad, empty apartment I always came back to. I *know* that quitting a month ago was the thing I needed to do if I wanted even a chance at having a life, but that doesn't make resisting the call of alcohol any easier. Throughout the meeting, I hear Frank's answers to people's stories, always so fucking positive or inspirational, they make me want to bang my head against the wall. As if life was a Disney movie and everyone always ended up perfectly fine.

Before I realize what's happening, people get to their feet and shake hands with Frank before leaving toward the frigid winter air. Thank God. I guess not everyone had to share after all.

I grab my coat on the floor and shrug it on, finally free to escape.

"Andrew?"

I freeze, eyes drifting shut. I know he's talking to me, but I haven't heard that name spoken to me in weeks. Even before everything fell to shit with my family, barely anyone called me Andrew.

Slowly, I turn toward the man. He looks just as cheery as he did when I walked in. "Can I speak with you for a minute?"

I don't answer, which he takes as a clear yes.

He looks around to make sure no one is close, then says, "I heard from the court officer that you'd be joining us today. I hope your first experience wasn't too bad."

I blink.

"Not a big speaker, are you?"

"There anything I can do for you?" I ask, the bite clear in my voice. I don't remember a time when all my sentences didn't come out this clipped.

"I thought we could have a chat."

My frown deepens as I try to understand what makes him think I'd be interested in that when I didn't give his meeting an ounce of attention. "Look, you know I don't want to be here. I know I don't want to be here. Let's cut the bullshit, yeah?"

He doesn't flinch. In fact, I'd swear his grin widens. "Well, too bad, my friend. I don't think you have a choice."

I lift a brow.

"You should probably go read the terms of your probation. It's not just showing up here. You also have weekly meetings with a sponsor." Then he points at his chest like he's a fucking prize.

A sponsor. I'd ask if this was a joke, but I know that'd be useless. "So? You like coffee?"

This might be even worse than that dumb meeting.

We only crossed the street toward the nearest coffee shop. I figured if I indulged him and chugged a drink with him, he'd be happy and call it a day, but apparently, that's not enough for him. He actually wants to talk, and talking is the last thing I want to do. I don't want to listen to his insufferable preachiness. I don't want to feel the judgment bleeding through his words.

No one could hate me more than I already hate myself.

We're facing each other in a booth, my cup empty while his is barely touched.

"So, Andrew. Tell me about yourself."

"It's Carter," I say. No way am I going to listen to that name for six months. The moment I joined my brother's band four years ago, I asked Yuri and Steve, the drummer and bassist, to call me Carter, and even Brandon obliged most of the time. Only my parents call me Andrew now, and since I don't speak to them anymore, the name is gone and buried.

"Carter. All right." He looks at me expectantly, but when he realizes I'm not about to start gossiping with him like a teenage girl, he shifts in the booth and cocks his head. "Fine then. We'll 'cut the bullshit,' as you suggested."

Now we might be getting somewhere.

"First meetings can be rough. I get that. The fact that you decided to come tonight, even if it was forced, means that you've made the decision to quit—or I hope it does—and that's the most important part of this journey." He dips his chin. "Congrats."

I swallow, body statue still.

"But before I let you leave, I want to know what your lifeline through this is."

My face must show I have no clue what he's talking about.

He leans in. "What are you going to hold on to when things get rough? Because they will. And you'll need something, or someone, that you'll think about to make you say no to that drink."

This time, when I don't answer, it's not because I don't want to. It's because I don't have anything to say. I don't have someone I'm doing this for or a goalpost that'll keep me on track.

I have nothing.

A few years ago, I would've said I had Brandon, who'd been by my side from the day I was born, but I can't even say that anymore.

I guess the only thing I could say is I'm doing it for myself because I've already hit rock bottom and I don't want to know what's even lower than that, and that means I have to get my shit together one way or another.

"I guess I'll start by telling you mine, then." He doesn't sound mad or disappointed as if having a one-way conversation doesn't bother him one bit. "I've had my last drink five years ago, and even now, it still happens that the only thing I want to do is drive to the nearest bar to get blackout drunk." His face transforms then, turning into a smile that should not be anywhere near the words he's just said. "And when that happens, I think of my daughter. I think of Lilianne."

Chapter 7

I'm not ready for this.

In hindsight, asking him to come live with me was probably a bad idea. I could've suggested we go to his place. Or better yet, offered that we pretend to live together while staying in our mutual places. There must've been a solution that didn't involve him moving in.

And yet.

As I plump a pillow on the couch for the seventeenth time this morning, the gold band on my finger catches my eye as it reflects the early spring light filtering through the window. I didn't take it off after we left the courthouse yesterday afternoon. I'm not sure why. I *know* this is not a real union. I *know* the vows we spoke were not true. But for some reason, they felt solemn all the same. Like even if I don't like it, a part of me truly is his from now on.

I've spent the entire morning cleaning around the house, partly because I needed to keep myself busy in order not to go into complete freak-out mode but also because I wanted the place to look nice for him. From an outsider's perspective, it might appear dated and unkempt, and the last thing I want is for Carter to hate his new home for the next two years, although he'd be wrong to think the place has been voluntarily neglected. Dad always wanted to do some work on the house one day, but wanting to and being able to are two different things. He was a single parent who had to drive me three times per week to the hospital and who always had to work overtime at his accounting firm to be able to pay all the medical bills his insurance didn't cover, so having a modernized house was never a priority. However, what this place lacked in beauty, it made up for with warmth. We were never unhappy here. I remember countless Sunday mornings kneeling over the shaggy living room carpet, completing puzzles while Dad sat behind me on the green-and-black checkered couch, going through his crosswords puzzle while an old vinyl of his played on the record player he'd kept from his teenage years. There was always music playing, conversations happening, or laughter ringing. I wouldn't have changed that shaggy carpet or that checkered couch for anything in the world. And selfishly, I want Carter to feel the same way about the house. Like maybe if he sees how comfortable we are here, he'll be able to overlook everything that needs to be done to it.

Even though I expected it, I jump to the ceiling when the first knock comes at the door.

I need to calm down. I can't keep being shocked when he shows up to his own place.

Forcing a calm smile on my lips, I walk to the door, and after placing my hair behind my ears, I open to him.

And lose my breath.

No one should look this good in such plain clothes. He wears his blank T-shirts like some people wear evening attire, like he doesn't need any artifice with his clothing because his face looks just that good. His strong nose might look overpowering on someone else, but on him, it only blends with his sharp jaw and smooth lips as if every single trait had been handpicked to balance the others and make a flawless whole. Today, his arms are exposed, and I get a glimpse of the dark patterns inked all over his skin for the first time. They automatically catch my attention, making me look for longer than is appropriate.

Stop watching him like that. He might be my husband on paper, but I still can't drool over his physique, as nice as it is.

"Hi," I say, and when he only blinks, I smile even wider. "Welcome in!"

He gives me the smallest of nods, then walks inside with a suitcase in tow and a duffel on his shoulder. Tough crowd.

I stare as he takes in the place, from the stucco walls lining the living room to the old-school wood paneling in the kitchen. Thankfully—*thankfully*—he says nothing as he turns back to me, and while I usually hate how expressionless his face is, today, I'll take it.

"So this is the common living area, I guess. Feel free to use whatever you like, whenever."

When he continues silently looking at me, I show him the staircase leading to the basement. "Want me to show you around your space?"

"Sure," he says, almost sounding relieved. I'd thought after yesterday, he'd be acting at least a little more comfortable around me, but while he was never the happy-go-lucky type, today, his stiff posture and avoidant gaze make him look even more closed off. Maybe he's just having delayed reactions, and only after we got married did he realize how big of a thing it was.

We go down the stairs, and once again, I stay back as he takes in the space I prepared for him. I made sure to clean out the clutter that had been accumulating in the guest bedroom at the far corner of the basement for years, and I even set up a living area with the television that used to be in my own bedroom so he could have a nice place of his own.

"I hope this is fine," I say, fingers twisted together in front of me, "but feel free to make any change you want."

"All right. Thank you," he says, slowly walking toward his room to drop his stuff, I assume.

I leave some space between us as he explores, but I remain down here in case he has any questions, like a good B&B host. However, I regret that decision the moment I hear a familiar voice upstairs.

"Hey, Lil? You okay?"

Carter turns at the sound while I freeze. Shit.

I've been dreading calling Finn since I decided to go through with the wedding, but I guess I can't escape him anymore.

Finn Olsen has been one of my best friends ever since the moment he sat on that dialysis chair next to mine, almost ten years ago now. He might've been older than me by a few years, but I saw the fear and uncertainty in his eyes when he stepped foot in the room for the first time, and since I was used to the entire process, I took him under my wing and made sure he was distracted. I was only fourteen years old, but I could tell when someone needed a pick-me-up, and that teenager sure did. Luckily for him, he only needed a few months of treatment in my unit, but we never lost touch after that.

And I'm pretty sure he will kill me once he learns what I've done.

Carter's watching me with a curious look, not moving either as if he's waiting for my instructions on the next steps to follow.

Without breaking our eye contact, I call out, "Coming up, just a sec." Then I whisper to Carter, "You stay here, okay?"

"What's going on?" he says, having the decency to whisper back.

"Nothing. I just have to deal with this, but I'll be right back."

Before he can say anything, I climb the stairs and hope he listens to my command. I need to explain at least a part of what is truly going on to Finn before he sees this stranger in my house and starts freaking out like the big brother he likes to pretend he is.

"Hey," I say, sounding breathless. "Didn't feel like knocking today?"

Finn stands from where he was leaning against the back of the couch, an eyebrow quirked up. "There a reason I needed to knock?"

"Because I'm a grown adult and could've had someone in here?" I say, keeping the question hypothetical for now.

"I *did* knock, but then I saw that other car in the driveway, and when you didn't answer, I got worried."

I probably should've thought about the fact that we often show up unannounced to each other's places before keeping a six-foot-two secret from him. I also should've considered that Finn would think another car in my driveway would be suspicious since I haven't had new people over since Greg and I ended things.

"Sorry, I was in the basement."

"I gathered," he says in a slow drawl, his face turning even more questioning. He knows I never go into the basement. Even though I'm a big girl and live alone in my house, basements still scare the living daylights out of me. "So who's there?"

"Huh?"

"The car. Whose is it?"

Of course he won't let me play dumb. Finn knows me too well for that.

Swallowing, I say, "Wanna go talk about this outside? Go on a walk?"

If there was a hint of calmness in his face, it's gone now. "Why? What's wrong?"

"Nothing's wrong." I walk toward the door.

"You're hiding something."

I don't bother denying it, and after slipping into my sneakers, I go outside. As predicted, he follows me. Once the door is closed, I go down the front steps and walk to the street, far enough that I know Carter won't hear us from inside even if his ear is right next to the window.

"So?" Finn says, making me turn and face him. "You're starting to scare me."

"Nothing to be scared of."

"Then why are you acting so weird?"

And that's when his eyes land on my left hand—more precisely, on the ring there. His face blanches.

Now or never, I guess.

Heart in my throat, I breathe out, "I got married yesterday."

A pause, then, "You did what?" His voice is calm. Too calm.

"I got married."

He blinks. Blinks again.

"I'm sorry, I think you're gonna have to repeat that again because *my friend* doesn't even have a boyfriend."

Not knowing what to say to that, I lift my hands in front of me. "Surprise."

Another long moment passes. "This is a prank, right? Something Lexie put you up to? Yeah, it has to be that."

"It's not a prank, Finn."

"Then I need you to tell me what the fuck is going on."

So I do. Well, the story I crafted, at least.

"We've been seeing each other for a couple of weeks on the down-low, and the other night he proposed on a whim and I said yes."

Finn stares at me for so long that for a moment, I think he's malfunctioning. "You want me to believe that?"

"Why not?"

"You, the person who never drinks and whose only brash decision in life has been to book a last-minute bus ride to Utah to join me on a ski trip, decided to get married to a stranger after dating in secret for no good reason?"

I don't trust my voice, so I simply say, "Mm-hmm."

"Wait!" I shout, holding his arm as he goes barreling up the driveway toward the house. "Calm down, you crazy slug!"

That gets him to listen. "Crazy slug?"

"He's not using me for sex." In fact, that idea never even crossed my mind, which probably makes me a little naïve, but too late to realize this now. "I'm doing promo for his band." Easier to explain it like that.

That seems to get him to calm down, but before we can continue our conversation, the front door opens, and out comes my husband, socked feet padding down the front porch. In a gruff voice, he says, "Everything okay here?"

I don't know what to expect from Finn, but he somehow finds a way to surprise me the most.

He laughs out loud.

"We're quite all right. Thank you, good sir."

Carter turns to me as if to confirm I'm fine, and while I appreciate the sentiment, I kind of want to burst into flames at the moment.

"We're good," I say. "Carter, this is Finn. Finn, this is Carter." I clear my throat, then say in a low voice, "My husband."

Even though he understands my reasoning, every bone in Finn's body screams his discomfort at the situation.

He trudges back toward the house, and while I quickly follow him, I'm not fast enough to put myself between the two of them.

"Pleasure to meet you," Finn says as he grabs Carter's hand and starts shaking. Carter winces, probably from a grip that's way too tight. "And if you even *think* of putting your hands on her, I swear to God I'll make your life a living hell."

Oh my God.

I don't know how to stop this, so I can only watch in horror as the two men continue to shake in the most awkward contact I've ever witnessed.

I only exhale when Finn finally lets go of Carter's hand. "Actually, I might let Lexie handle him. That'd be even worse."

I snicker. He has a point. I wouldn't want to go past him, but fighting his fiancée, who's an Olympic gymnast with a body made out of rock, would be way, way worse.

Finally, some lightness seeps into me. Finn knows, and the world didn't explode. And as annoying as he is when he gets all protective like this, I'm grateful to have someone like him by my side.

Finn hugs me quickly. "Come by the apartment later. Lexie will have lots of questions."

I'm sure she will. I don't expect Finn to keep this secret from his fiancée, and I know he's grateful I'm not asking him to. Plus, Lexie is like a tomb. Whatever you tell her to keep for herself will go with her to the grave.

I nod, and after throwing Carter one last murderous glance, Finn walks to his car and drives away. I don't even know why he came here in the first place, but I guess it wasn't important.

"Well." I spin on my heels to face Carter, chuckling awkwardly. "Welcome home!"

Chapter 8

For as many scenarios as I'd created about how living with Carter would be like, the reality still found a way to surprise me.

I didn't imagine we'd become best friends and have slumber parties every night, but I did expect some sort of partnership or even simple cordiality to take place between us.

I was dead wrong.

That first day, after Finn left and it was just the two of us outside, Carter didn't even look me in the eye as he said, "I'll be downstairs if you need me," before disappearing inside the house.

He wasn't joking. Aside from one or two exceptions when he had the vast displeasure of crossing paths with me, he's hid in the basement. Most days, I don't even know whether he's home or not. I feel like he tries his hardest not to make a sound in the basement, save for the rare flush of the toilet or the stream of the shower. He doesn't appear to be watching TV or talking on the phone with anyone. It's as if he wants me to forget he exists.

I don't, obviously.

Even when I try to relax and pretend like I'm alone in my place, it's just that. Pretending. I still enter the kitchen and living room warily as if I'll surprise Carter there and we'll need to exchange another awkward conversation that starts with me asking how he's doing and him finding some excuse to run away.

I don't want it to be this way. I know I'll never be able to walk around the place in my underwear while my hair dries in a towel wrap like I did before, but it doesn't matter. This could be more fun than a simple business arrangement. So last night, I tried to ambush him with food the moment he came back from work. I'd made enough quinoa salad to feed an army, but I still pretended it was a mere coincidence we were in the same room together at that moment.

"Oh, hey," I said. Then I turned to my food, and like the great actress I am, said, "You hungry? I think I made too much."

And what did this guy say?

"Thanks, but I'm good." And then, as if I were a carrier of all infectious diseases known to humankind, he and his rude ass escaped toward the basement, leaving me embarrassed and wondering what the heck I could've done to make him want to have this little to do with me. I understand that we never agreed to anything other than faking a relationship in public, but is basic politeness that much to ask for? Every time I speak to him, it's as if I've dropped a bomb in the room, and the awkwardness makes it hard to breathe.

However, being stuck in a car with him is worse than all those days combined. At home, I can pretend now and then that he's not ignoring me, he's only busy with other things, but here, there's no hiding how uncomfortable we are with each other. Or maybe *I*'m uncomfortable and he's simply indifferent.

Since we were both headed to the studio in Boston to meet with the band, I suggested we go together—mostly because my car's stuck in the garage thanks to a leaking engine—and while Carter didn't seem thrilled, he didn't deny me. However, it probably would have been better if he had.

"So," I say, unable to bear another second of this painful silence, only broken by the rock music playing from his Mustang's radio. "How should we play this?"

He quickly steals a glance before returning his attention to the road ahead. "What do you mean?"

Apparently, he was fine with the thick silence from before.

"Well, I can't just start posting about the band all the time out of nowhere. My followers need to know why I'm even with them to begin with." I readjust into the seat, then pull my phone out of my purse. "I was thinking of a boyfriend reveal. Or husband reveal..."

"No way."

This time, it's my turn to look his way. His hands are tight around the steering wheel, the muscles in his neck tense.

"Why not?" The second the words slip out, I regret asking the question. What if he's embarrassed about being associated with me? Maybe he was okay with marrying me so long as the whole ordeal was kept private, but the idea of having our faces attached together on the Internet is too much.

"I just don't do social media."

If that's a lie to protect me, I'll take it.

"We don't have much of a choice, though. It's our excuse for me being around." If I just started following a random band around with no relationship to them, it would look strange. "Plus, it wouldn't be very realistic for me to keep you hidden." If I could, I probably would. After having my previous relationship heavily displayed on social media, I'm not keen on doing it again, especially since I know people will probably bring up Greg in the comments one way or another, but again, we don't have a choice.

When he doesn't answer, I cock my head, thinking. "What if I don't show your face? Just, like, your hands or something?"

He throws me a glance, looking less against the idea than before but still not convinced.

"Please?" I say as a last resort.

With an exhale, he says, "Fine."

I smile, grateful even for this small win. "Great. Let's do it."

"Now?"

"Yes, now. It won't take long." I've already seen a few boyfriend reveals done this way before and it always looks cute. "I'll start with a photo post, and then I'll explain our faux love story in my next video. But for now, give me your hand."

He hesitates before extending his right hand, palm up. I take it, then flip it so it's facing down before dropping it onto my thigh.

He jerks at the touch. "What are you doing?"

"I told you, taking a picture. Jeez." You'd think he's some middle school kid who's never touched a girl in his life, although Carter's quiet confidence tells me that's probably far from the truth.

"Squeeze a little," I say. When he sends me a "what the hell" look, I add, "Girls love veiny forearms."

His nostrils flare, but thankfully, he does as I say, and the result through the camera is great. Delicious, even. Once I'm sure I've got the right angle, I place my left hand on his, showing off the gold band. I snag four photos. "All done."

I pretend not to be insulted when he rips his hand away before I've finished my sentence.

I start editing the photo, and a good moment passes before he says, "I don't think your friend's going to like that."

I don't automatically realize who he's talking about, and once I do, I laugh. "Don't worry about Finn." He'll get used to the idea. He loves to do the big, bad guy show, but in reality, he's softer than a marshmallow.

"He kind of made that hard to do," Carter says.

"Sorry about that, by the way. Finn can be a little...protective."

"Got that."

"But he'll be fine once he knows you better, I promise." Unless Carter decides he doesn't want to spend any time with my friends. Technically, now that Finn is in on the secret, we don't need to pretend to be a loving couple in front of him and Lexie. If Carter decides he never wants to see him again, he doesn't have to.

"Were you two ever..."

I lift my brows.

"A thing?" he finishes.

I snicker at the question but also at the thought that he decided to ask it. "No, no way." I tell him, just like I told Lexie when we met, that I've never seen Finn as anything more than a slightly annoying good friend.

Carter hums, and the rest of the drive to Boston is spent in our initial silence. I'd like to think that our micro conversation broke some of the ice, but that might just be me kidding myself.

Once the Mustang comes to a halt in front of an industrial building, Carter puts the car in park. "You do know his concerns were stupid, though, right?"

"Huh?"

"I'd never touch you or expect sex." He's still facing forward, not meeting my eye once. "That was never on my mind. Thought that was clear."

Everything he's saying is great—gentlemanly, even—but it still feels like a jab. It's not like I wish he would've wanted sex in exchange for his insurance, but did he really have to talk about touching me like that'd be the last thing he'd ever consider doing?

"Uh, yeah, sure," I babble. "I never thought that either."

"Good." Then he unclasps his seat belt and opens his door. "Let's go meet the guys, then."

"If it's not the lovely couple."

Three heads turn from the section holding two old-school brown couches at Bong's exclamation. While Carter simply walks straight to them without acknowledging the statement or the fact that I'm here with him, I give them a little wave, feeling way more embarrassed than I was when I first met them. I guess now's different, though. They know a lot more about me and my problems than they did then. That is, if Carter's told them the details of our deal.

This part of the studio isn't big, made of two rooms separated by a glass panel. This part of the room includes the couch section as well as the console where the recording technician does...whatever it is recording technicians do, and facing it is the actual recording room, with multiple microphones and instruments leaning against the walls. The room is decorated in a boho vibe, with mandalas hanging on the walls and warm rugs adorning the floors.

"I guess congratulations are in order," Ethan says as we reach them, his eyes only on me as he grabs my hand and brings it to his lips. "Mrs. Carter."

"Fuck off, Briggs," Carter says as he pushes his shoulder and takes a seat next to him. I'm not sure whether he's teasing or not.

"Come on, man. The amount of times you've given us shit."

Carter rolls his eyes but doesn't deny the statement.

"Have a seat, Lilianne," Emmett says when he sees I'm still standing awkwardly next to Carter.

"Lil, please. And thanks." I grab the spot next to Joe, who gives me a silent hi. I don't think I've ever heard him speak, but he doesn't seem to mind the chaos the other men bring.

"How'd you know her name?" Carter grunts.

"It's on her channel. Haven't you looked at it?"

I'm not surprised one bit when Carter shakes his head. Not even a little curious about the woman he married.

"So, Lil," Ethan says, clapping his hands between his knees. "First of all, thanks for doing this."

"Of course," I say. "I'm excited, actually. Never been on a tour before." I assume it'll be much different than the small shows I used to see at The Sparrow.

"Well, neither have we, so it's sure to be one hell of an experience."

Ethan then goes through the plans for the upcoming weeks. For the first three months, they'll only be touring in smaller venues in New England, so we'll be able to sleep at home most of the time. Then in August, we'll be going to the West Coast and driving to the different venues across the states in a tour bus.

"We should be gone for a few weeks. Obviously, you're free to hop on flights and attend shows here and there, but there's space for you on the bus if you want."

"I might take you up on that," I say, and I don't think I imagine the clench in Carter's jaw at that.

"Will you be there too?" I ask him.

Carter shakes his head, not offering more of an explanation. I guess it makes sense that the producer wouldn't need to be there for their tour, but I'm not sure how to feel about his future absence. It's not like he's the life of the party, but he's also the person I'm the most familiar with here, and living with only strangers for a week is something I never thought I'd ever have to do. Hopefully, they won't feel like strangers anymore then.

Nana better be proud of all this living I'm suddenly doing.

"It's settled, then," Ethan says before lifting his beer. "Welcome to the Crash & Burn fam, Lil."

The rest of the band members lift their glasses too, Bong shouting a "Whoop!" on top of it. I find myself smiling at the warm welcome they're giving me, not even caring that the least happy person in this room is the one I married.

Once they've all taken a sip, the band gets lost in mixed conversations, and while Joe and I remain pretty silent, I don't mind it. I take the opportunity to study these people I'll be spending a lot of time with in the upcoming months, but more often than not, my attention goes back to Carter.

We haven't been here long, and even so, I see a change in his demeanor compared to how he is at home. He looks much more at ease, even if that comfort is subtle. A slouch of his shoulder here and a huff at a comment someone made there. And while I know it's stupid, I still feel a pang of disappointment. I used to think I was an easily approachable person, but clearly I'm not. Something in me makes him uncomfortable.

A few minutes pass before I grab my phone and walk around to take pictures of everyone. If I want to uphold my end of the deal, I need content, and I want to figure out the vibe I'll be going for with my promo posts.

"Wait," Emmett says, jumping to his feet when he sees what I'm doing. "We can do better than that."

I lift a brow.

"If you're going to post about us, we should be playing instead of slouching around."

"Oh, I'm sure people would actually love seeing the behind the scenes," I say.

"Still," Ethan says as he too gets up. "He has a point. We can give you better photos than that."

"You're going to serenade me?" I ask the band.

"Damn right we are," Ethan says as everyone walks to grab their instruments.

I smile, excited to see what they're going to play. Even after only listening to them live once, I'm eager to hear more. As they get ready, I work with the lighting in the room to make sure the pictures and videos I get are the best they can be, and only once I take my position sitting on the couch's armrest do I notice Carter's eyes on me, watching. As soon as I meet them, they move to the band.

"Ready to get your mind blown?" Bong asks, bringing my attention back to what's important.

I lift my camera. "Bring it."

Chapter 9

If there's one thing that never fails to make me happy, it's people getting what they deserve.

And I mean that in all senses of the term. Sure, I do enjoy when good, old karma hits bad people every now and then, but more than that, I love seeing hard-working, kind people find happiness and success, especially after a lifetime of trials, and no one deserves that more than my closest friends.

"I suck at this," Lexie says, letting go of the bouquet of faux roses she was working on before dropping her head to the table, her short brown hair splayed around her.

"Stop it," I say, perfecting my own. "You're doing just fine."

"Why didn't I hire someone to do this again?"

"Because flowers are expensive," I answer as I tie the white silk ribbon at the base of my bouquet. Not that they really needed to save on their wedding. Ever since Lexie won a bronze overall medal in gymnastics at the summer Olympics last year, job offers have been raining on her, and as much as she continues to live a modest life, she could definitely splurge. I turn to her with a grin. "*And* because I convinced you that having a DIY wedding would be so much fun."

"Right, that's the actual reason. *However*, this is the least fun thing I've ever done." She throws a plucked plastic petal my way, making me laugh. "You should've gotten Finn to do it with you instead."

"Oh, please. As if I haven't convinced Finn to do plenty of stuff for the wedding already."

She perks up. "Really? Like what?"

"None of your business."

She rolls her eyes. "Fine then. If you won't tell me, then at least distract me with something else." Her flowers are completely forgotten now, and she's looking at me with strange interest, her hands flat on the table.

"Feels like you have something in mind," I say cautiously.

Lexie waggles her dark brows. "How's it going with the husband?"

I hold my sigh in. While doing wedding prep with Lexie has been a good distraction from my own life, she's brought me right back to one of the things I'd like to stop thinking about.

"It's…fine," I say, continuing to fluff the roses in the new bouquet I've started.

Lexie grabs the bouquet from my hands and throws it to the other end of the table.

"Hey!" I shout.

"They're plastic. It's fine." She leans forward so I can't escape her intimidating gaze. "Now tell me the truth."

This time, I can't hold off the long exhale. "It's been kind of horrible."

Lexie's body tenses. "What does that mean exactly?"

"No," I say, "nothing, like, *bad* bad. Just...we don't talk."

"Okay...?"

"Like, at all." I get up and walk to the pantry, then start pulling out ingredients by muscle memory. If Lexie won't keep me distracted with wedding prep, then I'll find a way to do it myself. I already cooked a white bean curry this morning for dinner, but I need more than that. "And it's not like I don't try. Every time he walks in, I try to make conversation, to get him to eat with me, to get to know him, but he always gives me one-word answers and then disappears downstairs."

"I'm not sure I'm following," Lexie says, still seated at the table. "That's a problem because...?"

"Because I guess..." Her question runs around in my mind until finally, the real reason I'm disappointed about this dawns on me. "I guess I might have been looking for more out of this arrangement than I thought."

"Oh, Lil," Lexie says, watching me with a pity I don't like. "Were you hoping that you two would, like, fall in love?"

I roll my eyes as I pour some flour into a mixing bowl, not measuring exact quantities but going with the feel of things. Life's too short to follow a recipe perfectly. "Don't be dumb. Of course I didn't." I bring the flour back to the pantry, then pause there. "But maybe I did hope we could form some sort of...friendship? Companionship?"

The truth is, I've been feeling so incredibly alone in this house. I do love it and all the memories it holds, but ever since I lost Dad, it feels like the ghost of him haunts all the empty corners. The more time passes, the more I notice everything I lost. In accepting Carter's offer, I realize I'd thought this emptiness could lessen with someone else there to converse with, but the only thing it's achieved is make me notice my loneliness even more. Obviously, I hadn't told that to Finn or Lexie because they'd make it their mission to make me their third wheel in order for me to never be alone, but that's the last thing I want. I love my friends, but they have their life, and I want them to keep it. I just wanted to have someone to keep me company too, even if it came in the form of someone who doesn't talk much and who seems to be in a sour mood twenty-four seven.

"And did you tell him that?" Lexie asks.

I shake my head. "I hoped my attempts at talking to him every single day would be good enough."

"He's a guy," Lexie says. "Obviously, that's not enough. You need to be clearer."

"So what do you suggest? That I go to him and ask him if he wants to be my friend like a second grader?"

Lexie shrugs. "Finn did that."

Of course he did. That's exactly the type of thing Finn would do—when he's not acting like a neanderthal, that is.

"Not sure Carter would like that as much as you did," I say, adding one too many chocolate chips in my cookie mix.

"I didn't like it at first, but it grew on me," Lexie says, smiling in a way that lets me believe she's reminiscing on the way they met. "You've got nothing to lose."

"I guess." Before I can add anything else, the front door opens and in comes Carter, an old backpack slung over his shoulder. He looks up quickly, and when he sees the two of us, his lips grimace in what I assume is a small smile before he escapes from our sight.

"Hey!" Lexie shouts, getting to her feet.

Carter steps back into view, looking even less comfortable now than he was three seconds ago.

"Wanted to introduce myself. I'm Lexie," she says as she hands him her hand.

"The one who's going to kick my ass?" Carter says, forcing a snicker to escape me. His eyes quickly flit to mine, and I'd swear I see a spark in the dark green.

"What?" Lex says.

"Ask Finn," I tell her, and she doesn't ask anything else after that, probably figuring out what went down a week ago.

"Well, I was actually about to be on my way to the gym," Lexie says as she grabs her stuff, minus the fake flowers, which I'm sure she's hoping I decide to throw away or forget about. "Talk soon?" Lexie tells me with her brows high, probably meaning this conversation isn't over.

Since I know she's not a fan of hugs, I keep my arms to myself and grin. "Sure. Next time we could work on the confetti?"

"Kill me now," she says with a wink, then walks out the door, leaving Carter and me alone in the kitchen.

I clear my throat, pointing at the mess I made on the kitchen counter. "I made dinner and dessert's almost ready, if you want some?" I hope my eyes don't betray the pathetic level at which I want him to say yes, just this once.

Even if they do, it doesn't stop him from saying, "I'm good, thanks."

Everything deflates in me, just like it has every time I've offered him to spend time upstairs with me this past week. I should be getting used to it, but every time, it seems to sting more than the last, especially since there's no kitchen downstairs, which means either he eats granola bars for dinner or he comes upstairs to cook while I'm asleep in order to make sure he won't cross my path.

Am I that hard to stand?

"Okay," I say. "Good night then."

"Night," he answers in a barely audible voice with a nod before disappearing into the basement, closing the door to the stairs behind him.

I return to my baking, finishing the batch of dough before I roll them into balls and spread them onto a pan. I try to keep my mind away from what just happened, but when I notice the balls of dough have been beaten down into flat discs, I realize I might be holding on to more frustration than I initially believed.

I start again, this time being careful not to hurt the innocent cookies. I hate being like this. Usually, I'm able to move on from the things that bother me, but it's not like I can avoid someone I share a house—and now a job—with.

Lexie's words come back to me. Maybe she does have a point and talking about it with him wouldn't be a bad idea. If he's simply clueless, we'll never have the chance to figure this out.

I put the cookies into the oven, and once I've closed the door, my mind is made. I can't complain about it if I don't try to do something first.

I only give myself time for a small pep talk, and before I can rethink this, I open the basement door for the first time since Carter moved in and go downstairs.

"Hello?" I call out before going down the steps in case he needs to cover up. When no answer comes, I finish the trek down.

The first thing I notice about the basement is how bare it is. I don't recognize anything that's changed since I cleaned up here, save for a pair of jeans laid on the floor and a computer monitor standing on the coffee table. Other than that, it's as if no one has stepped foot here since I did.

The second thing I notice is that it's empty. The door to the bedroom is open, showing an unmade bed and still-closed curtains. My annoyingly curious side wins, and just as I take a step closer to peek in, the bathroom door opens and Carter catches me red-handed.

"Sorry," I say, stepping back. "I called out, but you didn't answer, so I came down."

"Did you need something?" he asks in a bland tone, and I can't tell whether it's rude, bored, or simply neutral. I don't know him enough to be able to tell, which is part of the problem, isn't it?

"No. Well, yes." I tuck some of the strands that slipped out of my long ponytail behind my ears. "I wanted to ask if you had a problem. With me, I mean."

The second the words are out, I realize what a mistake I made. This is embarrassing as it is, but under his intimidating stare, there's no helping the deep flush that overtakes my face.

"Why would I have a problem with you?" he asks slowly.

"I don't know? Which is why I'm asking?" I wish all my statements didn't sound like questions. "You've been avoiding me ever since you got here, and if there's a problem, I'd like to know it so I can solve it. This doesn't have to be awkward."

"I'm not avoiding you," is his simple answer.

"Yes, you are." I try but failing not to laugh. He doesn't seem to find it funny at all. "You've barely acknowledged me since moving in." Surely it's not all in my head. "Maybe it's because of the weird way we met, and if it is, then I want to apologize and make it right. Start again." I add a smile at that to show I genuinely want that, but of course he doesn't return it.

"I'm not avoiding you," he repeats, still standing in the bathroom doorframe and ignoring about half of the things I've just said.

"Fine," I say. "You're not avoiding me. But you *are* avoiding spending time with me, and I'd like to know why so we can move on, and, I don't know…" Once again, I think back to Lexie's advice, and at the cost of sounding like a total loser, I say, "Be friends, maybe?"

A long breath comes out of his lungs as he drags a hand through his hair. "Look, I have nothing against you, okay? But this is a business deal, not an actual relationship. We don't need to pretend otherwise."

I take a long time to answer, mostly because I don't even know where to start. Every time I open my mouth to say something, I stammer, confused between all the emotions I'm feeling. Shame. Anger. Hurt.

In the end, what I land on is, "I wasn't trying to pretend anything, just wanted to be decent." I can't look him in the eye anymore, my heart thrumming in my chest. Nose prickling from my overflow of emotions, I say, "Don't worry, though, your message has been heard, loud and clear." Before I make an even bigger fool of myself, I turn around and go back upstairs.

The second I cross the threshold of the basement door, I force my mind to blank and forget about it all. I won't allow myself any more time to be sad about this. About *him*. That man doesn't deserve another single second.

I arrive back in the kitchen just in time to pull the cookies out of the oven, looking perfectly golden and crisp. And when I bite into one and then another, I focus on only tasting the chocolate and not the bitterness still residing in my throat.

Chapter 10

The venue almost filled out for the first official show of the tour.

I wasn't sure what to expect before coming tonight, but this wasn't it. I've done my research on the band during the past few weeks, and while I've seen they have a decent amount of regular followers and listeners, I did not think it'd be enough to fill a concert venue, no matter how small. Shows how little I know about this industry.

I'm up to the challenge, though. I've looked up what other influencers have done to blow up smaller artists, which of my posts surrounding music lead to the highest engagement, what people like to know about musicians that will make them buy tickets for their shows. I'll obviously let their music speak for itself, but I'll also show everyone's personality so that listeners feel close to them in a way. Tonight's the first time I'll share snippets of an official show, and I plan on giving enough to pique interest without showing too much. I want my followers to be curious, to want more.

I'm nursing a soda while standing at the back of the room. As much as I'd love to be in the front row, this will allow for the best shots. The venue is one large room without assigned seats, which has already led to a bunch of people huddling in front of the stage.

Even if I'm not the one going on stage in a few minutes, adrenaline pumps in my veins, the way it does every time I attend a concert. There's nothing like the feeling of a crowd singing along to a song everyone loves, a feeling of familiarity instantly being built between all these strangers for a few minutes. Everyone's energy seems to be high, and when the background music cuts off and the room suddenly darkens, the tension in the room increases tenfold. I whistle with my fingers as Crash & Burn walk on stage, and even though I've now seen their set a few times, I still get chills at the first note of the guitar that announces their debut's intro track.

I allow myself a full minute of enjoying the show before pulling my phone out and getting to work.

I find different view points across the room to record videos, then post a story and get some more footage for future posts. A few minutes into filming, when the band has played two songs and Ethan has paused to introduce the band and welcome the audience, a tingle builds at the base of my spine, tuning up my awareness. And of course, when I look to the left, I see the one person I've been trying to avoid all week.

Ever since Carter made it clear he wants absolutely nothing to do with me, I've listened to what I'd promised myself and steered clear. Most of the time, I made sure to be out of the common areas of the house at the time he came back from work and to be in my room when he left in the morning. Sure, it's tiring to avoid him, but I think it's necessary, at least for now. Our paths crossed once or twice, and I did exactly what he'd wished for: I acted as if he wasn't there. No hellos or good nights, no invitations for shared dinners or even acknowledgments of his presence. He wanted nothing, and that's what he got. At some point, I won't have a choice but to talk to him in order to get pictures together, maybe a video or two, but that day is not today.

Even though he's in my peripheral vision, I don't do myself the disservice of looking his way. I'm sure he looks painfully handsome, probably wearing an all-black outfit and his usual scowl. Not when I'm having such a great time. I don't even know why he came tonight—a producer doesn't have to attend their artists' shows—but I'm not about to ask.

When I force myself to forget about his presence enough to regain my focus, I resume filming, all the while moving my hips to Emmett's bass. Their music is catchy yet unique, a blend of The Killers and Fall Out Boy, with something utterly theirs. Ethan has a perfect rasp that has us begging for more, and the rest of the band keeps up with him and brings even more energy to the scene. At The Sparrow, I've seen multiple bands that were looking to build rapport with the crowd but ended up stealing their energy, but here, it's the opposite. Crash & Burn are powering them up. It doesn't matter that the crowd doesn't know the lyrics to the new songs the band is testing; they're loving every second.

I am too. My hair is a tangled mess around my shoulders, sweat drips under my black corset-like tank top from all the body heat around me, and I realize I haven't felt this alive in a long while. My smile is wide as I sing out to every song.

At some point, I realize I'm no longer filming straight, so I give up and discard my phone in my pocket, then squeeze myself through the crowd so I can get closer to the stage. The room is warm and smells of liquor and sweat, the floor is sticky under my block heels, and I couldn't care one bit. I forget about every single worry I have as I dance, sometimes by myself and sometimes with strangers. I don't have to keep up any pretenses here, where no one knows me, so when a guy comes close behind me, his hips brushing my back and his blue eyes twinkling with wicked delight, I don't push him away and share the song with him.

As the band leaves the stage and quickly comes back for their first out of three encore songs, there's another tingle at the base of my neck, and sure enough, when I glance behind me, I find Carter's body in the crowd, his gaze on me. The eye contact only lasts a nanosecond, but it feels much longer and makes me feel out of sorts. When I return my attention to the stage, I'm out of breath.

I try to enjoy the song, but soon, I overheat, like a sudden wave of steam has been dumped on me. The room also begins to blur, a key sign that I'm about to pass out.

Not wasting a second, I start pushing my way out of the crowd. Faintly, I hear someone calling after me, but I can't turn around to answer. I need air.

Sounds blast left and right as flashes of light slash through the room, dizzying me even more. I blink deeply, the stars in my vision blending with the strobes. Nausea rumbles in my stomach as I try and try to catch my breath, to no avail. Voices shout and sing everywhere, sounding both close and far.

After what feels like an eternity, I finally cross the venue's doors and walk into the May air, a warm breeze brushing my hair out of my face.

I only have time to sit on the sidewalk before everything goes dark.

"Fireball? Wake up. Come on, Lilianne, wake up."

I weakly shake my head against the brushes of fingers against my damp forehead, the world still fuzzy.

The moment I open my eyes, though, everything comes back to me, clear as crystal water.

The pavement is cold against my back as I pull away from Carter's touch. "What are you doing?"

"Jesus! What are *you* doing? You scared the fuck out of me," he says, sounding breathless. For the first time since we met, I think I see something other than boredom, annoyance, or perfect neutrality in his gaze. "Did you take anything from one of those guys? Did someone slip you something?"

I frown. Since when does he care?

I try to sit up, but he quickly pushes me back down. "No, wait here. I'm calling an ambulance."

Oh, hell no, he isn't. I don't need that extra bill, especially for something as small as this.

Pushing his hand, I lift myself into a seating position, then push my hair away from my forehead.

"Thanks, but I'm fine." I might have overdone it, but I'll go eat something and drink some water and should be fine.

"The hell you are." Carter looks genuinely shocked that I'm suggesting this. "You just passed out."

"My blood pressure drops sometimes." I slowly get to my feet, only needing to close my eyes briefly to stabilize myself. "It's not a big deal."

"We're going to the hospital," he says, not listening to a word I've just said.

"No, we're not. This is nothing. Happens all the time," I say, not even lying.

"I don't care. I don't like it."

"Well, you don't have to like it, do you?" I cock my head, chest tight. "We're nothing to each other, remember?"

He sighs, so deep it seems to hollow out his chest.

"I'm going back inside," I say, not feeling like rejoining the crowd just yet but wanting to stay here with him even less. As if he has any right to act worried about me now when he's dismissed me time and time again. "You do whatever the hell you want." The emotions enveloping my voice surprise me. I thought I was getting over it, but apparently, I'm still very much on edge.

"Lilianne, come on—"

"Have a great rest of your night," I say, not even looking at him before I walk back inside, hoping he won't follow.

Chapter 11

I'm missing a necklace.

I was speaking with Lexie this morning about what I should be wearing as accessories for the wedding. When she asked me, her sister, and her sister-in-law to be her bridesmaids a few months ago, she only asked that we wear whichever green dress we wanted but didn't mention anything about accessories. When I asked her about it, she said to wear something that meant something to us, and I immediately thought of the beautiful jade necklace Nan gave me from her jewelry collection when I graduated from high school. It'd look beautiful with the mint green dress I chose, elevating it while remaining modest. And right after thinking that, I realized I haven't seen that necklace in a long, long time. I could obviously do without it for the wedding, but it's a family heirloom, and I want to find it at some point.

I've spent my every waking moment since my call with Lex turning the house around to find it, but no such luck. The worst part is I don't remember when or where I saw it last, so I don't even have an inkling of where it could be. It can't be in the basement since I emptied it of my stuff before He Who Shall Not Be Named moved in, so it has to be somewhere here.

There's one part of the house I haven't touched, and I was really, really hoping I wouldn't have to. I don't see why the necklace would be in Dad's room, but there's a chance he might have picked it up at some point after I'd left it in the bathroom or something and could've forgotten to give it back. It might even be in the laundry basket I know is still in his room, untouched for the past two years. I'd made my peace with never seeing the clothes in it again, but that necklace is too important for me to accept its loss forever.

There's also a possibility I could've left it at Greg's at some point, but there's no way in hell I'm contacting him. So this is my second to last resort.

I stretch my fingers from where they're balled into fists as I stand before the master bedroom. It's been too long since I've walked in there. I've put it off as long as I could, and the more time passed, the harder it's made it to open the door.

It's just a room.

It almost feels as if someone else takes control of my body to take that final step and turn the doorknob.

After two years, the room smells a little stuffy, but mostly, I'm hit with the smell of Dad's shampoo, like a punch to the gut, stealing my breath away.

God. It's as if he's still here.

The step inside feels like walking through a time machine to the day I found out he'd been in a car accident and had passed from his injuries. The moment the police officers had left my house after gifting me with their condolences, I'd closed the door to the room and never dared open it again. The bed has been quickly made, sheets hanging off one side under the duvet. A pair of jeans hangs over the back of the La-Z-Boy in the corner of the room. The laundry basket is indeed there, holding the outfit I wore to the dialysis ward Christmas party the week before he died. If I stayed in this room, I could pretend he's just gone to pick up some milk from the grocery store down the street. He'll be back in ten minutes, bellowing as he opens the door, "Hey, Bean, I'm back," a pack of chocolate chip cookies in his bag because he wouldn't have been able to stop himself from grabbing it for me.

My breaths come in faster and faster as I continue looking around, finding him in every corner and yet knowing this is all I have left of his life.

Screw the necklace. I don't need it.

My throat is dry as I step backward, almost tripping on a pair of shoes before I shut the door, breathing fast. Exhaustion pushes at my shoulders, feeling heavier than they were mere seconds ago. I let my forehead drop against the closed door, and when I feel the threat of tears, I squeeze my eyes shut.

Turns out two years wasn't long enough for me to be ready.

I'm not sure I ever will be, and sometimes, that's what scares me the most. The bright pain of losing him has dulled, of course, going from a burning, oozing wound to a scar that lances with certain movements. Still, sometimes I remember that I'll never see him again, and the pain that rips through me could make me topple over, and what will happen if that feeling never goes away? What if I never get over this loss?

I let out a shaky breath, then turn toward the living room, but I'm stopped in my tracks when I find a pair of hazel eyes staring me down.

"What's wrong?" Carter asks, a small crease between his brows the only indication that he might be feeling something other than boredom.

I shake my head. I'm not handling him right now. I don't know what he might find to say but don't think I'm strong enough to want to find out. Not today.

Without acknowledging him, I walk over to grab my purse and shoes. I need to leave now anyway if I don't want to be late for my shift.

"Where are you going?" Carter asks. Of course he picks the day I want to be left alone to decide to make conversation.

"Work," I answer simply, not wanting to get into it with him right now.

"Do you need a lift?" he asks.

My hands curl. I forgot my car still isn't back from the garage.

"I'm fine." I'll walk. Or run, rather, with ten minutes to spare and a few blocks to cross. I slip my feet into my sneakers.

"I—"

"Can you not?" I snipe before he can finish. Then I escape outside, and he thankfully doesn't follow me.

Tonight's shift makes me question my decision to keep this job instead of quitting and agreeing to do the collab with that company making weight loss pills that are actually laxatives. At the time, I felt like it was unethical to use my low BMI that's due to my chronic illness to sell some magic weight loss pill, but after another night of Jayson groping me left and right, who pretended he needed to touch me to walk by or grab a glass, it makes me question if ethics are *that* important.

My feet are killing me as I lock the door behind me, and the twenty-minute walk to get back home makes me regret not asking Nan to borrow her car tonight. I crack my neck left and right, then bring the trash to the dumpster, and the moment I round the corner of the building and headlights blind me, I almost jump out of my skin.

There are two options that come to me: the first is that I'm about to be kidnapped or killed and thrown into a ditch. The second is that Jayson decided to wait for me to ask me to go home with him. I'm not sure which option I prefer.

But neither one happens to be true when the car pulls up beside me and I recognize it as the vintage Mustang that's been sitting in my driveway for almost a month now.

I don't move as Carter pulls the passenger windows down and says, "You coming?"

"What are you doing here?" I ask.

"You're not walking home alone at three a.m.," he says like that's an actual explanation.

"I've done it before."

"Well, not anymore."

I lift my brows. "I'll do whatever I want, thank you very much." Then I start walking away. Who does this guy even think he is?

The car follows me. "Can you just get in?"

I continue walking. "Why do you even care?"

"Why are you so stubborn?" Of course he wasn't about to pretend like he cares.

Still, I stop in my steps. I'm tired, especially after the breakdown I had today, and if I can get to my bed faster, it's worth more than my ego.

Without another word, I open the door and get in.

Carter doesn't drive away until I catch his look and put on my seat belt.

"Are you cold?" he asks, messing with the temperature controls.

"I'm fine," I say, knees tucked close to the door to take the least amount of room in his space.

Hard rock plays from the speakers, but even so, the silence between us feels like a third person in the car, thick and pulsating. I should've walked home. Now I can't help but think about how he found me earlier today and probably decided to come pick me up out of pity.

Two streets away from home, I feel Carter glance my way. I keep my gaze out the window.

"Are you going to talk to me at some point?" he asks, something I never would've guessed would come out of his mouth.

"Why would I?" I'm not usually this petty, but something about him, whether it's his arrogance or his hot-and-cold moods, brings it out of me.

"You talk to everyone, always," he says. "I've seen you."

I grind my molars together, hating that he has a point. Hating that he's seen enough of me to know that.

"I thought you didn't like that."

"I never said that."

"Could've fooled me."

A deep sigh comes out of his mouth, and he turns the music off.

"Look, I'm sorry about that night. It's not you. It's never been about you."

I let out a humorless laugh.

"It's not," he repeats, his face still devoid of expression but voice sounding determined. With his eyes on the road, he says, "I'm not big on the whole...extrovert stuff."

"You mean being civil with someone else?"

He sends me a glare that'd make me smile if it were in any other context. "I mean getting to know others. I'm...used to being on my own." His throat bobs, the only indicator that this might mean something to him. "And you caught me on a bad night, but again, not on you."

I'm not sure what to say to all that, so after going over my options, I settle on, "Okay."

"Okay?"

"Yeah, okay. I get it." I look out the window. "I can be a bit much sometimes."

"That's not it," he says.

"It's fine," I say, forcing a small smile. I remember all the times Greg made me feel like I was asking too much. *Being* too much. If my own boyfriend thought that, I can see how it could be baffling to a stranger, especially one who seems to be the definition of antisocial.

"I really am sorry I hurt you," Carter says, and I have to admit he sounds genuine.

"You didn't," I lie.

"Pretty sure I did."

I give him a side-glance. "Fine. Maybe you did a little."

I'd expect him to smile at my admission, but what was I thinking? This is Carter. Smiling doesn't exist in his muscle memory.

"Are we gonna be good now?" he asks.

"Sure." And I mean it. He might be asking for it out of pity, but at this point, I don't care. It's exhausting to avoid someone you live with, and the energy I've spent being mad would be better used elsewhere. We can coexist in neutrality. We don't need to be friends, and I won't ask for it again, but we also don't need to be enemies.

"Good," he says, then turns the music back on.

While the short rest of the drive home remains silent, it's much, much lighter.

Chapter 12
Carter

Three and a half years ago

He's doing crosswords.

Or at least I think that's what those are. I can't really see, with the cover of his old-school puzzles book folded over itself, hiding what he's actually doing.

It doesn't matter. Whatever it is, he's using it to ignore me.

Today didn't start out well, and it certainly isn't getting any better. For one, the Grammys are on tonight, and ever since I woke up, I've been teetering between hoping Fickle wins the awards it's been nominated for and wishing we lose in all categories. On the one hand, maybe losing would help my brother see that this band was a terrible idea anyway and take our breaking up easier. Maybe even find it in himself to forgive me for leaving. On the other hand, if we lose, this is it. We'll have had the lifespan of one album, and if this one doesn't make it, then this all truly amounts to nothing. Everything I've sacrificed for it, useless.

I'm not sure if Brandon will be there tonight. It's always been his dream to attend the Grammys, to become famous for his music, so I hope for his sake he does. Mom and Dad will for sure go with him, shaking hands left and right with old acquaintances, in their element.

I was never going, for obvious reasons. The moment I left and triggered the bomb that blew up our four-person band, I forfeited that right. I'm not even going to watch it on TV. If this were before, I'd drink enough that I could pass out and miss it, but now, I'll need to find another way to make myself ignore the ceremony. I quit the band because I couldn't be in it and stay sober. If I drink anyway, what was the point?

So I spent the day restoring an old wooden table I'd found on the side of the road, needing to busy my hands with something now that they don't have guitar strings to mindlessly pick at. I left my phone at the bottom of my socks drawer, put my headphones on with a seventies rock album at the loudest setting, and sanded. And sanded.

And then, I remembered I had to come here. Did I want to go out where I could spot snippets of the award show playing at a restaurant television? Fuck no. But I also didn't want to have a judge go back on their lenient decision and send me to jail, so I kicked myself in the ass and drove here, to that same boring twenty-four-hour diner we went to last time.

The moment I sat down, Frank smiled at me like he was genuinely happy to see me there. It made me jerk back. I couldn't remember the last time I'd been with someone who wanted my company. Granted, I'm a pissy, lonely drunk, and I was drunk the majority of the nights last year, but it still surprised me.

"Carter," he said, once again dressed like he was about to join a church choir. "How are you doing? I'm glad you came."

"I'm fine," I lied. I didn't add that I didn't have a choice to come.

"Good. That's good." He went over a few other polite niceties, then asked, "Were there any harder moments this past week?"

My jaw clenched. *How about every single second?* It'd be useless to say so, though. I was surprised he'd even try to have an honest conversation again. Last week, after he was done telling me how his daughter was the one thing that kept him from going back to drinking, he asked me again what my anchor was, but I didn't feel more inclined to speak, especially since I didn't have a clear answer to give him. He left looking slightly less encouraged, but today, we were back to square one.

I stared at him with my mouth shut, hoping he'd get the hint and call this meeting a day. However, when I didn't answer, he said something like "Okey dokey," dug out this stupid book, and opened it, solving his crosswords or sudoku or whatever he was doing as if I'd suddenly disappeared from his sight.

And now here we are, thirty minutes later, and he still hasn't looked up from his book, save for when he asked the waitress to refill his coffee cup.

It's pissing me the hell off.

I don't know why. It's not like I want to listen to his inspirational quotes and life stories, but seeing how he's just…given up on me makes me mad. It's selfish and pretty fucking stupid, but I can't help it.

"Is this some kind of twisted game to make me speak?" I finally say.

"What?" he asks, not even looking up.

"Some reverse psychology shit so I decide to open up?"

"And why would I do that?"

I make a gesture like, *how would I know?*, and I'm pretty sure it makes me look like a stubborn child who's been refused dessert.

"I have no purpose in playing games with you, Carter." Still, he keeps his eyes on his paper, reading glasses perched on the bridge of his nose. "You want to waste our time? Be my guest." He doesn't sound angry, or sad, or even bored. His voice is completely bland. I wish he'd get angry, decide to argue. I'm itching for a fight, for a reaction, *anything*.

"Then why are you still here?" I snarl. Is he bearing the brunt of the discomfort and anger I felt throughout the day? Maybe, but I'm not stopping now.

"Doing what I signed up for. I said I'd spend an hour a week with you, and I don't go back on my word." He shrugs. "You don't want to talk? Don't talk. It doesn't change anything to me. Good luck because you're going to need it, but go ahead. Either way, it doesn't matter. I'm just here to help if you decide you need it."

This is bullshit.

Frank doesn't say anything else as he continues writing with his sharpened pencil, and now that we're back in silence, my thoughts swim back to what's happening tonight. It almost feels like my body is in two places at once, here with him and there with the people I used to consider closest to me. I'm not sure what place makes me feel worse.

And it all comes back to alcohol. I should've been able to be there tonight. If I didn't have this problem, I wouldn't have needed to escape everything I had. Plenty of people have a couple of drinks without going overboard. If I was able to control myself, I'd be able to go to shows and after-parties and big events without fearing I'd lose myself and do something messed up like drive my car while drunk out of my mind and hit some unmoving object. I'd be able to play shows without feeling this pull toward the bar at the end of the night. I'd be able to enjoy what I had and not fuck it all up. I wouldn't need to be sitting with some middle-aged guy at a nasty diner across the country.

"How is talking supposed to solve anything?" I spit out, picking up the conversation where it left off.

Frank's head bobs up as if I've finally captured his attention. As if I've finally taken his bait. And fuck me, I think I might have.

"You want the honest answer?" he says, closing his book and putting it on the table. Crosswords.

When I simply stare, my face feeling warm from all the emotions boiling inside and looking for an outlet that doesn't exist, he says, "It won't."

"I'm sorry?" He's been on my back all this time to talk.

"You're right." He puts his hands on the table. "Laying it all out to some random man won't magically solve all your issues."

I don't think he's ever annoyed me as much as he does right at this moment.

"But it just might be the one thing that will keep you from tipping over the edge. It was for me." His gaze turns upward as if he's getting lost in thought. "Alcoholism is a pretty lonely thing. We spend so much energy hiding our problem, making sure that our loved ones don't know how much we're struggling."

He drags a hand over his mustache. "And we think our experiences are unique, but really, they're so common it's almost embarrassing. And I can't erase the mistakes you made or the people you hurt because of alcohol, but I can help you think of ways to repair your wrongs, and most importantly, I can let you know that you sure as heck aren't alone."

Alone.

It resonates in my head as if he's shouted it inside my empty corpse and there's nowhere for the word to go, echoing forever.

When wasn't I alone? When I was a kid and my parents would leave me and Brandon alone for weeks with nannies? When I was playing shows all over the country and it felt like I was in a different world from the entire crowd? When my friends and family decided they wanted nothing to do with me the moment I decided to step away from the thing that was making me sick?

Frank's looking at me so intently, I want to hide under the table. I don't like the way it feels, like he knows exactly what I'm thinking and how I'm feeling even when I haven't said a word. I don't understand how he's smiling once again. This man, who I've been an ass to, who owes me nothing, and yet who's there when so many ran at the first opportunity they had.

He grabs his book and slides down the booth. "I think we're done for tonight, but you should probably think about this." When he stands and I remain there, it doesn't matter that he probably measures five-seven and I usually have two heads over him: it still feels like he's way, way bigger. "No, talking to me won't solve your issues. But maybe it'll help you see that it's possible to get to the other side of this thing."

Chapter 13

The next day, I find Carter in the same spot in the parking lot, waiting to drive me home from work.

And the next day. And the next.

It doesn't matter that I haven't asked him once for a lift. Every night, he's there, even when I finish a little early.

During all those drives, we remain silent, and while it's never uncomfortable—soft music playing as Carter drives with one hand on the wheel and the other propping up his head—I don't know what they mean. It's confusing. I've had a full schedule at the bar since we didn't have any shows planned, so other than during those moments, we haven't seen much of each other.

However, tonight, as I exit the bar with Jayson right behind me, the back of his hand accidentally brushing my ass, I couldn't be more thankful to spot Carter's car in the driveway, one tattooed arm hanging out of his window.

I've had a feeling since the shift started that tonight was going to be the night my boss would truly shoot his shot, and I wasn't ready for all that would entail. More than that, I hated the thought of being alone in a hidden parking lot at 3:00 a.m. when I rejected him.

"All right, good night," I tell Jayson over my shoulder, already walking toward the Mustang that feels like a beacon of safety.

"Wait," my boss says. I wince. "Don't leave so soon."

I don't turn around. "I'm pretty beat, actually." When I go to take another step, a bony hand wraps around my wrist, sending a frigid flood down my body. I *knew* he'd do something like this. I pull against it to see how tightly he's holding me, which somehow is amusing to him.

His voice grates against my skin as he chuckles. "Come on, don't—"

"Take your hands off my wife. Now."

We both startle at Carter's voice that seemingly comes out of nowhere. His car door has been left open behind him and while he's walking and not running, the giant footsteps he's taking bring him to where we're standing in a second.

My breaths come in ragged, either from the threatening feel of Jayson's fingers or from those words coming out of Carter's lips.

"Wife?" Jayson says with nervous laughter as he finally lets me go. I take a step in Carter's direction, wanting to put as much space between us as possible. "She never said she was married."

She. Like some person whose name doesn't even deserve to be mentioned.

"So that gave you free rein to touch her?" Carter still sounds calm, but this is nothing like his usual aloof self. His body radiates lethal coolness.

Jayson lifts his hands in front of him. "Sorry, man. Didn't mean no harm."

Carter's jaw clenches, the only sign that he's about to burst. "Apologize to her. And next time, keep your fucking hands to yourself."

Jayson stammers something unintelligible, and I'm too tired to try to play nice with him. Instead, I put a hand over Carter's tense forearm. "Come on. Let's go home."

He stays put for a moment as if he has more to say, but when I pull on his shirt, he throws Jayson one last murderous look and follows me to his car.

We remain silent as we get in and pull out of the parking lot, both of us probably needing a second to cool down. I could nag him for probably getting me fired, but honestly, I'm thankful for him stepping up for me. He's got more balls than I do, that's for sure.

"Is this fucker always there when you work?" is the first thing Carter says to me after another five minutes of silent driving.

"No. Well, sometimes he's there during my shifts, but he never stays until close time. Tonight was the first time."

He makes a noncommittal sound.

"I don't think he'd have ended up doing anything, but thanks for intervening anyway. I appreciate it."

"You were uncomfortable. He should've seen that."

That, we can agree on.

We finish the drive in silence, Carter yawning twice before we finally get home, fatigue written all over his face.

I unclasp my seat belt and turn to him, deciding this has gone on long enough. "I'm really thankful for tonight, but how long are you planning on doing this?"

"Do what?" he asks before exiting the car.

I follow him out. "Coming to pick me up in the middle of the night."

He doesn't stop walking in front of me as he says, "When are you going to stop walking home in the middle of the night?"

"I usually go with my car."

"Fine then. I'll stop when your car's back."

Which won't be for another two days. Apparently, keeping my dad's 1995 Ford was not a sure way to have a reliable car.

"And when I know that creep's not there with you," he adds. I'm not about to tell him he's my boss and he's there most of the time. I think Jayson will probably have learned his lesson tonight.

"You don't have to." I don't know if it's coming from a place of guilt over rejecting me at first or a strange sense of duty, but it's only making me feel bad about keeping him awake.

Carter stops in front of the door, head hung between his shoulders, defining the muscles in his back under his black T-shirt.

Stop ogling.

"Would you question it if it were Finn or Lexie doing it?"

Surprise must be evident on my face because when he turns around, he raises a brow. I never would've thought he'd remember their names.

"Maybe I wouldn't," I say. "But it's not the same thing. They're my friends."

"So?" he says, not contradicting my statement.

I lift a tired shoulder.

"You're still mad. That's why you're against it."

"I'm not."

He gives me that same eyebrow quirk.

"I swear I'm not. And I'm not against it. I just..." I walk to open the door, the early summer breeze cool against my face at this time of night. "I don't like you feeling like you owe me something." I'm in his debt enough. I've seen the first insurance payment go through two days ago, which means he followed through with his end of the deal, and the relief that inhabited my body the second I saw that amount felt like breathing for the first time with eighty pounds off my shoulders.

"You don't owe me anything," Carter says. "I'm just trying to be a *decent* person." Even though his face doesn't let up anything, I'm pretty sure I hear a hint of humor in his voice.

My lips twitch up. Using my own words against me. A good one.

"Fine. *Thank you*, then."

"You're welcome," he says as he crosses the threshold, then removes his boots and places them right next to where I've left my own shoes. The picture is so domestic, it's almost caricatural.

As I take off my coat and tie my hair in a bun, unable to stand it being loose a second longer, my stomach grumbles so loudly it makes Carter glance my way.

"I haven't eaten in twelve hours. Sue me."

He shakes his head with round eyes as if to say he wouldn't dare, and I bypass him on my way to the kitchen. I don't usually cook after an evening shift, but I know I have no leftovers and I can't go to bed like this.

I scavenge through the cupboards until I find a can of white beans and a jar of sauce. I pull a pan out, turn the stove on, and jump when I hear, "What are you making?"

It almost feels like seeing a ghost when I turn and find Carter sitting on my kitchen countertop, watching me. That's definitely a first.

"What are you doing here?" It seems I keep asking that question as of late.

"Should I leave?"

"I—No, of course not," I babble, still uncertain whether this is real or I'm already asleep and dreaming. I'm not about to complain about it, though. Not when that was the exact outcome I was wishing for a few weeks ago.

Carter dips his head. "So?"

I look back at my pan. "Oh." The sauce is sizzling, so I pour the contents of the can in. "Just beans in pesto." My voice is hesitant when I ask, "Want some?"

Perched on the counter, he looks younger than he usually does. From looking at his ID when I filled out the marriage license, I know he's almost thirty, but here, in the dim kitchen light, with his head cocked and his hair a little mussed as if he'd been sleeping before coming to pick me up, he reminds me of a kid waking up for a piece of cake by the refrigerator light in the middle of the night.

"Sure," he says, once again surprising me. Who is this man and what has he done to the grumbling guy who moved in with me?

I decide not to make a big deal out of it. He might return to his basement exile tomorrow, and this would only be a blip in our cohabitation, but if this is the only thing I get, then I'll take it.

Carter remains silent as I stir the sauce and hum one of the Crash & Burn songs I listened to tonight. When I heard it play through the speakers from the local radio station the bar usually tunes in to, I almost dropped the beer I was holding. I don't know if the few posts and videos I've shared of them have even made a difference, but I like to pretend they did. I've never been part of a team as a kid, being homeschooled most of my teens, and even though my role is minimal, the band has succeeded in making me feel like I'm a small part of them now.

When the beans are done, I place them on two plates and sprinkle spices on top before adding pieces of pita bread and forks. Then I bring Carter's plate to his hands and join him on the countertop, facing him.

He thanks me and we both start eating in silence, cicadas singing through the screens of the windows I forgot to close.

"I have a question for you," I say, making him look up faster than I expected. I gathered Carter isn't the type to share everything about himself over mimosas, but now that I take a good look at him, I figure I've underestimated it. He's not a simple closed door, more like a fortress he'd never want anyone breaching. Still, I'll try my best.

"Hm?" he says, ever so eloquently.

I kick my feet so they lean against the opposite cupboards. "What have you been eating for the past weeks? Have you been using the kitchen in secret?"

He visibly exhales.

"I, uh…" He scratches his jaw, the beard slightly longer than it was a few days ago. "I got a microwave and ate instant ramen."

A moment passes. Then two.

And then I burst out laughing, head thrown back, a deep belly one I can't control. "Oh my God," I wheeze. "That's so pathetic."

And then, the most beautiful thing happens.

The corners of Carter's lips turn upward.

It's nothing big, something you'd probably miss if you didn't know him, but now that I've seen the ways his face can remain still as a statue, his smile is *everything*. It doesn't matter that the change is subtle, that it's only noticeable in the crease at his chin and the twitch of his left brow. It's as if a light has been turned on.

The sight makes something *whoosh* in my stomach, like bubbly liquid fizzling from my belly all the way to my chest.

I can't stop laughing, but this time, it's not only out of laughter; it's also out of sheer happiness, that maybe the two years we're forced to spend together aren't doomed after all.

Chapter 14

The type of information I've shared on my platforms over the years is kind of contradictory.

On the one hand, I've always been fully transparent about my medical journey. When I was put on a trial for a new drug that might have beneficial effects in the slowing of FSGS—or focal segmental glomerulosclerosis—I shared the entire experience with my followers, and I also cried on my channel when I learned it had done nothing for the auto-destruction my body was wrecking on my kidneys. When I learned that a kidney had been found for me and that it was a match, I shared the news on my pages almost right after telling Nan and best friends. It didn't matter that there were chances it might end up falling through—a living donor changing their mind, a deceased donor's organ not being usable after all, someone else needing it more urgently than me—I wanted to let them all know. It's always felt as if they've been part of my struggles and successes, being the best support group a person could hope for, and I didn't want to keep any of it from them. If the happiness over the good news was to last for only a few days, then I wanted them to have those days, too.

However, as much as I've kept this side of my life open to the public, my personal life is something I've tried to keep for myself. With Greg, since he was also an influencer, we shared a lot about our relationship online, but the moment we broke up, I took a step back. I didn't share details of our breakup, didn't talk about the trauma of trying to date again after a previous relationship had messed with everything you thought you knew and liked about yourself. I barely mentioned the passing of my father.

So I shouldn't have been surprised when, even weeks after my initial marriage announcement, my inboxes and comments sections, even on sponsored posts, continue to be flooded with demands for information on my husband.

> @TS1989: WHO IS HE?!?!?!

> @Flowersinbloom27: Bitch you can't just drop this and leave

> @Samseaberg: You don't even need to show his face, we know he's hot af just by looking at THAT HAND!!!

That last one made me laugh. I looked again at the picture I'd taken of Carter's hand draped on my thigh, and that person was right: the sight of those long fingers and strong veins does something to me, too.

I tried to keep it on the down-low, to go on with my regular posting schedule, but it's not working. I need to give them something, or else I fear they're going to revolt.

I walk out of my bedroom/office and head over to the kitchen, where I stop in my tracks and take in the scene.

Carter is standing in front of the stove, cooking something that smells heavenly, his wide back to me, tattooed arms on full display. The sight is nothing out of the ordinary, and yet it makes my mouth dry. The art is all in black and white, traced in fine lines. There doesn't appear to be a theme to the tattoos. A lion's head, mid-roar is drawn next to a mechanical clock that blends into a pair of wings and a pickaxe. I don't know if they all have meanings or were picked randomly, but they are true works of art.

I clear my throat, then get back in motion, trying to forget how insanely attractive this man I'm married to only on paper is. "What are you making?" I ask.

"Lentil spaghetti sauce," he says. "Although I can't promise it won't taste like shit."

I can't stop my smile from growing. I didn't want to hope he was cooking for the both of us, but a part of me obviously did.

"Not a big cook?" I ask, hopping on the counter like we did a few nights back. Something shifted between us that night in the dimness of our kitchen. Since then, we've lived our own lives as usual, but every evening I've been home and made dinner, he's joined me there and ate with me. Usually, the television was on and we didn't chat much, but just knowing he was there felt great.

"Usually I do okay," Carter says as he drains the pasta in the sink. "But I've never cooked a vegetarian recipe before."

Thankfully, his back is still to me, so he doesn't see the way my smile grows even more.

"I'm sure it'll be good."

He looks over his shoulder. "You have a lot of faith in me."

And I realize I do.

Not only in regards to his cooking abilities but about everything. I've been living with a man I know practically nothing about for weeks, and yet I've never felt safer in my own house. He might not be Little Mr. Sunshine, but for all his faults, he's never once scared me. Since I've been living on my own here, I've spent so many nights jumping up because I thought I'd heard a sound, tiptoeing through the house with a heavy water bottle I could swing around as a weapon. I haven't slept this well in years. Maybe I'm too trustful of Carter, or maybe he just gives me a sense of security.

He finishes making the sauce, then serves two plates on the kitchen counter, our dining spot of choice. We never make it to the formal dining table.

"So," I say after a few bites of delicious pasta, pausing the show he was watching, one about a rock band in the seventies. "I have a favor to ask you."

He hums, continuing to eat.

"I was wondering if you'd go on a live stream with me."

A choking sound comes from his throat, and after I tap his back twice, he swallows forcefully. "Why?" he rasps out.

"Because my followers have been asking day and night about you, and I think if we give them a few crumbs, they'll let it go." I take a sip of water. "Plus, it'll make the whole thing more believable."

"I don't know," he says, now picking at his food. "I told you I don't do social media."

I almost feel bad at how uncomfortable he is, but not enough to let it go.

"Come on! It'll be fun. And short, I promise."

"What would I need to do?" he asks, and I grin.

"Nothing. Just, like, answer a few questions. Look cute."

His eyes roll upward, then he says in a lower, almost shy, voice, "I don't like being in front of cameras."

"Gotta get used to it, mister up-and-coming producer of the year." When he doesn't react, I nudge him with my knee. "It'll be fine. I'll do most of the talking." Then I bring out the big guns. "Please?"

He side-eyes me, then sighs. "Fine. But no Twenty Questions, okay?"

I jump to my feet, plate in hand. "Scout's honor." I scurry to my room to prepare the setup, fluffy socks sliding against the parquet floorings of the hallway. "Thanks again for the food!"

Thirty minutes later, we're ready for showtime.

"You nervous?"

"No," he says, clearly nervous, hands clasped tightly.

I hide my smirk. "Good."

As I adjust the camera one last time, I roll my shoulders back, feeling some tension there. Even though I've done this kind of thing hundreds of times before, I feel tightness in my stomach at the thought of doing this. Now it will really, *really* be out there.

On the camera, it's obvious we're sitting way farther apart than a couple usually would, so I say, "Scoot over."

He does, only in the opposite direction.

"I meant closer to me, dummy."

Once again, he listens, a twinkle in his eyes. "Bossy when we're nervous?"

This time, I'm the one who shoots him the stink eye.

"All right, you ready?"

The moment he says yes, I turn the live stream on and start my usual welcome spiel.

"Hey, everyone. So, as you may have seen, I dropped a little bit of a bomb two weeks ago, and while I initially wanted to keep this a secret, I don't think I can any longer." I turn to Carter, who's looking straight into the camera like I would at a grizzly bear. I kick him under the frame, making him snap his head my way. My smile must look incredibly fake as I widen my eyes at him, hoping he'll start acting a little more natural if we want this to actually work. "This is Carter, my husband, and we're going to answer a few questions you have for us today." Then I take his hand in mine. It's stiff as a rock, but I don't let it go, and eventually, he seems to relax, his fingers becoming softer between mine.

Thank God.

This is the first time we hold hands, and for some reason, it doesn't feel as strange as I would've expected it to, at least for me.

"So let's see what we have." I start scrolling through the comments on the live, ignoring the hundreds of exclamations and going right to the questions, reading them aloud.

"How long were you together before getting married?" I read, and immediately I realize what a crappy idea this was. We didn't even think to get our stories straight beforehand. I turn to Carter, who's watching me, and now, instead of being nervous, he almost looks amused as if he knows I'll be the one to have to get us out of this mess.

Sucker.

I smile again, hoping the heat in my face isn't too obvious on people's phones. "We actually just met a while ago, and we didn't date long before knowing we wanted to marry each other. Right, boo?"

He blinks, then grits out, "Love at first sight."

I almost laugh at that. *Sure.*

"All right, next question." I scroll through a few I *really* don't want to answer, like why I never spoke about him before or what details of our wedding I can share, and wait until I find a good one.

"Oh, here's a good one." I turn to Carter, doe-eyed. "Carter, what did you first notice about Lil that made you fall?"

I expect him to grit his teeth and answer something stupid, but once again, he surprises me by actually appearing to think about it. Then he says in a rough voice, "Her hair."

Automatically, I bring a hand to my ponytail. Most of the time, having long, thick hair annoys me, but I do love the way it looks. Apparently, Carter might too. Unless he's acting.

I go to turn to the phone to scroll some more, but Carter interrupts me by putting an arm around my shoulder, tucking me closer to him. "What about you?"

A wave of warmth drenches my body, feeling every hard line of him against me. The smell of his laundry detergent and bodywash fills my nose, making me want to tuck in even closer. His arm feels like a weighted blanket over my shoulders, and the little arm hairs that come in contact with my neck make me shiver. He's decided to up his acting game, apparently. And then, I think of the question he's just asked and burn even more.

"I noticed his voice," I say to him more than the followers. It's not even a lie. He cursed at me before I ever saw him, and I remember how hot that voice sounded.

His cheek twitches. He's probably remembering the same scene I am.

Then the heathen decides to drag a finger down the side of my throat, making me inhale deeply.

Holy shit. This is nothing, and yet it feels so freaking sensual, especially done in front of an audience like this. He must notice the way his touch affects me because the look he sends me is pure evil. "What about my voice?"

That little shit.

Since we met, I've seen multiple different facets of Carter, but this teasing side is new to me, and I hate it almost as much as I like it.

I could lie, but I decide I can do better than that. Instead, I lean closer to him and whisper, loud enough so everyone can hear, "I don't think I can answer that in front of an audience."

When I pull away, I notice I'm not the only one who's flushed now, his pupils so wide the murky green of his irises has almost disappeared. He seems to have finally forgotten the camera, his attention only on me, his finger still tracing subtle lines on my skin. I don't know whether I'll be thankful for the loss of this overwhelming sensation when the live is cut off or if I'll crave more. It doesn't matter, though. For now, it feels like I've gotten the upper hand, even if only in appearance. I smile triumphantly, then return to my feed of questions.

We answer a few more, although the next ones I select are tamer. I'm hot enough as it is, and I think Carter's suffered enough too. I only let it last a few more minutes, but I can see this little broadcast has done its job. Comments flood the chat, showing things like *Look at them!* and *Please, I want someone to look at me like that too*, so I'd say we did a pretty good job convincing people.

When we finally wave goodbye—or rather, I wave and Carter gives his classic nod and moody look—I turn the live stream off and let myself sprawl back on the couch, eyes closed. It feels like I've just run a race, and I'm not sure why.

I expect Carter to berate me after putting him on the spot, or maybe even leave downstairs without a word, but he surprises me by saying, "Boo?"

I laugh, straightening my body. "I panicked, okay?"

"Uh-huh," he says, not making a move to leave. He also doesn't bring up whatever happened back there, and I don't plan on doing so either.

"I have to say, I'm glad we have more proof of our relationship out there," I say, undoing my ponytail that was giving me a headache, and when I catch his gaze tracking the movement of my fingers running through my hair, I try not to think about his statement from earlier. "I've kind of been worried about getting quizzed about you at some point and not knowing the answer and then getting arrested for fraud by the FBI or something."

"Is this what actually keeps you up at night?" This earns me another twitch of his lips, one that feels like a precious treasure I'll need to polish and hold on to so I can examine it further when I'm alone. "You don't think the FBI has bigger fish to fry than spying on you?"

"How would you know?"

Another fraction of an inch up. "You won't get arrested."

"Again, how would you know? Ever been arrested?"

Something changes in his face as he remains silent.

I gasp. "Oh my God, you have! What for?"

"I thought we weren't playing twenty questions."

"We're not. This is one."

He blinks, not finding me funny at all. When he sees I'm not budging, he drags a hand over his jaw. "Can't we start with an easier one?"

"You haven't, like, hurt anyone, right?" Maybe my initial reaction of feeling safe with him was a bad one, after all.

"Course not," he exclaims, face twisted in disgust, and for some reason, I trust it.

"All right. Then..." Something easy. "Favorite color?"

Even that takes him a moment to answer, like he has to think about it. I have a feeling getting answers out of him will be like prying bricks out of a wall.

When he finally answers, he stares right at me. "Blue."

Huh. I would've expected something like black, considering that's all he wears, but I'll take it.

"See? Wasn't that hard." I shift onto the couch so I'm sitting on my heels, facing him. "Now another."

"Fireball..."

"What? I need to know more in case I get interviewed by an FBI spy." I grin, knowing very well this is a ridiculous excuse, yet also grasping at any straws that would allow me to know more about the man I married.

He rolls his eyes, a move that must be part of his DNA, and mutters something under his breath.

But still, he indulges me.

Chapter 15

"Lilianne Valeria DiLorenzo, what the hell have you done?"

The tone my grandmother uses is even more frightening than her words, especially since this is the first thing she utters the second I pick up her call.

"Nan?" I ask, afraid that something tragic happened and I missed it.

"Please tell me this was a prank and you didn't get married in secret."

My jaw hangs open and I let myself fall backward onto my bed, my laundry forgotten on the floor. "How…"

"I watch those videos you make. You know this," Nan says, almost obviously rolling her eyes at me.

"No, I *didn't* know."

Shit. Of course I didn't know. If I did, I wouldn't have boasted about my new husband online before calling her. Not that I actually planned on telling her anything. I knew that lying to Nan would be close to impossible, but sharing the truth wasn't an option either. I was secretly hoping I could prevent Nan from ever learning about Carter's existence or the fact that we're married. That was probably hopeful naiveté on my part.

"I can't believe my only granddaughter had the guts to get married without even telling me. Is that a way to treat an old lady?"

Dramatic as ever. "I'm sorry, Nan, I—"

"Don't apologize. Make it up to me instead." She huffs. I can imagine her pacing inside her studio apartment, curlers in her hair and a flowery robe on her back, holding a pencil between her index and middle finger to help with the urge to pick up a cigarette instead. She only smokes on special occasions, as she likes to say, but it's not the temptation that's missing. Although maybe today, she settled on an actual one and opened the window so as not to get the residence administration on her back. That would be just like her. "I'm waiting for you and whoever this man is to be at my place at noon, and you better not be a second late." Then she hangs up, leaving me babbling into the disconnected call.

This is bad. Really bad.

If there's one person I can't say no to, it's Nan. First, because she wouldn't let me, and second, because she's the only family I have. Even as a child, I hated disappointing her, and the feeling has never gone away.

Which is why I immediately leave my room and holler, "Carter?"

It feels strange to be calling for him. I've never done so. Even though we eat most of our meals together, or at least side by side while I watch my TV show and he does what I think are sudoku puzzles on his phone, we rarely seek each other out, unless it's to ask if he's seen my hat somewhere or if I've touched his keys. Plus, we're rarely in the house at the same time, but it's Sunday morning, so it just so happens that we're both here.

Loud footsteps echo from the kitchen, all the way down to the hallway, and in seconds, he's in front of me, eyes wide. "What? What's wrong?"

"Oh," I say at the sight of his alarm. "Nothing. Well, nothing that bad, sorry."

His body visibly relaxes.

"Although I'm not sure you should be relieved yet." I take a careful step his way and try to give him my most charming smile. "I have another favor to ask."

"So, before we go in, I need you to promise to act the shit out of this," I tell Carter as we get closer to Nan's retirement home.

I have to force myself not to ogle at him while he drives. Ever since he came back from the basement dressed in a black crewneck and clean dark jeans that make his ass look ten out of ten, I've been trying my best not to drool over him, but it's more difficult than you would think.

He throws me a quick look. "What's up with that?" he asks.

Hoping he didn't bust me staring at him, I say, "She can't know the truth. Ever."

"You think your grandmother would blab about us?"

"No. I think the truth would devastate her."

Outside the window, the overflowing trees create a blur of color that's almost neon green. Spring has always been my favorite season for that reason. Everything is so vibrant, so electric. It feels like the entire world is coming back to life, more intense than ever before.

Carter doesn't say anything, but I can feel in the silence that he's waiting for me to elaborate. And after more than a month of being married to him, I guess it's time I tell him at least some part of the story.

"I've been sick pretty much my entire life."

While Carter's attention remains ahead, his grip tightens around the steering wheel, balancing his fingers.

"Diagnosed in childhood with a disease that pretty much destroyed my kidneys little by little until they were unusable and I had to go on dialysis. Started it at thirteen years old, three times per week, four hours per session. There was nothing else to do while I was put on the transplant waitlist to receive a new kidney.

"As you can imagine, all those treatments cost a pretty penny, and it's always just been me and my dad. He had good health insurance that covered most of the costs, but he still had to work twice as hard to pay for the difference."

Carter's throat bobs. He doesn't turn when he asks, "What about your mother?"

"What about her?"

"Where was she?"

"Left when I was two. Said she was destined for more than motherhood." My voice is calm, so unlike how it was at some point. "It used to haunt me when I first got diagnosed. Every time I sat in that dialysis chair while kids my age went to school and attended dances, I'd think about how my mother might've been a match. If she'd stayed, maybe she could've given me one of her kidneys and life could've gone back to something close to normal, but she was never there for me to even ask."

After a pause with only the sound of the engine between us, Carter says, "I'm really sorry, Lilianne."

"*Lil*. And it's fine." I inhale a deep breath. "It's fine. I've made my peace with it. And I did end up receiving my transplant after all without needing her help, so that's the best outcome I could've hoped for." My lips turn down, and I have to force my voice to remain steady. "I'm just sad my father never got to see it. He died before he got the chance to live the moment we'd been waiting for for years."

I wish this didn't make me so emotional, but I can't help it. Every year, when I baked Dad a cake for his birthday, he told me he'd wished for random things while blowing his candles, but I always knew it was a lie. I don't think he ever spent one wish—birthday cake, eyelash, shooting star—on something other than my transplant.

When I got the call that they had found a match for me almost four months after his death, my first reaction wasn't to jump around, but to break down into sobs because he'd missed it by so little. The one thing he wanted more for me than even I did.

I blow out a breath, blinking fast, then I clear my throat. "Anyway. So after an operation and expensive anti-rejection medications I still had to take, my medical debt started building up, and without my father's insurance, there was no way for me to be able to continue paying it forever—which is where you came in." I don't know why Carter's gaze makes me blush just then, but it does. "And while my life is just fine, I know my nan would feel terrible to know I got married because I was struggling financially instead of asking her for help. I know her. She'd have moved out of her residence and into a cheaper one to help me, and I couldn't have lived with myself."

There. It's done. Now Carter has most of the pieces of the puzzle and he can do whatever he wants with them.

When he remains silent as he turns onto the nursing home's parking lot, I start questioning whether he needed to know all that. Maybe he's judging me for lying to my grandmother. Maybe he thinks it's stupid that I didn't try harder to find a job with benefits when I need them so badly. Maybe he even thinks he's regretting marrying me now that he knows I'll be using his insurance policy a lot and it might raise suspicions on the legitimacy of our marriage.

However, he qualms all those doubts when he parks the car and exits before rushing to open my door, extending his hand my way. I hesitate, gaze going from his long fingers to his serious brows. We haven't touched since the livestream a few days ago, and that was only pretending.

My hesitation doesn't last long, though. I trust this man, for whatever reason, and if he wants to take my hand, there's no reason for me to say no. His palm is warm against mine, and once I'm out of the car, he lets go of my fingers just to wrap his arm around my waist, making my breath catch in my throat. Then, with the most serious face, he says, "All right, wife. Let's give that woman the best show she's ever seen."

Chapter 16

"Weren't they amazing?"

I pull my hair away from my sweaty neck and into a high ponytail, chest still pounding after dancing for the entire two-hour show. Next to me, Lexie and Wren look equally disheveled and equally awestruck. While I don't get to see Wren as much as I do Lexie since she lives with her husband, Aaron, in Boston, I love her just as much. She has health struggles of her own and understands me in ways that are sometimes difficult to explain.

"Yeah," Lexie says, fanning herself with her hands. "Been a while since I danced that much." She was right there with me taking videos of the show and posting them on her social media, which is going to be a win for the band since she has even more followers than I do.

"You're more than welcome to join more shows during the tour." I hook my arms with theirs as I lead them toward the backstage area, where the band's planning to host an after-show party.

"Might take you up on that," Wren says. "Also, if I wasn't happily married, I would comment on how hot that lead singer is."

"And if I wasn't getting married in a few weeks, I'd be telling you the same thing," Lexie adds as we make our way through the rapidly filling VIP room, all of our eyes finding Ethan, a cocktail in one hand and the other resting on some girl's thigh.

"What about you?" Lexie asks, taking a sip out of her vodka soda. "Isn't your marriage...open?"

I did tell her that—and told Wren too, when I ended up confessing the whole thing during one of our regular phone calls. I trust her and Aaron as much as I do Lexie and Finn.

Ethan's boisterous laughter resonates through the room. He's sitting with the rest of the band, in the middle as usual, a leader with them just like he is on stage. With his boyish features and easy personality, he has everything needed to be the face of a band that'll make it big. However, when I look at him, I feel nothing, except maybe a sense of friendship. Nothing about him makes me catch my breath or feel even an inkling of lust.

"That'd be a very bad idea." I grab a water bottle from one of the ice-filled tubs spread throughout the room.

"Why's that?" Wren says, doing the same.

"We kind of work together, for one." Carter might be the one who officially "hired" me, but every member of Crash & Burn considers me the band's media person. "And I don't think I could do it while being married." It doesn't matter that everything about the arrangement is fake and I don't owe Carter faithfulness—especially since *we* don't even sleep together. As stupid as it sounds, I made vows and I don't think I could break them in good conscience. Plus, I haven't been with anyone in almost two years. What's two more?

With a devilish smirk, Lexie asks, "Why? Think your husband might be jealous?" Then her gaze moves to a spot behind me, and that is when I feel it: that telltale pressure on my back as if my skin has been grazed.

I glare at Lexie, who's still grinning like a cat before peeking behind my shoulder, and sure enough, there he is. The one man who actually makes something flip inside my stomach with a single look, no matter how annoyed it makes me. He's standing alone in a corner of the room, back leaned against the wall, posture almost casual, but not. I've spent enough time with him in the past weeks to know when Carter is truly relaxed and when he's trying to appear so. And now, with his gaze straight on me, I know this is pretense.

Not knowing what the protocol is for meeting your fake husband out into the wild, I settle on a smile and a wave, which he doesn't return, only giving me a barely there dip of his head.

My ponytail flies as I whip around and ask, "How long has he been here?" He wasn't even supposed to come tonight. Or at least I assumed he wasn't. I attended the last two local shows on my own, so I didn't think of asking him if he was planning on being here tonight. He has no reason to attend the shows unless the band's planning on recording right before or after them.

Wren and Lexie both shrug, but while Lexie only gives me a shit-eating grin, Wren answers, "A while."

I don't know what that's supposed to mean, and I don't think I'm going to ask.

"And here he comes." Delight coats Lexie's voice.

"Time for us to leave anyway," Wren says, bumping Lexie. "Aaron and Finn are waiting for us."

"Traitors," I hiss before giving them both a big hug. "I still love you."

They turn to leave right as Carter says, "Looking at anything interesting?"

I turn, only to find him much closer than I initially thought. I have to crane my neck to see him in full, all furrowed brows and tight jaw—the man's going to have the deepest frown wrinkles when he's older.

I smile at him, not even having to fake it. I don't know when having him around went from being awkward and tense to like I was hanging out with a good acquaintance, but I'm so glad it did. Then I process his words and follow his gaze, which is stuck on Ethan, who's cackling once again.

My forehead creases at the way he's glaring. Is he...is he jealous?

Do I want him to be jealous?

"We were just commenting on how loud he is," I lie for some unknown reason. The girls were right. I did say we could date other people. Carter probably has. He might even have hooked up with some in my home. Still, I don't feel like telling him about the conversation we were having.

Carter hums, attention still lost somewhere in the room, and to make sure we can move on from the subject of Ethan, I say, "Didn't know you'd be coming tonight."

He shoves his hands in his pockets. "The house felt lonely."

It takes a second for me to wrap my head around his words, and my face lights up. Four words that are so simple, and yet I think it's the most true, personal thing he's ever said to me.

"You ready to go?" he asks.

"Oh." We didn't come in the same car, so I'm not sure why he's asking. "No, I'm gonna stay a bit."

"All right then," he says in that gruff voice of his that always finds a way to crawl under my skin. "See you at home."

"Wait." I grab his arm, then realize we might not be at the stage of casual touching yet when his muscles tense under me. I let him go. "Stay." I'm not sure what pushes me to say it except that it seems like we've just gotten to a good place and I don't want him to feel like he has to run away because I'm there.

He glances around the room. "Not really my scene."

"Just a few minutes."

His gaze flits to me, a muscle ticking in his jaw. "Five."

"Ten."

"No."

"Twenty, and that's my last offer." I wink, then lead him to where the band is sitting before he can change his mind.

"You're unbelievable," he says, following.

"Why, thank you," I say with a dumb smile. "Now sit down and have fun." I lean closer to him so I can whisper, "I think you might need it."

"I can't believe you thought they wouldn't find out about it," Emmett says thirty minutes later with a dumbfounded expression.

Everyone laughs at that comment because really, Bong *should* have expected it.

"I don't know, man, I'm not good at that kind of stuff," Bong says, letting his head hang back.

"Good at not dating two girls who are related at the same time?" I say with a chuckle at the same time Carter deadpans, "You're a dumbass."

The laughter that comes out of Emmett is so high pitched, it makes the whole situation even funnier.

The room is full of maybe twenty people who are either chatting in different corners with a drink in their hands or playing a game of poker on a table at the far back. Music is playing loud enough to create a warm ambiance but low enough that we can speak without it being a cacophony. I'm sitting next to Joe, with Carter leaned against the armrest next to me, arms crossed, his bicep brushing the top of my head with each of his movements. Everyone seems pretty buzzed, except for Carter and me. While I ordered a cocktail that was "as light as you can make it," Carter got himself a soda.

When I raised an eyebrow at him after ordering, he said, "I don't drink." And that was that.

Admittedly, I haven't attended a lot, but tonight's my favorite after-party of the tour. The energy is palpable in the air, like everyone is still reeling from the adrenaline rush of the show. Even Carter seems to have gotten more relaxed, which should probably earn me a trophy.

"Can I join you for a minute?"

We all turn to a man who must be in his early forties, with black gelled hair and thick-framed glasses, wearing a dress shirt and jeans that are a little too skinny for my taste.

"Vince, hey," Ethan says, lifting his beer at him.

"Great show tonight, guys," Vince says, making eye contact with each member of the band. "Looking promising for the rest of the tour."

"And hopefully the sales will follow," Bong says.

"Cheers to that," Ethan says, once again lifting his drink to all of us. When his eyes meet mine, he stands. "Oh, Vince, this is Lil. She's the one I was telling you about. Lil, this is our agent, Vince."

Vince turns to me. "Right. You're the one who's been putting Crash & Burn on the map."

I stand to meet his extended hand and shake it. "Nice to meet you. And I haven't been doing much." Which is pretty much the truth. Except for posting here and there and attending shows to gather content, I haven't done anything, only showcasing their talent.

Heat builds behind me as a heavy arm falls onto my shoulders, fingers tickling my arm. I don't need to look to know whose arm it belongs to. I recognize his smell—bergamot and something spicy. I recognize his presence too, like something my body is attuned to.

"Carter," Vince greets, voice solemn.

The grump doesn't say anything, probably only giving him one of his usual nods. Goose bumps rise on my arms as the tips of Carter's fingers trace my arm, the movement so careless, so small, yet it feels like my entire nervous system redirects to this patch of skin, like I consist of only this.

"Your girl's somewhat of a big thing, apparently," Vince says.

Carter's body moves even closer to me, the heat of his skin making me burn as his free hand falls onto my hip and carefully squeezes.

I feel like both tensing away from him and leaning into his touch. He hasn't been this close since our livestream, and I hate that I like it. Hate that I wish, even for only a second, that he didn't have to wait for an opportunity to fake our relationship to touch me.

And yet I don't know why he's faking so well right now. This is different than when we pretended for my grandmother. Then I did my best to act as in love as possible with a brush here and a squeeze there, trying to fool someone who could easily read through me. We touched because it was necessary, and it seemed to work. Nan didn't bat an eye, only gushing over how handsome Carter was and how she would "never forgive me" for not telling her about him first. But here, we could easily convince Vince that Carter and I are a real couple without touching. He doesn't know us. We could be a private, modest couple.

Yet modest is the opposite of how we are right now. Carter is so close that the whiskers of beard scratch my temple, hands tracing shapes on my body that feel like they're being tattooed on my flesh.

I'm warm. Too warm.

I also don't want this moment to end.

"By the way, Vince, about the tour..." Ethan begins.

Their manager ends up taking a seat next to the singer, and while I go to sit back in my place, Carter gets ahead of me and steals my spot.

I watch him for a moment before he subtly taps his thigh.

Oh God.

This is a bad idea. I'm already too riled up. I don't know how much longer I'll be able to pretend his touch doesn't affect me.

I can't hesitate too long, though. There are still people in the room who, for all intents and purposes, believe Carter and I are married, and it wouldn't make any sense for a wife to refuse to sit in her husband's lap.

In the end, he doesn't allow me to question it any longer, instead tugging me by the hand until I fall back onto him, his scent enveloping me even more than before.

His breath tickles my ear before he whispers, "Relax."

I turn, then whisper-hiss, "You relax."

"Thought you wanted this to be believable. Not afraid of FBI spies anymore?"

That man. That freaking man.

I last all of one second of seriousness before elbowing him, then lean my back against his chest, the picture of a perfect couple.

"Good girl," he whispers against my skin, then once again rests his hand on my hips, the contact as electric as ever.

My whole body is stiff as a rock. I shift on his lap, trying to find a position that allows for the least contact between our bodies, but in such a small seat, there aren't many options.

He squeezes my hip in a contact that probably looks loving but that feels like a warning. "I'd stop doing that if I were you."

"Hm?" I say, turning to him with my hair curtaining us away from the rest of the crowd.

He inhales sharply. "Stop. Fidgeting."

And that's when I feel it.

He's hard under me.

If I was hot before, I'm now a furnace, body frozen over him.

"Want me to get up?" I whisper-shout.

He clears his throat. "Please don't."

There's something in his voice that sounds a whole lot like embarrassment. It makes me smirk. Suddenly, I don't feel like the vulnerable one in this scenario.

"You started this, you know," I tell him.

"Oh, believe me, I know."

"That'll teach you," I say. Then, because I apparently love torturing him, I shift slightly, making him hiss through his teeth. His hand clenches tighter around my hip, but it doesn't succeed in keeping me still.

"Hey, lovebirds, what are you whispering over there?" Bong shouts at us.

I straighten, but my gaze shifts behind me. "Carter was just telling me about some water damage at home. A *big pipe* leaked, apparently."

Carter sputters something that he covers with a cough while Bong says, "Shit, really?" The rest of the guys chime in on their meager experience with plumbing, but my attention rests on Carter, who gives a small shake of his head.

"What did I do to get tied to a brat like you again?"

I grin. "I don't know. Must've been really good in a past life." Then, for good measure, I shift again, ever so slightly.

"All right, you're done," he says, making us both climb to our feet, keeping me in front of him.

I laugh, then go to walk away. "Oh, wait, I need to—"

He clamps an arm around my middle to keep me close as a shield, then says in a low voice, "You're the devil."

He's way too fun to mess with. I look up at him, then whisper, "Aren't you lucky to be stuck with me then."

Chapter 17

Carter

Three and a half years ago

If I can say one thing about Frank DiLorenzo, it's that he doesn't give up easily.

After that second meeting in the diner, I don't magically begin to pour out my life story to him, but I try to be less of an asshole about the whole thing, and that seems to be enough for him. As payment for me being civil, he tolerates us talking about literally anything else, so long as we meet once a week. He doesn't even rat me out to the judge about my lack of trying, so for that, I'll do all the small talk in the world. I begin by humoring him with answers when he comments on the Sox's shitshow of a season, and when he brings up his favorite movies during the next meeting, I can't help but butt in with my favorite picks—mostly because of their insane soundtracks—and somehow, during that one-hour session, he doesn't need to open his crosswords book once.

The following weeks look something like that too. We meet in a café or a restaurant, he asks me how my week has been, and when I say, "Fine," he opens his book, then begins chitchatting about life. Sometimes I join in, sometimes I only give one-worded answers while I, too, mess around in a sudoku book I bought at the convenience store down the road, and those sessions are fine by me.

I still attend the group meetings once every two weeks, but there, I can blank out and pretend I'm not there. All in all, things are fine. I don't feel like any of it helps keep away from drinking—that is out of sheer will alone—but it's not so bad either.

Except today, poor Next-Door-Neighbor Frank finds me in a mood I wouldn't wish upon anyone. It's not his fault, but I can't do anything about it. Not when I'm this fucked-up inside.

It started off with something so stupid, it shouldn't even have caused a reaction. I got a box of things in the mail. That's it. A box of things.

Except those were things I'd left behind when I escaped California and booked a one-way flight to Boston.

Once I was cleared by the medical staff and was able to leave the hospital after my accident, arm in a sling and soul shattered, I decided that had to be my wake-up call. I didn't even stop by the hotel where the band had been staying. I knew I didn't have enough self-restraint to go back there, to see the boys probably high out of their minds, still partying, and be strong enough to leave. So I got a taxi straight to the airport and booked a flight to the farthest place in the States that came to mind. I didn't know anyone in Boston, and that was just as well. All the people close to me were related to my career as a musician in one way or another, which meant no one was left when I quit.

And because I left so abruptly, I never went back to pick up the stuff I'd left in the hotel room. I never even emptied my studio apartment in LA—my landlord must've given my old furniture away to goodwill by now. I'd forgotten all about those things I'd left behind until I received the giant box to my new address here. I opened it up to find bunched up clothes, my computer, and most importantly, my favorite guitar.

It used to be, at least. Ever since my father sat me down at four years old and decided I would become a guitar player, not a day went by when I didn't play. That specific guitar is the one I bought the day we signed our record deal.

This morning, seeing it in its case almost made me want to puke. I both wanted to tug it close to my chest and throw it out the window. I slowly opened the case and dragged my fingers over its silk-soft black wood, chipped around the body from so many sessions of heavy playing. I hadn't touched a guitar in over four months. My fingers itched to pick it up and play.

My relationship with the instrument has always been strange. When I was a kid, I made myself sick over it. My parents said I'd be good, and so I would be. I'd play all the time. When my classmates attended birthday parties, I played. When they won spelling bees, I played. When they hung out over the weekends, you guessed it: I played. I didn't care how much it overwhelmed everything in my life. When my mother would look up from her phone and pause a few minutes to listen to me play, then come to kiss the top of my head and tell me how good I was, it was worth all the sacrifice in the world.

Then, when I got old enough to understand that my mom and dad sucked at being parents and didn't actually want kids, only little music prodigies like the clients they focused all their energy on representing, I decided to say fuck it. They wanted me to play? I would do everything I could not to. I wouldn't bend over backward to please them anymore. It made no sense. They'd never *see* me, and I recognized that now. The thing was, at that point, I was addicted. The guitar was my safe space. It was what I did when I wanted to drown out my parents' shouting matches in the kitchen, or when I wanted to comfort myself when I realized I was seventeen and didn't have a single friend, like a goddamn loser. Plus, I was good at it. Playing brought me some sense of comfort I'd never found anywhere else. So, at that point, I started playing in secret. Hiding from my parents because I didn't want them to think I was their little puppet anymore, but I also couldn't walk away from it. I didn't want the guitar to be theirs anymore. I wanted it to be mine and mine alone. I could play for hours, and nothing could ever come close to it.

At some point, when I realized it was the one thing I was good at and Brandon asked if I was ready to go all in with him, I did what any sane person would do: I said yes and followed him wherever he wanted. I wasn't dumb enough to say no to that, even to piss my parents off.

Our band got a surprisingly good start, even with two players who had contacts in the industry, and soon enough, we were signing contracts and playing gigs with big names and being invited to parties, and I lost myself in that. In a way, the guitar led me to where I am now, which is an alcoholic who has nothing and no one, except for this one man waiting for me at the café table, sitting by himself. The one who somehow hasn't given up on me yet.

Seeing my guitar this morning only reminded me of everything I lost along the way. Most importantly, I had to give up the one thing that ever made me content. I can't play anymore—it's too tangled up in my mistakes, in my drinking.

The fact that no note was in the box didn't help either. I know Brandon's the one who sent it. He's the only one who has my new address, purely for business purposes. We still had contracts and engagements going on when I left. I can see my own fault in that, in destroying everyone around me by trying to save myself, but it still hurt when the only person I'd ever felt was actually on my side decided I wasn't worth a single word to him.

I spent the day looking at that guitar still sitting in my living room, almost like a living entity that was taunting me with everything it had ever given me before taking it all away. Every glance made me tenser, turning me into a roiling cloud of anger.

And I wanted to drink. I wanted to drink so fucking bad it physically hurt. I kept thinking about that bottle of gin still hidden under my kitchen sink, and I could picture draining it so easily. I craved the burning in my throat, the haziness that would get over me almost instantaneously. The only thing that kept me from doing it was the idea that *this* was all I had. My sobriety. I'd left everything for it. How sad would it be if I didn't even have that?

Still, I shouldn't have come tonight. I'm too on edge. I can see this when I sit in front of Frank and realize my hands are still shaking.

He briefly looks up from his crosswords. "Hey, Carter." Then he does a double take. "Everything okay?"

I don't answer. If I say something, I have a feeling it'll all come out like a nuclear bomb touching ground and hitting everything it can reach, and he doesn't deserve that. Logically, I can see this.

But when he asks again, "What's wrong?" I can't help it.

"Everything, Frank. Every. Fucking. Thing." I drag a hand through my hair that's in dire need of a trim, strands falling over my brows. "There's no point anymore, so I won't talk to you about weather or a fucking cookie recipe. I'm done."

I expect him to explode back, the way my own father does. I start a reaction in chain, a kindle that eventually becomes a forest fire. I give it bad, he gives it worse. Of course, that was back when he still talked to me. My brother might have yelled at me with expletives and insults when I left, but at least he cared enough to say something. My parents didn't even bother with a call or a text. I'd failed—worse, quit—at the one thing they'd ever expected from me, so what was left after that?

However, Frank does the opposite of that. Instead, he closes his book, leans forward, and says, "No point in what, Carter?"

So that's the part he stuck on.

"In everything," I say, maybe sounding dramatic, but I don't know how else you could see my situation. I have no family, no friends, no career, no prospect for the future, not even the hobby I used to love. I have money from the royalties we made, but what worth is that when I've got no one to share it with?

I have nothing.

"You seem angry," he says in that annoying, calm voice of his.

"No shit."

"Who are you angry at?"

The muscles in my jaw tighten so much, pain rises to my forehead and then to my scalp. My hands bunch, my feet push against the floor, and my shoulders squeeze up to my ears. The tension has to release one way or another.

"The entire world," I say, loud enough that a couple a table over looks up at me. I ignore them, focusing on the way Frank's stare holds mine as if he wants me to stay, to keep on talking. I realize just then I've fallen right into his trap, but I can't make it out. Not anymore. He wants me to talk? Fine. I'll talk. "I'm angry at everyone who's ever crossed my path. I'm angry at the people who offered me drinks when I was already trashed. I'm angry at the girls who climbed me during parties when I was too drunk to even realize what was going on. I'm angry at my parents for not preparing me better for what was to come."

He looks at me so long, not even blinking away at the awkwardness of the held eye contact, that I let myself say the most accurate part of my answer, in a voice that's barely a whisper now. "I'm angry at myself."

I'm the one who decided to join the band. I'm the one who never said no when I was offered a drink. I'm the one who lost control so much that I had to break the one thing my only brother had ever wanted. I'm the one who ruined all the relationships around me.

I'm the problem.

And when Frank nods along, with his preppy sweater and his square glasses, looking like the most squeaky-clean human you could come across, I spit out, "Don't act like you know the feeling."

He stops moving. His body remains still for so long, I think I might've broken him. Then his lips quirk up.

Strangest man I've ever met.

"You think I've never been angry at myself?"

To be fair, I don't know that. I *can't* know that, mostly because I've never allowed him to actually start a conversation for us to get to know each other. I didn't want him to know me, and I didn't particularly want to know him either.

But now he's got me wondering. He's in AA. He used to have an alcohol problem. The probability of everything not being as it seems is high.

"Son, you don't know how many days I've spent hating myself." He shakes his head, still smiling, but this time, it looks sad. "Every time I hid in the pantry to gulp down vodka I'd hidden in vinegar bottles while my daughter was playing Barbie in the living room next door, I wanted to die. I really, really did. Her mother had left me, and I couldn't cope, and I let myself drown while I still had my daughter to care for. She saved me from it, that's for sure, but even still, I'm so angry at myself for all the times I failed her, even if she never noticed."

I swallow.

"Being angry is part of the recovery. You'll never be more angry with anyone than you will be with yourself. It's the sad truth of it. But you wanna know something?"

I feel like a kid watching television, entranced by the shiny new toy being shown off, unable to blink away. I don't answer, but he must see how he's got me in the palm of his hand.

"It gets better. At some point, the anger dulls, and you learn to forgive yourself." He twists his coffee cup in a clockwise motion, over and over again. "It never truly goes away, but eventually, you see that some of the things you said and did were part of the disease, and you decide to move on from them."

I don't answer now either. I can't find the words to say just how badly he's hit the nail on the head and how much more I want from him. Suddenly, I want to hear all about what's going to happen next. He's gone through it, and it looks like maybe he's not as different from me as I thought he was. Maybe he fucked up just as badly. I don't know that he ruined his family like I did, but at this point, I can't get any lower than I am, and if he has something that can make me want to live even an inkling more, I'd say I want to hear what it is.

Frank leans back in his chair, looking smug. I can't fault him for it. He did make his point, in the end.

"Now, are you ready to get your head out of your ass and get to work?"

This time, I don't hesitate. I have nothing else to lose.

"Yes."

And so we truly begin.

Chapter 18

I wake up to a ruckus coming from down the hall.

I worked yesterday and didn't get home until three thirty in the morning, so even though my phone tells me it's 8:00 a.m., I still want to bang my head against the wall. Whoever's making all that noise better be happy I'm not grumpy in the morning.

Slippers on, I trudge over to where the sound is coming from, then stop dead in my tracks when I find all the honey-colored cabinet doors ripped off their hinges, Carter piling them on the floor, one of them still hanging halfway onto its hinges. Every inch of my messy cupboards is exposed, threatening to send me into a panic. *I really should have done a better clean-up before he moved in.*

"What's going on here?"

He looks up from where he's crouched in front of the island, noticing my presence for the first time.

"I'm removing the cabinets," he says, then goes back to unscrewing a door as if that was the most normal answer in the world.

"I can see that," I say, stepping closer to him while rubbing sleep off my eyes. "The question is why."

He lifts his head. "I opened a cupboard to grab a cup and almost left with the door, and I thought that was enough. Found a sanding machine in the garage." He lets out a grunt that has no right to sound sexy as he throws the door on top of the others. "I'll sand and paint them before reinstalling them properly."

Something clenches in my chest. That sanding machine. Dad bought it a few years ago, thinking he could do some of the work in the house by himself, but my health took a turn for the worse at that time, and he never got to pick it up again.

He never will either.

A crease forms between Carter's brows. "Hope you don't mind." Then he turns and looks up at the kitchen, which looks like a whole mess. "Yeah, maybe I—"

"Thank you," I say, voice choked up for some reason. Maybe because he's getting a step closer to achieving what Dad would've wanted for this place, or maybe because he's removed a huge weight off my shoulders by taking the lead on this project I knew needed to be done but couldn't get myself to pursue, or maybe just because he's taking his precious time to do this for me. "I really appreciate it."

"Course," he says, still frowning, studying me for a moment, then another. Finally, he breaks the contact to look at his phone, then stands. "I'll have to finish this later, though. The band's recording today."

"Can I come?" I ask, partly because I have no plans and partly because I have a feeling if I stay here alone and continue looking at this ongoing project, I'll feel never-ending grief I'd rather avoid.

Carter pauses wiping his hands to ask, "You want to?"

"Sure. It'll make good content." Anything to get me out of this place. I go get a cup from the—now open—cupboard to make some tea. "Oh, I could make it some sort of interview too afterward."

"Sure, yeah." He scratches his head. "I need to stop by my place while we're in Boston, though."

"Boston?"

"Yeah."

"Your job's in Boston? Like, you drive there every day?"

A pause, then, "Yeah?"

"And you have a place there."

"Are we just stating facts here or…"

"Oh my God, why didn't you tell me?" I never even thought to ask him where he used to live. Since we met so close to here, I assumed he was from the area too, but I should've thought it through. Carter works for a record label, and clearly, there are no record labels in the small towns of Vermont.

"Lilianne, it's fine."

"This makes no sense. You should go back to your place. We'll keep up with the pretense another way." Even as I say the words, they taste bitter in my mouth. As strange as it felt to have him in my space initially, I think it'd be hard to go back to the way it was. Waking up in a small space that finds a way to feel so incredibly vast. Losing the safety net I've started to feel when he's around. Not being able to see his "kill me now" face every time it's my turn to pick a movie to watch while we eat dinner—apparently, Mr. Carter only likes movies when they have "great soundtracks or interesting acting." Of course he couldn't enjoy films for their plots like any normal human being. Just for that, when it's my day, I always pick the most random movies I can think of, usually ones with terrible artistry that I still enjoy thoroughly.

"I don't mind the drive."

"Carter." I stand straight, only realizing how close we are to each other when I feel his breath on my forehead.

His thumb lightly chucks my chin. "Lilianne," he says in that infuriating way, never once having shortened my name. "I'm fine."

"I don't want you troubling yourself." *For me*, I refrain from adding.

"I'm not." His mouth ticks. "The company's okay here." Then, before I can react, he's stepping backward with a stern, "We're leaving in ten. Better get changed."

I look down at my clothes, realizing I'm still in the Christmas pajamas I wear year-round, those that are a size too small but that I can't get rid of because they're too soft. Appropriate when I used to be alone in here, but maybe I should've thought twice about coming out in them today.

Except when I bring my attention back to Carter, it's to find his eyes skimming me over. The shirt barely covers my stomach, leaving a slit of skin that he seems to have gotten stuck on. He's only wearing jeans and a black T-shirt, and yet I feel naked next to him. I pull the hem down, breaking the strange trance he seemed to be in as if restarting normal speed after a slow-motion scene.

Carter looks back at the kitchen, studying something. "Meet you at the car." Then he disappears down the stairs.

I remain in place for a long moment before rushing to get ready, wondering whether I imagined it all or not, and what it'd mean that I hoped it was real.

"What are you doing?"

"What does it look like I'm doing?" I ask as I shut the passenger door behind me.

The building Carter has parked in front of is in the older part of the city, and while it's nothing fancy, the place looks well-kept, with four stories and a dark-brown brick exterior. Children are drawing shapes in the street with multicolored chalk, while an elderly couple is rocking in their chairs on one of the upper balconies.

Carter doesn't move from his spot next to the car, staring.

"I'm coming in," I end up saying.

"You don't have to," he says, which I translate to *please don't come inside my place*.

"If you thought I wouldn't get my nosy ass into your stuff to discover all your deepest, darkest secrets, then you're wrong, *boo*."

His face loses some of its color, which only makes me grin. "Come on. Show me what Andrew Carter's natural habitat looks like." I start walking toward the building, and eventually, he has no choice but to follow.

"Less messy than yours, that's for sure."

I gasp audibly. "I'm not messy."

He throws me a look.

"I'm *not*," I repeat as he opens the front door and leads us through an old but cozy lobby to the elevator. He presses the button and the doors automatically open.

We step inside. "Tell that to the hundred chocolate bar wrappers strewn all around the house," he says.

"I like to snack. Sue me."

He snickers, a side of his lips curling up, and just like the last time I saw his face light up with a smile, a *whoosh* goes through my chest.

"What about the socks you keep littering all over the place?"

"I'm always cold and like to be prepared." The elevator doors open, leading us to a narrow corridor with only three doors. I straighten my shoulders. "Plus, I'm not the one we're supposed to be roasting today. That's all you."

Carter takes the lead, stopping in front of the first apartment we come across. Then he unlocks the door and opens it to me.

I'm not sure whether I'm disappointed or pleasantly surprised that I have nothing to roast him about, after all. Carter's place is…lovely. I expected a bachelor pad or, based on the way he brought nothing to the basement, an air mattress thrown on the floor with a television and nothing else. But that's as far from the truth as possible. Natural sunlight wafts in, illuminating the dark leather couch and kitchen table in buttery yellows. It's a small space that's not cluttered but that also feels lived in. Apart from the open-air kitchen and living room, there seems to be one other room at the other end of the hallway.

I take slow steps, soaking it all in, trying to memorize every detail. Knowing Carter, I'll probably never get a glimpse of his universe like this again, and I don't want to miss anything. Not the live plants decorating the space. Not the neatly stacked books in the hanging shelves, or the checkered rags in the kitchen, or the guitar leaned on a stand in the corner of the living room.

I let my hands drag over the strings, picking at a few to play a false note. "You play?"

He tracks the movement of my fingers as he says, "Used to."

The black-on-black instrument is so him, I can almost picture it. The way he'd look with the guitar in his hands, careful, focused, face tight as he'd play every note with diligence. He'd forget about the world like he does when he's watching one of his historical fiction movies or when he's looking for the missing number in his sudoku square like it's a mathematical equation that will determine the fate of the world. Sometimes, he doesn't even notice I'm watching, too lost in his own mind, his pen always tapping the same corner of his jaw where a small mole resides, a bull's-eye for his fidgeting.

"Why'd you stop?"

I'd swear I don't imagine the faraway look in his eyes as he says, "Another life."

I hum, then continue exploring, not wanting to dig into something he'd clearly rather keep hidden. We've come to build a careful kind of trust, one that's constructed brick by brick but that could easily crumble with the wrong question. I've come to see he doesn't want me to be hunting for answers, but by catching information here and there and holding onto it, I'm getting better and better at figuring out who Andrew Carter truly is.

"I'll be back," Carter says before disappearing into what I assume is his bedroom, probably doing whatever it was he needed to do by coming here.

My feet take me to the books, my curiosity piqued, and I chuckle when I start reading the titles.

"Who would've known you were such a nerd?"

The grump comes out of the room with a stony face, making me laugh even more.

"Big fan of hobbits?" I follow him to the patio door.

He spins on his heels. "I've seen the kind of books you read. You're really not in a place to judge my hobbits."

My jaw drops open. I thought my discreet covers made me subtle when I read steamy romance books, but I guess they didn't.

"Opened them up to read?" I ask.

"No need. You should see the way you blush when you get to *those* parts."

Of course that is when my body once again decides to betray me by making my face burst into flames. Stupid pale skin and stupid vascular dilation.

Amusement is written all over his face even without a smile as he turns around and opens the patio door. The bastard knows he's right.

"What are you—" I lose my words as I try to wrap my head around what I'm seeing.

A large, likely handmade wooden bird feeder is hanging from a hook on the patio ceiling, and here is Carter, putting what looks like bird kibble into the feeder. Almost immediately after he steps back, a brown bird flies to the feeder, picking at a few bites before flying off. Carter doesn't look away, an expression of peace—or is it contentment?—overtaking his face. Like this is his safe place.

I can't stop staring as Carter puts food into a second feeder, then picks up a watering can that's exactly like the one Nan owns and starts watering his plants, both inside and outside the apartment. This man, who shows such a tough exterior and an unapproachable air, comes back to his Boston place to keep the birds fed and the plants watered.

I misjudged him. I really did.

When he's done, he comes to get me with a, "Ready?"

I nod, then follow him out. Only once we're in the elevator do I say, "I really like what you did with the place." We're both shoulder to shoulder, staring at the metal doors, unmoving.

"Thanks."

"And with the feeders. Built yourself a real little zoo up there."

He exhales in what can be considered a laugh, then shifts on his feet. "I was a little lonely."

I hold my breath, waiting for him to say something else to erase that moment of vulnerability he just had, but he doesn't. As if it needed to come out, like he's waited a long time to tell someone how those birds that come and go might have been his saving grace.

I don't want to speak for fear of breaking the rare, fragile bubble he's just blown around the two of us, one that might burst the second those elevator doors open. Instead, I take a step closer and, still facing the doors, let my head lean to the side, just enough so it can rest on his musky-smelling arm, his skin warm against my temple.

Maybe he and I aren't so different after all.

Chapter 19

"Cheers to a second record!"

We all clink our glasses at Ethan's celebratory statement, the Irish pub loud and alive around us. It's packed for a Tuesday night, probably because of the live music happening in the opposite corner of the restaurant.

"Thanks for allowing me to experience this with you guys," I say before I take a sip of my ginger ale.

They've only worked on one song today, but they're off to a great start. As amazed as I was to see them in concert, witnessing their creative process in the studio is even more impressive. The way Joe would come up with a random guitar riff on his own, and Ethan would find lyrics on the spot, and Bong would test two or three different beats on his drums, and suddenly, there was a chorus. A *good* chorus. I'd never witnessed such raw talent in the same room, and I spent the entire day with my jaw open, forgetting to record content because I was too busy trying not to fangirl.

But my biggest surprise of the day was Carter. The ideas he came up with, the instructions he gave that instantly elevated the melodies, the sheer focus in his eyes as he put the headset on and dipped his chin slightly with the music only he heard... I couldn't tear my eyes away. It was mystifying to behold his talent, to realize how he'd sometimes make something out of nothing as if using magic. It was all too much for someone who's trying her damnedest not to be attracted to her fake husband. I'd rarely seen anything sexier than Carter acting the perfect, professional producer, so into his job that an earthquake might have ripped through the room and he wouldn't have noticed. Attending today's recording session was both one of the most fun experiences of my life and a big, big mistake.

Still, I shot content for him too. After all, he's the one who's supposed to benefit from this arrangement. He told me earlier how he's been offered to produce for another promising band as if he wanted me to know that a part of our plan was working. I might have shrieked a little.

"Of course," Ethan says, then turns to Carter. "The first album could've put us on the map, but this one will really define us as a band."

"If the first one doesn't flop," Joe says, making us strain to hear.

"Don't say shit like that," Bong answers. "We're doing well." Then he leans his head on my shoulder. "Partly thanks to our beautiful Lil. You got me twenty thousand new followers."

I laugh, resting my head on his while I feel Carter reaching behind me to Bong, then lightly pushing him away. "Keep your paws to yourself."

"There's the caveman I was waiting for!" Bong replies.

"Fuck off."

This exchange only makes me laugh more.

"What's so funny?" Carter whispers in my ear from his seat next to mine, voice gruff, sending a ripple of chills down my back.

I turn and almost jump at the realization that he's this close. Our noses are almost brushing, his breath warm against my skin.

"You," I mouth.

Like this, it's as if we've cocooned ourselves from the cacophony of the table and the restaurant, like we've become invisible to everyone else.

Clearly, though, we're not.

"Hey, keep it to your bedroom."

My face flushes faster than the time it takes for Bong to finish his sentence, and I spin back to face everyone, doing my best to act as if the words he just used have disappeared into thin air. Meanwhile, I wait for Carter's rebuttal of Bong's statement, hoping I won't hear disgust or incredulousness in his voice at the thought of truly being with me. Since he's been nothing but the perfect gentleman at home—at least in terms of physical contact and sex—I don't know how he views me, but I like to think he acts this way out of respect and not because he couldn't fathom being with me.

However, the only thing Carter ends up saying is, "Again, fuck off."

I chuckle, but this time, it's not as lighthearted. Everyone seems to be wondering why he didn't outright deny it, including me. The longer the guys stare at us with weird smirks, the warmer I feel.

"Did you guys know Carter plays the guitar?" I blurt, hoping something, anything, can take the attention away from me.

It works.

Faces turn from confusion to amusement. "Dude, are you serious?" Emmett asks me, putting his beer down with a heavy thud.

"Yeah?"

He turns to Carter. "You haven't told her?"

"Told me what?"

"Nothing," Carter says, voice low.

"Nothing? Dude. Please." Emmett's eyes meet mine. "Your husband was the guitarist for Fickle."

"Fickle?" I ask.

"Just a Grammy-nominated band that earned more recognition in its three years of existence than most musicians ever will in a lifetime."

I turn to Carter, expecting him to be rolling his eyes or telling Emmett to stop messing with me, but the only thing I find when I look at him is perfect neutrality, only hindered by a light flare of his nostrils.

"Is that true?" I ask.

"It's been a long time," is his dumb answer.

"So?" I can't believe I didn't know something so important about the man I've been living with for the past two months.

"So it doesn't matter anymore."

I huff. Only a guy would say something like that.

As if realizing he spoke too fast, Emmett changes the subject, bringing up the next few venues we'll be going to. Everyone joins in, save for me. Instead, I pull out my phone and begin my research. And while Carter sits right next to me and has his gaze turned down toward my screen, he doesn't try to keep me from doing it.

I spend the next fifteen minutes scrolling through articles on Google and then videos of the band playing on YouTube. At some point, I undo the band's name and type Carter's instead, and when I land on a scratchy phone video showing a man I barely recognize partying in a hotel room, with longer hair and a blazed out look as he holds a forty-ounce bottle in one hand and a joint in the other while slurring the lyrics to a song, Carter says, "Can you close that?"

I barely recognize his voice, and when I notice the begging look on his face, I oblige.

He might not have told me about that time in his life, but I have a feeling he doesn't tell anyone.

My mind is reeling when we get back into the car and start our drive home.

Searching the band online should've enlightened me, but it only brought forth more questions. There is so much online about the band, their rise to fame about six years ago, and then the sudden breakup three years later, but there's nothing about why they parted ways or what the members are doing now.

Well, I know the answer about at least one of the members.

"I can't believe you kept all this from me," I say after fifteen minutes of silence.

He doesn't need to ask what I'm referring to. "I didn't actively keep anything from you. I just never talk about it."

"Why?"

He sighs, rubbing his hand down the steering wheel. "It wasn't a great time in my life."

Probably referring to the video I landed on earlier.

"I still think you should've told me," I say, not wanting to bring up something he clearly didn't want me to find.

"Why? So you're ready for your FBI interviews?"

"Stop messing with me. It's important."

"No, it really isn't."

"To me, it is." I swallow. "I want to know you."

I don't bother being embarrassed at how true my words are. At this point, he probably knows it all.

His knuckles blanch for a moment. "You do. More than you think."

As much as I want to say that I've only scratched the surface of who he is, I have a feeling he's telling the truth. For him, what he's told me *is* a lot.

"Why did you guys break up?" I ask, going from another angle. "Seemed like you were doing well."

"That's a long answer."

"We have time."

He still doesn't explain, which probably means the problem isn't the length of the explanation but his keenness on sharing it with me.

I decide against asking for more, not wanting to make him clam shut, but after a long moment of silence, Carter says, "We were a ticking time bomb. It was…unhealthy. For me, at least. I decided to leave, and the band unfolded after that."

Okay. That's something, I guess.

Carter's jaw clenches and unclenches as he continues driving as if fighting himself over what he does and doesn't want to share. I don't say anything else. The only way for me to truly know him will be if he wants it so.

I should want to stay away, should stop looking for things he doesn't want me to have, but I'm hungry for all the scraps he can give me, and I can't stop, as pitiful as that makes me.

"I can't believe you've lived so much already," I say, hoping he'll be thankful for the slight shift in conversation.

"I'm older than you."

"Okay, grandpa."

He hooks one brow up.

"You're what, five years older than me? And it's as if you've lived an entire life already."

"It's not all it's hyped up to be."

"Still. You did it." I lean my head against the window while my fingers mindlessly tangle my hair in a braid. "I've barely started living mine."

"What is it you want to do that you haven't?"

"Everything?" I smile, although there's nothing funny about this. "I'm grateful for everything I have, but sometimes it feels like I've spent my life wishing for the day I could do whatever I wanted with no limits, and now that I'm here, I've barely scratched the surface." Living your dreams when you're crippled in debt, working two jobs while pushing through endless grief will put a hold on your dreams, that's for sure. "I'm not sure I'll ever be able to catch up on all the things I want to do."

"Tell me."

His hazel gaze is warm on my skin, tracing a pattern from my forehead to my neck and back to my eyes.

"I want to travel. I never left the country, do you know that? Never got on a plane." I look outside the window, at the lilac and fuchsia sunset, soaking the inside of the car in a lavender haze. "I want to see what the world looks like outside of New England. I want to get drunk without fearing it'll send me to the hospital. I want to find a new hobby. Get a tattoo. I want to figure out what I want to do for the rest of my life. I want to fall in love with someone who actually loves me for me."

I stop myself when I might've gotten a little too vulnerable, especially with someone as emotionally stunted as Carter. Still, it was the truth. After the two years I spent with Greg, begging for a minute of his time, pretending to be someone I wasn't to fit whatever mold he wanted me to, I know I either want the real thing or nothing at all. I realized too late that the way he felt toward me was more pity than love. It's clear to me now, but at the time, I took every scrap of attention he threw my way, even if it never made me feel loved.

"You'll do all those things," Carter says. There's no trace of doubt in his voice. He says this the same way he talks to the guys in the studio when he gets an idea, like he knows what's best and nothing could change his mind. "Maybe we avoid the alcohol if it's bad for you, but there are some pretty good mocktails. Trust me." He shrugs a careless shoulder. "Otherwise, you *will* do them. We'll figure out a way to make sure you do."

We.

Such a simple word. Two letters that could mean nothing.

And yet, in this context, those two letters mean everything.

Chapter 20

When Carter walks up the stairs from the basement, I'm waiting for him.

He wasn't expecting this—clearly. He's wearing joggers and a white sleeveless T-shirt showcasing all those beautiful dark lines adorning his arms, his hair is mussed, and a crease from his pillow lines his cheek. For a moment, I'm taken aback at how normal he looks. Every time I see him, it's as if he's prepared for whatever could happen, always slightly on edge, and now, I've caught him off guard. For the first time, he appears entirely...human. He's never gotten up after me, which probably explains why he let himself be this casual in the house, but I'm not going to complain. In fact, that little pillow crease makes me grin more than I'd care to admit.

Carter stops in his tracks when he sees me, hand stuck midway through his hair. "Hey." He sounds confused, maybe even a little shy. I eat it up.

"Hey."

"What's up with the smile?" he says in his gruff voice. Guess he's not a morning person.

Lucky for him, I am. "I have something I wanted to show you."

His brows draw together like I said something ridiculous.

And then, doubt creeps over me.

Maybe this was a bad idea. I got a little carried away yesterday when I thought back to what had been collecting dust in the garage and could finally be put to good use. I didn't watch more videos of Carter or his band yesterday, wanting to respect the privacy he'd asked of me even if he wasn't there to see, but my curiosity never dimmed, and the idea came to me late last night. I never stopped to think about whether Carter would actually like it.

"Lilianne? What's up?"

Right. Guess it's too late to turn back now.

I clear my throat. "I found something in the garage—or rather I went looking for it—and I thought it might be useful to you."

Carter doesn't budge, doesn't even blink as I move to my left and show the eighties' acoustic guitar Dad had kept in pristine condition over the years. "Ta-da!"

My smile slowly slips as he remains silent. The only indication he's still alive is the tick in his jaw. "It was my dad's. After seeing yours at your place, I remembered I still had it in here somewhere." I knot my fingers behind my back. "Thought we could put it to use again."

His gaze remains on the scratched acoustic guitar. "I told you. I don't play anymore."

I nod, then do it again, and again. "Right. You're right." I'm not sure why my chest feels this tight, but I try my best to hide it. "I'm sorry. It—"

"Don't." He takes a step my way. "Apologize, I mean."

I nod again as if this is the only thing I know how to do.

His gaze is heavy on mine before he decides to step closer to the instrument, his fingers hovering over its neck in an almost caress. There's reverence in the way his hand moves. I can almost imagine him doing it on my skin, down my back. How it'd feel to be touched this way.

"He never taught you?" he asks, pulling me out of my inappropriate daydreams.

"Always said he would one day." I go to say more, but I feel like if I continue, the words won't come out well. He never will teach me, after all.

Carter glances up, eyes searching, the color so dark I can barely see any green, then brings his attention back down. Fingers hover once more, his body looking like it's fighting a battle with itself, one I know nothing about.

It feels like a lifetime passes before Carter actually touches the guitar. When he does, it feels like a heavy tension slips out of the room through cracks in the wall, like a commune bated breath has been released. He doesn't look at it anymore but grips its neck tightly, lifting it from its stand.

"Let's do it," he says.

"Huh?"

"I don't play, but that doesn't mean you can't." Carter takes two steps toward the living room couch, his easy hold on the instrument looking like second nature to him.

"Oh, no, it's okay, I—"

"Didn't you say you wanted to try *everything*?" He lifts the guitar, holding me accountable with a single annoying glare. He got me and he knows it. "Then get your ass on that couch and start living, Fireball."

For some reason, his words make me laugh. No one ever puts stuff in my face. So long as I was spending time in the hospital or recovering post-surgery, people would treat me with kid gloves, looking at me like I was a fragile flower a wind gust away from shriveling.

But not Carter.

"Fine." I go to the couch and grab the guitar he's holding out to me. I never thought this would be the outcome of taking the guitar out of the garage, but it doesn't matter. It will be used one way or another.

"All right, so to get through a song, you need to know your chords first." He sits next to me, and the way he looks at the instrument now, in my hands, is different from how he did before. There's a new lightness to his demeanor. "Let's start with a basic one." Then he proceeds to explain to me where all my fingers need to rest on the strings so I block the right ones and hopefully produce the right note. However, it's tight on the twin couch, and from the side, it's hard for him to reach around and place my fingers properly.

After three failed attempts and the most horrendous false notes ever head, he mutters a, "Fuck it," then rounds the couch so he's standing behind me, his tall frame wrapping around my shoulders like the warmest of blankets.

"There." Easily, he settles my fingers in the proper position, his touch as careful around my hands as it was above the guitar earlier. "Now strum."

I do, producing a C chord that finally sounds right. A high-pitched sound comes out of me, one I wish very much I could've kept back. That is, until I hear Carter chuckles. I lean my head back, neck almost bent in half as I look up to find Carter pinching his lips.

That little scoundrel, hiding his smiles from me.

I grin at him long enough that eventually, he lets some of it out.

Whoosh. A Christmas tree being lit on.

Mission accomplished, I straighten and try to strum my C chord by myself, and after two more tries, I get it right.

"Show me more," I ask him, and he does.

He proceeds to teach me the hand placements for a few more chords, then to play them in a specific order. I do, taking so much time to position my fingers between each note that the song is barely recognizable. However, when I repeat them a few more times, I finally recognize The Beatles' "Let It Be." A song I remember Dad and I belting out in the car more times than I can count. One I've always loved so much.

"See?" Carter says, pride thick in his voice. "Easy."

I did it. It might have taken me an insanely long amount of time to get these four stupid chords in a song, but I did do it.

I look down at the pale brown guitar, brushing my thumb over a scratch under the strings, one that probably came from a night of music with friends during Dad's early adulthood.

He might never have had the chance to teach me like he wished to, but got to it nonetheless.

I blink fast against the tears that suddenly rush up, part sadness and part deep, flowering happiness.

"What's wrong?" Carter asks, suddenly standing in front of me, his voice louder than usual. This man is too good at reading me.

"Nothing," I say with a shake of my head. And then, when I see his nervous expression—one I never thought I'd see on his face, never mind for me—I can't help myself.

I climb to my feet over the couch so I can hug him properly.

Like this, I'm barely taller than him, which allows me to wrap my arms around his neck and pour everything it is I'm feeling about this moment into the embrace.

At first, he doesn't hug me back, and I don't even care. A unilateral hug is what he deserves for gifting me this, whether he wants it or not. After a few seconds, though, there's a barely-there pressure around my lower back. He's giving the weakest hug I've ever received, one that feels a little like he's restraining himself, or maybe like he's forcing himself to give me a little something, but again, I don't care. This isn't about me. It's about him, who's just given me so much. And if I can only explain my full gratefulness by squeezing the air out of his lungs, then I will.

"Thank you," I whisper against the silky scent of bergamot in his neck. For taking his time for me. For granting another one of Dad's wishes.

For caring.

Chapter 21

"This place is a pigsty."

I look up from my book, with the smutty cover on full display—what use is there to hide them from him anymore? "I'm sorry?"

Carter's sitting in the rocking chair Nana always monopolizes when she visits but that he's adopted in the past weeks. Now he doesn't only eat with me when I'm home, but he'll also join me in the living room sometimes, either to watch whatever movie I've put on while working on edits or to read in his chair. Every time, I almost feel afraid to move or make a sound as if it's a fluke and he'll leave once he realizes I'm here. But somehow, he never does, even when I end up getting comfortable and start talking his ear off about which influencers are dating or fighting online or about how *Twilight* is a cult favorite for a reason.

"We need to clean around here," he clarifies.

Six words I never thought I'd hear out of a man's mouth.

I start to look around, and now that he's said it...yeah, it's pretty bad.

I've never been a neat freak, but when I lived alone, the house remained more or less clean, mostly because I couldn't make much of a mess on my own. However, now, the place looks lived-in. There are blankets messily thrown onto the floor from two nights ago when Carter reluctantly joined me on the couch to watch the third *Twilight* movie (hence the discussion on its cultural significance) and we ended up going to bed at 3:00 a.m. after watching the next two movies, his arm draped on top of the couch, sometimes brushing my neck and making the blankets unnecessary. Music sheets are strewn across the dining room table from the time Carter decided to teach me the basics of reading music, and then from the time he showed me how to play my father's old partitions on the guitar. An umbrella is leaning against the door, still dripping water onto the welcome mat from last night. I'd opened my car door after coming from a show, prepared to run across the driveway in the rain, only to find Carter there, umbrella above him and ready to shelter me from the summer storm. Dust covers the floor from when Carter patched some small holes in the walls over the last week.

I like the way the house looks now, as messy as it is.

"There must be at least twenty half-drunk glasses of water strewn across the house," Carter says, bringing me back to earth.

I flip my gaze to him. "I like to stay hydrated."

"I can see that."

My eyes narrow. "Why don't you mind your business and start cleaning, then."

Humor colors his cheeks, and just as asked, he gets up and starts putting the place in order, which in turn makes me feel lazy, so I join him.

We spend the next two hours cleaning the entire living area from top to bottom, one person doing the dishes while the other dries, then one picking stuff up before the other vacuums and mops. I put a 2010s music playlist on the speakers and can't help myself from dancing as I clean, and while Carter doesn't participate, he hums to the beat a few times.

Thankfully, the house is small, and we're able to do a lot in a short amount of time.

"Now on to the rooms," Carter says, a rag on his shoulder and bright pink scrubbing gloves hanging out of the pockets of his sweatpants. He shouldn't look this good while cleaning, and yet I have to stop myself from ogling him. This scene is so casual that for a moment, I lose myself to the fantasy. This is just another Sunday morning with my husband. We've done the laundry and the cleaning, and later tonight, we'll spend an evening out and make love in the kitchen because we weren't able to wait to get to our room. This is our life.

Except it's not.

I clear my throat. "My room's fine."

"I'd bet everything I own that there's another army of water glasses in there."

My mouth curls up. How spot-on.

"Let's go," he says, heading toward the first closed door in the hallway.

"Not this one," I interrupt before he can turn the doorknob. I'm not ready to go back into Dad's room yet. I'm definitely not ready to clean it up either.

He pauses, hand a twist away from opening up to a scene of preserved grief, and the look he gives me says he knows exactly what I'm doing. Still, he doesn't insist, slowly letting go of the door with a nod. I'm so relieved, I don't even worry that he moves along right to my own room.

"Yep, even worse than I thought," he says once he opens the door, bringing back some of the lightness that has seeped out for a short moment.

"It's fine," I say, automatically bending to pick up stray clothes from the floor. I don't even have it in me to be embarrassed about the state of my room—the one place I do get pretty messy. Carter has witnessed too many mornings of me walking into the kitchen with my hair all over the place and drool probably stuck to my chin for that. It's nice, really, not to have to pretend in front of him. No need to make an effort in a fake relationship.

I remember with Greg, I would wake up earlier than him, go put on some makeup to give my skin some color and make sure my lips weren't too chapped when he woke up. Some days, I'd pretend I was going to run errands when I actually had medical appointments, and I'd lock myself in the bathroom to take my medications. I never wanted him to feel like I was too much to handle. It's probably a good thing he dumped me for good before my father died because I don't think I would've been able to keep up any pretense at that time.

"I don't understand how much water such a small body can actually drink," he says as he continues to add glasses to the already massive pile he's holding.

"I spent years restricting my water intake because my kidneys couldn't handle it. Now I drink it like it's liquid gold."

Carter pauses in his movement, assessing, as if he's suddenly seen my body for the first time. When he spends a bit longer on my arms, I lean down to pick up some more clothes, all the while pulling my sleeves down to my wrists. I've never liked how thin I was, and while I've been able to gain some weight after my transplant from a diet that was much less restrictive, I still feel like I'm too bony every time I look at myself in the mirror.

When I straighten up, he takes a step forward. "You know what?" He hands me the glass that was the closest on my nightstand, the one I brought with me to bed last night. "Drink up."

I grin, grabbing the glass and taking a large gulp that does still taste like heaven, even two years post-transplant.

Then we're back to our cleaning routine, me shifting to the music, Carter mumbling under his breath every time he finds something that "doesn't belong in a bedroom." Every time, I pretend I don't hear him and fight back laughter.

"Where do the pajamas go?" he asks as he picks up a large T-shirt I always use as a nightgown from *the chair*—the one no one has sat on in years because its sole purpose is now to hold my clothes.

"Bottom drawer," I say over my shoulder, noticing the neat way he folds the washed-out shirt.

A drawer rolls open while I fill up the hamper with loose socks, and only when I notice the room has become eerily quiet do I turn around.

And die on the spot.

Carter is leaning over the bottom drawer of my nightstand—*not* my dresser—which I only use to store one thing.

My toys.

Carter seems transfixed, gaze lost in the pile of vibrators.

"Oh my God, not that drawer," I say just as he leans forward to pick up...yep, he picked *that* one. The gigantic pink dildo Wren and Lexie gave me for my birthday last year as a joke. The two heathens had dared bring that thing to the restaurant, and I'd almost passed out from laughing so hard.

I cross the room in two steps, then grab it from his hands and clutch it to my chest.

However, he's stronger than me, and when he says, "Oh, but I wasn't done with it yet," he easily steals it back.

"Give it," I say.

His large hand dwarfs the toy as he inspects it, turning it at different angles. When he finally looks up from it, I'd swear there's a sheen of something new in his eyes. Something that almost looks like lust. But just as rapidly as it appeared, it's gone, replaced by pure delight.

"Who knew cleaning could be so informative?"

"Carter, I swear to God."

I try to sound intimidating, but clearly, it doesn't work because he only returns to his study of the dildo.

"Realistic, isn't it? All those veins..."

"Give it back."

His smirk is devilish. "Or what?"

I decide to skip the answering part and go straight to grabbing it from his hands. Sadly for me, he's faster and taller than me, and he decides to go for a playground move: lifting it above his head where I can't reach.

"You asshole," I say before jumping on him.

He doesn't expect it, wobbling as I climb his body like a tree, one arm clamped around his neck while the other is extended, trying to reach that fucking dildo. My face is burning, but I don't know if it's from exertion or embarrassment. Obviously, I was wrong to think I couldn't dig myself deeper in front of Carter. And for some reason, I don't really care.

I start laughing as I push my foot into his side, making him lose his balance, enough that he shouts an "Oh, fuck," before falling backward, arms gripped around me. Thankfully, my bed is there to absorb our fall.

I'm now sprawled onto him, eyes level with his, and I'd swear I've never seen him so gleeful.

"Give it back, you brute."

"Not sure." His nose scrunches in the cutest way. "I kinda like it."

I try to grab it from where he's holding it behind my back, but again, he brings it above his head.

"I will literally kill you," I say, unable to keep a straight face.

"A real fighter, aren't you?"

When I narrow my eyes, it makes him laugh, his lips splitting into the biggest smile I've ever seen on him, teeth glinting in the afternoon light. One of his canines is a little bit crooked, I notice for the first time, and it only makes his smile even more endearing.

Whoosh.

I can't not return the smile. Happiness looks so freaking good on him.

"You know I will get this toy even if it kills me, don't you?"

His shirt rides up as he brings the dildo higher above his head, exposing some of the dark hair creating a happy trail at the bottom of his abdomen. My breath stutters, and I force my gaze away. I need to think of a strategy.

He expects me to reach for it again. Which is precisely why I don't, instead digging my fingers into his sides. Just like I expected, his muscles contract as he starts cry-laughing.

Knew it. He's ticklish.

"Oh my God, stop," he wheezes out.

"Give it." I giggle.

He resists another second before dropping the dildo to the floor. "White flag."

I keep on going, just a little more.

His body shakes under me, and I only stop when his hands grab my wrists and hold them next to his head. "You little devil."

"You deserved it."

He breathes fast under me, hair ruffled, looking more alive than ever before. His dark hazels stay on me, moving from my gaze to my nose and finally landing on my lips.

Only then do I realize just how entangled we got. My hair is hanging in ribbons around his neck, arms bracketing his head, and my ass is right on his groin.

I swallow. He's hard under me, and just like last time, I can't help but move over him, just a little. His breath hitches.

I should get up. He should push me off.

But the way he stares at my lips makes my own gaze drop to his, parted, and when his tongue darts out to wet them, I know I've lost the battle.

I can't help myself from crushing my lips to his.

Immediately, his hands let go of my wrist and climb to my head, where he cradles me and tilts me at an angle so his tongue can meet mine, forcing a moan out of my mouth.

He's both taking his time and giving me his all, deep, languid kisses that make my toes curl coming again and again. He kisses like he wants to devour me whole, like I'm the only thing he could ever want for.

And I give it back, shot for shot.

My nipples harden against his chest, and since I'm not wearing a bra under my loose sweatshirt, I know he feels it too. He groans softly, tightening his fingers in my hair, pulling just enough that the sensations become almost overwhelming. He knows what he's doing, rocking under me, tracing lines with his pinky under my jaw, all the while getting me drunk on the taste of mint on his tongue.

And then his hands are moving down my back while his open lips brush my chin, my neck, my throat. When his fingertips lie against the small of my back, I arch even more against him, and he climbs back to kiss me once more. His large hands splay across my back, palms grazing the sides of my breasts, leaving me panting.

I've never been this riled up by a kiss, this electrified. I thought I'd been kissed properly before, but I was very, very wrong. I had to be because those guys never came close to making me feel like how I do when Carter drags his teeth against my bottom lip, passionate, applied.

Those guys were little bar shows, but he's the goddamn stadium tour.

Our breaths come in fast as I stroke his tongue with mine, but it's not enough. A switch has been turned on in my body, and I need more. I shift to the side so his hand can cover my breast. Just as his fingers reach my nipple, a hissing sound comes out of his mouth, and then his hand pulls back. He's completely let go of me, his kissing paused.

And suddenly, I realize what we just did. What I have just done.

This is a fake marriage. We can't be kissing. We can't be doing anything *more* than kissing. I know myself. I develop feelings easily, and our relationship is tangled enough as it is. If we continue, I know I'll fall, and that'll only get my heart broken.

Plus, he clearly thinks this was a mistake too. It's written all over his face.

In one quick move, I'm off him, tucking my hair behind my ears. "I'm so sorry."

He sits up, trying to subtly adjust himself in his sweatpants. Then he drags a hand through his hair. "No, it's fine, I—"

"I shouldn't have done that," I interrupt. "I got caught up. It really doesn't have to mean anything."

"Lilianne..."

"No, I'm serious." I force a smile on. "A stupid slip of the mind. Let's just forget it."

He blinks. "Right."

"Great," I say, sounding maybe too cheerful, but that's better than letting my face show all it is I'm actually thinking. "I think we did enough cleaning for the day. I'll go start on dinner."

I give him another smile, and before he can answer, I leave, pretending with all I have that I'm simply walking away and not escaping him.

Chapter 22

"You done with those fries?"

I don't give Carter the time to answer before I steal one and chump on it.

"You're not even done with yours."

"Yours taste better."

He rolls his eyes but doesn't say anything more, allowing me to continue stealing from him.

After we left the recording studio at noon, Carter told me he knew this great spot not far from there and led me to eat the best bean burger I've ever had in my life. I don't know why he knew about this vegetarian place, but I sure am not complaining.

"I like what you did with the strings arrangement today. It was..." My words die out as I notice the expression on Carter's face, so different from what it was mere seconds ago. It looks as if he's seen a ghost.

I've seen him in a lot of bad moods since we met—from his casual "don't talk to me" air to answering in grunts or not answering at all. Now that I know him, I mostly notice this level of grumpiness when he's talking to other people. Even so, I don't think I've ever seen him quite like this. Not even angry or annoyed, but distraught.

"What's up with you?"

"Nothing." He shakes his head. "Let's just go."

I frown. "I'm not done eating."

His hand reaches for mine, but I avoid it, not wanting a touch that could trigger memories. "I'll get you another burger somewhere else," he says. "Let's go."

"Why?"

"No time to explain." He tries to get me to stand up again.

"Andrew Carter, will you just sit down and tell me what the hell's going on?"

His jaw flexes, then he quickly looks over his shoulder as if ensuring no one's listening before he says in a hushed voice, "I forgot something at the studio."

"Has anyone ever told you you're a horrible liar?"

He sighs, then runs a hand through his hair. "I think my brother just sat down back there."

My brows climb to my hairline. "Brother?"

I don't know why I'm surprised. It's not like we've talked much about our families or our lives outside of the little bubble we seem to have built for ourselves at home. Still, I would've thought he'd have brought up the fact that he has a brother—or maybe even siblings—at some point during all the months we've spent together.

"Yes. Is that enough for you to agree to leave now?"

"Why don't you want him to see you?" I ask, ignoring him. Then I realize my error. Maybe he doesn't want to hide from him. Maybe he wants to hide *me*.

"Because Brandon is—"

"Andrew?"

If Carter's face was tight before, it just turned into a glacier.

I feel helpless as I see the walls erecting right back up around Carter, all those bricks I carefully took out one by one.

"It really *is* you," the guy—Brandon, I assume—says as he reaches us. He doesn't look anything like Carter, with almost black eyes, straw-colored hair, and a narrow jaw. I can see he's handsome, in this pretty Ken doll way, but he's got nothing on his brother. "What are the odds? Seeing my brother during a work trip."

"Hey," Carter says, the word seeming to physically pain him.

"How are you doing?" Brandon opens his arms wide, and when Carter doesn't throw himself in them like they're in some theatrical family reunion, he wraps Carter in a quick embrace, clapping his back twice with a strength that makes me wince.

"Fine," Carter says, not even bothering to pretend like he cares how his brother is doing.

"You live here now?"

"Yeah."

Again, I'm hit by how little I know of him. I didn't even know he wasn't a Boston native until this moment.

Brandon's eyes narrow, and I want to disappear as the two men fall silent, the tension nearly unbearable.

Finally, Brandon breaks the stare down, but only to fall on me. "Where are my manners? I'm Brandon. Andrew's older brother." I don't miss the way he emphasizes *older* as if that makes him superior. "And you are?"

"Lilianne," I say, shaking the hand he's extended my way.

I don't know what else to say, until Carter's arm wraps around my waist and he adds, "My wife."

A wave of heat rushes over me, one I've been trying my hardest to avoid since the kiss. We moved on since that day in my bedroom, never once bringing it up again, acting as if it never happened, like promised. So long as we keep our distances, I can pretend. My body doesn't become attuned to his the moment he steps into a room. I don't have the urge to turn toward his voice like a flower rotates to face the sun. I can forget about it all.

And yet the second he squeezes me against his hard body, claiming me in front of his brother like I'm something he can be proud of, all those efforts go to waste.

Brandon's head jerks back as if he's been hit. "Wife?"

Carter doesn't answer, only squeezing me tighter. And for some reason, it doesn't feel possessive or defensive, but more like he needs me as a buoy.

I'll gladly save him from rough waters anytime.

I put my hand over the tense grip he has on my hip. "It was sudden," I say, smiling like a lovesick fool who had no choice but to marry the guy she fell hopelessly for. "We couldn't wait to get married and decided to do something small, just the two of us."

Not a lie per se.

I don't need to hear Carter's words to feel his relief that I took over the conversation.

"Huh," Brandon says, looking us up and down. The over-the-top cheeriness is gone, replaced by a coldness that makes me glad for Carter being so close to me. He hisses through his teeth, then asks Carter, "That the reason you left?"

Carter tenses. "Don't."

"Don't what? Keep you accountable for fucking it all up?"

"That's it, we're going." Carter leans over to pick up my purse and strings it over his arm.

"Same fucking Andrew, heh? Running like a coward the second shit gets hard."

I don't know what he's talking about, and frankly, I don't give a rat's ass about it. I take a step closer, ignoring Carter's hand tugging on mine. "I don't care who the hell you think you are. You don't talk to him like that. Ever." I might be half his weight and a head smaller, but he could be a giant for all I care.

Air puffs my chest as I get ready to hand his ass over to him, but once again, Carter pulls me away. "Let's go. It's not worth it."

"Got your girl fighting your battles for you now? New low, even for you."

"He doesn't need me to do shit for him," I hiss in that asshole's face. "The difference is he actually has someone there for him." I make a show of looking around. "Where's your person?"

His nostrils flare. Bingo.

"You're right," I tell Carter over my shoulder. "Let's leave." But not before I *accidentally* step right onto Brandon's toes.

We don't look back at where his brother curses before we walk out of the restaurant hand in hand.

"I don't know how you kept your calm," I say as we sit down on a quiet patch of grass in Boston Common. We walked in silence from the burger joint to here as if we both needed some time to process the chaotic moment that had just happened. The park is full on this beautiful June day, groups of young people playing Spikeball to our left while women push strollers down the path to our right. The weather is perfect, with a cool breeze coming from the water making the heat bearable, the beginning of a promising summer. "I'd have blown a fuse if I were you."

"I saw that."

I push his foot with mine, then try to fight the scowl that's threatening to overtake my face as I think back to how that prick acted. "I didn't like the way he talked to you."

The left side of Carter's lips ticks, the way it does when he's refraining himself from smiling too big. "I saw that too."

I groan.

"I underestimated you, Fireball. Or maybe I got it right with that name."

"I don't like people attacking the ones I care about," I say. And that's the simplest truth. I *care* about Carter. Even if our marriage is a business arrangement for him, it's more than that to me. I care for him the way I care for Finn or Lexie, the way I care for Nan. It doesn't even matter if it's only one-sided. I can't lie about it.

"Brandon's been a dick for a while now," Carter says. "I don't mind whatever he says, but I appreciate the sentiment."

I bring my knees closer to my chest. "What happened between you two?"

The heaviest sigh leaves Carter's lips. "It's complicated."

"I'm sure it is. But I have time."

I expect him to brush me off. To say he doesn't want to talk about it and would rather move on from the whole ordeal. And I'd understand, too. I would never hold it against someone not wanting to share whatever haunts their nightmares.

What I don't expect is for him to start talking. And talking. And talking.

I'd read more about the band online after learning of its existence, even finding some Reddit threads on theories about the band's breakup, but as I listen to Carter, I realize I had barely scratched the surface.

It's as if a dam has burst open as he tells me about the band he had with his brother and two of their friends. He doesn't talk about Fickle like the band that made waves during its years of existence, earning awards and major recognitions, but as the garage project he had with his friends and brother. He tells me how Brandon had this idea for an album and Carter agreed to join, not believing in it at first. How they rose to fame almost overnight, something that shouldn't have happened and that didn't allow any of them to adapt to it. How they suddenly had shows and fans and parties with all kinds of excesses. How when he decided to walk away, his brother decided to hate him, and their parents with him.

"They can't hate you," I say once he's done. He might have been difficult to figure out at first, but no one who knows him—*actually* knows him—could hate him. No one could be indifferent toward his quiet humor or his subtle attentions that add up to so much. He may hide it well, but this man cares. So much so, in fact, that he might not show it more for fear of it not being returned.

"You don't know my parents," he says.

"Haven't had the pleasure, no."

He turns to me. "You're not missing anything, trust me. They're two people who should have never had kids."

"So that's why you didn't tell them about us?" Or the us we're showing to the world. "Because you're not on good terms anymore?"

"'Not on good terms' is putting it mildly. We don't talk at all."

I pull at blades of grass under me, then begin braiding them. "When Brandon showed up, I thought you'd kept me hidden."

"No," he says, shaking his head. "Or rather, yes, but not because I wanted to hide you from them. I wanted to *spare* you from them. You're so much better than them." His gaze is lost in the direction of the pond where swan boats are floating all around. "You deserved better than being thrown into that pack of wolves."

I try not to smile at that. I try very, very hard.

But I lose spectacularly.

The rest of the afternoon slips by as we people-watch and lie on our backs under the setting sun, talking about his childhood and mine, about what he liked about growing up in San Francisco, about what kind of students we were. It's so easy all of a sudden as if he needed a kick start before being able to tell me simpler things.

Next to us, a girl starts strumming her acoustic guitar with a group of friends sitting beside her, shading their faces as they watch her play.

"Would you ever go back?" I ask Carter.

His head turns to me, cheek brushing against the grass. "To what?"

"Playing. Touring." With or without his brother.

He shakes his head.

"Not even with Crash & Burn?" I haven't forgotten that we're supposed to leave for the "away" part of the tour in less than two weeks. Carter said he wouldn't come, but I'm still holding out hope he'll change his mind.

"Touring's not for me anymore," he says, not offering more of an explanation.

"Hope you won't miss me too much when I'm gone, then."

He hums, then looks back up at the sky. After a pause, he says, "You don't have to go, you know. The exposure you've given the band is already huge."

"It's part of our contract."

"And I'm saying it doesn't have to be anymore."

I twist my lips as I study him. "This leg is too big for them not to promote."

Carter doesn't say anything.

"No, I'm still going," I decide. I made an engagement, and I'm not stepping back. Plus, I actually want to experience this. I bump him with my hip. "But thanks anyway for offering. Glad to know you thought the deal was worth it."

He hums once more, but as we pack up and walk back to the car, I have a feeling I didn't give him the answer he wanted.

Chapter 23

It's been days since Carter told me about everything that went down with his brother and his parents, and I haven't been able to stop thinking about it.

Our childhoods couldn't have been more different. It's painful to think his family literally abandoned him after he made a decision for himself. I don't know what particular event drove him to leave the band, and I couldn't care less. He didn't deserve to lose the people who were supposed to love him no matter what. And from what I gathered, his family didn't seem that great even before the band's downfall. What parent could value their child's professional success over their happiness? I almost want to fly over there myself to shake them. My mother might've walked out on me, but with the father I had, I see Carter's the one who got the short end of the stick. Dad never made me feel like I needed anything more, and that's out of sheer luck.

I've been standing in front of his bedroom door for who knows how long, clenching and unclenching my hands. As much as I want to turn around, one thing keeps blaring through my mind: I can't keep ignoring it, ignoring *him*. Every day I continue walking in front of this door without going in is another day I don't honor my dad. Hearing Carter's story was the wake-up call I needed. With everything he gave me, he deserves to have his life recognized, not forgotten, no matter how uncomfortable it is for me to go in there.

"What are you doing?"

I don't need to look to know Carter is walking in my direction. I could recognize his voice, even his presence, with my eyes closed. I've gotten so used to having him around, I've learned his tells, learned the pattern of his footsteps and the way he breathes. And even without all of this, I learned how *I* feel when he's around as if his aura reaches mine, calming and rooting.

I swallow. "I think it's time."

"Yeah?"

I look to my right, where he's now standing, head tipped down to gaze at me. I never told him what the room truly means to me, but somehow, he knows.

"Yeah." I'm not avoiding it any longer. Dad would want me to donate his clothes, have them be of use to someone in need. He'd want me to use this space for something else. He'd want me to deal with my grief.

"You don't have to be there for this," I add, not quite sure whether I say it for him or for myself. I don't know how I'll handle dealing with this stuff. I might not be able to keep a straight face, and Carter probably doesn't want to have to deal with me being a mess.

As I should have expected, Carter doesn't answer. Instead, he takes a step forward and opens the door for me. No time allowed for me to back down or chicken out. Pushing right through.

Just like the last time I walked in, I'm first hit with the nostalgia of seeing his room as if he were still there, living in it, and then with the scent of him. I inhale deeply, closing my eyes. God, what I wouldn't give to smell this on him, his pullover retaining the scent of the detergent as he whizzed past me on his way to get dinner out of the oven. To get one last hug from him.

"Guess being a glass hoarder is familial."

I open my eyes, following Carter's gaze to where it's landed on the five almost empty glasses of water standing on the bedside table.

My smile grows slowly as if testing the waters of whether I actually want to go there. Eventually, though, I can't control myself and burst out laughing. Carter's lips tip up, small but so very there, and I don't think I've ever felt more grateful for him than I do now.

I haven't quite caught my breath when I step inside, but the lightness in my chest makes it so much easier. Carter knew what he was doing.

I look around, this time not with a feeling of grief that threatens to drown me, but with purpose. We need to clean this space, just like we did the entire house before. And Carter's right: Dad was as messy as I am.

I breathe deeply as I look at the clothes I recognize and the trinkets I missed, then say, "All right. Let's do this."

"Music on or off?" Carter asks, his phone already out but paused. He'll leave me in silence if I want to, and yet he knew I wouldn't. Knew music would help me get through this.

"On," I say, then grab his phone and find a playlist of seventies rock that my dad would've known every single word to. And then, we get to work.

I can't stop laughing.

"Please stop," Carter says, voice ice cold.

"I can't," I wheeze out. Maybe I could if he removed that stupid hat, but for some reason, he's kept it on, even though it looks like he'd rather die than wear something so ridiculous for a second longer.

"Lilianne, for the love of God," he chastises but still doesn't pull it off.

"Just one more second, please," I say before looking up at him and bursting out in another fit of laughter. When I found the boater hat at the bottom of Dad's walk-in closet, I immediately put it on Carter's head before he could say no, and the image was too good to be true.

"I'm giving you two more seconds and then I'm done."

I don't waste the opportunity, grabbing my phone at the speed of light and snapping a picture of him, stone face and all, with the hat flattening all his hair. There. Now I can laugh about it forever.

"You're impossible," he says as he finally takes the hat off. He'd already kept it on far longer than anticipated.

Cleaning up this room has been an interesting experience, that's for sure. At times, I found items I had fond memories of or things

I'd been looking for—Nan's necklace *was* here, after all, under a pile of papers on his desk—and at other times, I fell upon stuff I'd forgotten he owned, and the thought that some of my memories of him were already slipping away almost brought me to my knees multiple times.

All in all, though, it was survivable, and I only have the big man in front of me to thank for that. It's as if he can sense my mood and know when I need silence or when I need a breather. Observant as always. Something I don't think he even recognizes in himself.

"Okay, back to business." I return inside the closet. We've emptied most of the room in the past three hours, from bedding to clothes we could donate and the few things I decided to keep, and now we're stuck with the little knickknacks. Most of them are useless, but I'd feel terrible throwing them away.

There are a few boxes of things at the bottom of the closet we still need to sort through, so I go to grab one but find it stolen from my hands at the last second.

"I can carry my own boxes."

"I know," Carter says, still bringing it all the way to the bare mattress.

"Thank you," I grumble as I get to it, then start triaging. Thick biographies that go straight to the *donate* pile. A sweater from our trip to Ogunquit I decide to keep. Random paper documents I'll go through later.

Then my hand lands on a booklet, and I freeze when I pull it out of the box.

An Alcoholics Anonymous flyer.

I blink, turning it over in my hands as if I'll find some kind of information about why Dad had this in his stuff. Maybe some kind of message he'd scribbled behind a flyer while talking on the phone.

Nothing.

Frowning, I put it down, then return to the box, only to be met with more of the same.

A Member's-Eye View of Alcoholics Anonymous

A.A. At A Glance

Living Sober

My fingers trace the title of the last flyer. My father never drank in excess. In fact, I don't remember when the last time I saw him drink alcohol was.

I shake my head as I continue going through file after file on dealing with alcoholism, getting a sponsor, and even becoming a sponsor.

"What's all this?" Carter asks from the other side of the room.

I open my mouth to answer, but no word seems to come out. I look up at him, probably resembling a fish out of water.

My silence seems to trigger something in him because immediately, he's in front of me, picking up one flyer, then another. His throat bobs.

"He wasn't an alcoholic," I tell Carter, not because it'd have been shameful if he was, but because he couldn't have been, simple as that.

"Lilianne..." He takes a step closer, pity clouding his eyes.

"He wasn't." I pull out even more documents and books from the box as if wanting it to finally be empty. If it's all out, then I can't be surprised by anything else, so I grab and grab. My hands are shaking as I throw them with the others. "I knew my father. He wasn't an alcoholic."

He repeats my name, this time with a softness that brings tears to my eyes like he's seeing something I'm not. Then his hands land gently on mine, stopping me in my movements.

"Knowing someone doesn't mean they can't have struggles you don't know about."

"But he wasn't struggling," I say.

His gaze falls to the pile of flyers on the mattress, then comes back to me. "I think maybe he was."

I shake my head. It's not possible. "And how would you know that?" I shouldn't be snapping at him when he's only trying to help, but he doesn't *understand*.

Carter rubs at the back of his neck as he looks at the ceiling, his face losing some of its color, something I've never seen on him, except maybe on the day we got married. I've just struck a chord I didn't know existed, and for whatever reason, I wish I could take it back. His always calm exterior crumbles under my eyes, something I hate because I know he must hate the feeling in return.

Silence ensues, and I almost feel bad about rebutting him this way. The thick tension between us remains for so long I think he's going to move on to another subject and trudge on, but he surprises me by saying, "Because I struggled with it too."

I force myself to remain as neutral as possible even though deep inside, my jaw falls to the floor. Carter's like a rock. He doesn't seem like someone who can struggle.

And yet he says, "I stopped drinking when I got into a drunk accident. Had to face that I had an alcohol use disorder. Was forced to join the AA, and it's probably what saved my life in the end."

I blink, not knowing what to say. Is that what made him leave his band? What came between him and his brother?

It all clicks into place. His partying. Saying touring was bad for him. His family not understanding.

Carter sits on the bed, his movements still so careful. "But you could ask everyone I was close with at the time, and they wouldn't have a clue what I'm talking about." He cocks his head, a movement that makes him look younger than he is. "You can know someone without knowing all their struggles."

He has a point. I know he does. I've lived with him for months and never knew he had an alcohol problem.

My thoughts start to jumble left and right, memories clashing in my head. The times my father said no to champagne for New Year's Eve countdown, and I thought he was just accompanying me in my forced sobriety. The times I walked in on him and it looked like he'd had a really rough day, but he pretended like nothing was going on the second he saw me. The multiple times he had appointments he had to attend during the evening, without a clear explanation.

I grind my teeth, then put the flyers back into the box, dumping them all into one pile. There must be another explanation. Because if this is true and Carter's right, then it means there was a gigantic part of my father's life I never knew, and I can't accept that.

"I think that's enough for today. What do you think?"

"Lilianne, I—"

"I'm fine." I put on my bravest smile. "And thank you for sharing. Really." With a hand on his knee, I say, "I'm so glad you're doing better, and if you ever struggle again, I'll be there. You won't be alone." I hate to think he got sober by himself. I've heard how hard it can be even with a strong entourage, so him being forced to do it without anyone around... He's so much more than what I'd initially believed. An entire universe.

I give his knee one last squeeze, then get up. "But I still don't think my father went through the same thing." Maybe, at some point, he thought he drank too much and decided to slow down, but he didn't suffer from alcoholism. I would have known.

I spend the rest of the day trying to convince myself of it.

Chapter 24
Carter

Three years ago

"You did not just get this one in."

I smirk at Frank's shocked face. I don't know why he keeps on being surprised when I beat him by about eighty points during every one of our games. He should be getting used to it at this point.

"Talent, old man," I say. Then, because I'm a sucker and like to rub it in, I grab the basketball that bounced my way and turn around to throw it backward. I hear it hit the board then bounce to the side, probably narrowly missing the rim of the net. Frank still looks impressed, so I shrug and walk away as if I'd put it in.

"Good game," I say, extending one hand his way while wiping the sweat off my forehead with the other. It might be late at night, but the September air still feels sweltering, the suburban town having forgotten it's supposed to be fall.

"Appreciate the lie," Frank says, his hands on his knees as he catches his breath. His cardio's gotten better since we started playing, I'll give him that. Even then, I make him run enough that he ends every game this way.

We didn't plan on playing regularly, or at least I didn't. The first time Frank suggested it, I even laughed in his face.

"I'm not joking," he'd answered with an almost offended expression.

"You have to be."

I'd been having a rough day. Rough week, really. I'd attended two months of meetings by that point, and I didn't feel any closer to a better future than I did on day one. I still felt angry and regretted every single choice I'd ever made. Apart from the meetings, I pretty much spent all my time doing sudokus, reading books, and waiting for time to pass, each day feeling longer than the previous one. I didn't know how to find a job when I had no qualifications or experience, and without friends or family, I had no one to hang out with. It was my new routine: waiting. But that particular day, my mother had texted me for the first time since I'd left California, and it was to say that if I'd been planning on attending my father's fiftieth birthday (I hadn't), I probably should reconsider. She added that *the situation wasn't ideal* and *she didn't want to have anything ruin the party*. The ruining thing being me.

That day, I'd gotten the strongest urge to drink since I'd gotten sober, and that was saying a lot considering I spent the majority of my days battling the urge to soften everything by grabbing a bottle at the corner store. Frank had eventually gotten me to admit I still had a bottle hidden inside my place—apparently, that's pretty common for people in recovery—and to get rid of it, but going out to grab another one would've taken no effort whatsoever.

I'd resolved to stop by the store when I came back from my meeting with him, but that never happened. The second I walked into the pizza place we'd agreed to meet at, he took one look at me and figured something was wrong, and faster than I care to think about, he got me to spill everything. I expected him to be disappointed, or even angry that I wanted to give up, but the only thing he said was, "What's your favorite sport?"

I didn't understand, but after he asked again, I answered, "Basketball." I'd played a little in high school, and while I didn't particularly like it, I was tall and athletic enough that it came easy to me.

"Great. Let's play, then."

He actually wanted us to play, even with my eight inches and eighty pounds on him. It felt cruel. But he hadn't relented, and eventually, I had to give in, and we found ourselves in an open school gymnasium not far from there. Frank was horrible, out of shape and uncoordinated, but he took my mind off things for long enough that when I drove back home, I passed by the liquor store without stopping.

"Same time next week?" I ask now as I grab my stuff. My skin is still warm from all the running I've been doing, and my head feels clearer than it has in days.

"Wait. I have something for you before you leave." He goes to the side of the court to grab his bag that I keep calling a man purse but he insists on calling a satchel. "Don't hate on it till you've tried it," he always says, making me snicker every time.

Frank leads me to his car in the parking lot while digging through his bag, his salt-and-pepper hair plastered to his forehead. The bright spotlights surrounding the outdoor basketball court illuminate the empty lot, enough that I can examine Frank's car while he opens the driver's door and leans inside. It's an old Ford station wagon, and as you could expect from a man like Frank, multiple family-friendly stickers occupy the back windshield. One in particular catches my attention.

My daughter needs your help! Have an extra kidney? Get tested to see if you're a match and save her life! Below's some kind of phone number and a name that's too small for me to read from here.

"Your daughter's sick?" I ask with a frown. He's been talking about her for months and never once mentioned it.

When Frank pulls out of the car with one of his hands balled around something, sadness I've never seen on him shadows his face. His throat works as his gaze follows mine to the handmade sign on his window. "Kidney failure. She's been on dialysis for eight years now."

"I'm so sorry, Frank." I feel like such a dick all of a sudden. All those times he's said he could be with his daughter and he was with me instead. If I'd known, I never would've wasted so much of his time. Or maybe I would have. During those first meetings, he could've been Mother Theresa helping little kids left and right, and I still would've been an asshole. I wasn't ready for help then.

The person standing in front of me is the only reason I am now.

Frank nods. "It's been a rough few years, but she'll make it out of this." He smiles then as if he's not living through one of the hardest things anyone could encounter. "She's a strong kid."

"If she's anything like her father, I'm sure she is."

This is as close to a compliment as I've ever given him, and the way his face lights up makes me feel like a dumbass for never thanking him properly for everything he's done for me.

Then he looks down at his hand as if he's just remembered what we're standing here for. "There you go." He extends his fist to me, then gestures for me to hold my hand out. I reluctantly do so, not sure what's going to come out of there.

The object is so light when it lands in my palms, it almost feels as if there's nothing in there. But when I take a look and notice the embossed lettering spelling *6 months* over the blue chip, I know it's very well there.

"Congratulations on six months sober, Carter."

I don't look up. The chip tips from my palm to my fingers as I trace its borders and letters. I can't believe I didn't notice it this morning. My sentence is officially up. I did it.

When I finally look up, though, it's not with a triumphant smile but with a grimace. "I don't feel like I deserve this."

Frank's brows mirror mine by dipping down. "Darn right you do."

"You should be the one getting a medal or some shit. I haven't done anything."

"How can you say that? You've stayed sober for six entire months. That's huge!"

"But I'm still at the same exact spot I was when we started." No job. No future. No interest. My best friend is a forty-something-old man, for Christ's sake.

It hasn't hit me before today just how stagnant I've been. I guess knowing it's been six months already is like hitting a wall. I'm exactly where I was when I landed in Massachusetts.

"No, you're not. You've made so much progress."

"But my life is still…blank." I guess that's the perfect word for it.

He leans back against his car. "Isn't that a good thing? You can start fresh." Frank knows most of what happened in California. How I lost control with alcohol. How each show led to a party, which led to me getting drunk. I spared him the part where I'd end my nights fucking any girl who was willing before falling asleep right where I was. Bed. Kitchen floor. Bathtub. It didn't matter. I also told him the story of how one night, I decided to pick up my car keys to drive to a convenience store a few streets out to grab some more liquor for a party the band was holding in Brandon's hotel bedroom. I ended up slamming into a lamp post and falling asleep right there. The cops found me and arrested me before bringing me to the hospital. It still doesn't make sense to me how lucky I was on that night. I got out of my totaled car without a scratch on me. Most importantly, though, no one was around. Me, fine, but I don't think I could've ever forgiven myself if I'd hurt someone else.

Frank knows how that was my wake-up call. How when I sobered enough to realize what had happened, I decided I was done with it all. I made sure I could have a virtual sentencing, and once I knew I could, I grabbed a cab straight to LAX.

But even if Frank knows all of this, apparently, he doesn't get why I can't just get over it and move on. I never planned on "starting fresh." I just planned on running away so I could stay as far away from my demons as possible. I never thought beyond that.

"I don't know where I'd even start," I say, arms crossed.

"You love music, don't you?"

"I can't play anymore." Besides, during those months on tour, I had no pleasure in doing it. It felt like a task, just like it had when I played as a kid so my parents would clap and finally give me the attention I'd been craving. There was none of the tingly feeling I used to get in my fingers when I played and knew I *had* it. I played so I could get drunk afterward, or I'd already be drunk by the time we made it on stage. If I'm honest with myself, leaving the band didn't take my favorite thing away from me. I lost it way before then.

He shrugs.

"Then do something else with music. Write. Compose. Produce. Just do something with that talent I know you have."

I'd be lying if I said those things never crossed my mind, but I don't think they ever did as seriously as they do now.

Produce.

"You're young. You're bright." He puts his hand on my shoulder and squeezes. "Don't waste that because you made some mistakes in your early twenties."

I don't know what to say to that, especially with the way my throat suddenly burns, just like it does when you've inhaled deeply and are waiting to blow all the air out. I nod instead, and he seems to understand that this is all he'll get.

"Now, you've done your six months, so by the law, you're free of me."

My throat—my entire body—feels even tighter. He can't leave. He's the only person I have.

"You can decide to walk away and never look back. But if you want to continue beating my old butt at basketball and nagging at me for my pressed shirts, I'm all for it."

Who would have guessed six months ago that this offer would make my body feel a hundred pounds lighter?

I flip the coin once more between my fingers before pocketing it.

"Yeah, I think I'll take you up on that."

Chapter 25

This is the part of the tour I've been anticipating the most.

Attending local shows has been incredible, and I've spent so many great nights singing and dancing to the songs I now know by heart, but I'm ready to experience this next part. I also can't wait for those three weeks away from the bar, even though I haven't picked up many shifts in the past months. Following the band has consumed a huge chunk of my life. My channel has slowly drifted from "day in the life" content to being very music-focused, but so far, my followers don't appear to mind. In fact, they seem to have fallen in love with each member of the band, for different reasons. Ethan for his charisma, Emmett for his teddy-bear-like persona, Bong for his humor, and Joe for his quiet but awe-inducing talent. Of course a lot have also been following my husband's and my "love story," and while I hate lying to everyone, there's no hiding the success this promotion has brought the band. Ethan told me a week ago that the ticket sales have skyrocketed in the past months, almost doubling the audience from the first shows of the tour. I also received DMs from multiple followers saying they discovered the band's music because of my posts and now have become die-hard fans. I can't take the credit for it all, of course, but knowing that it's made a difference makes accepting the emotional challenges that have come with this arrangement worth it.

Case in hand: I'm happy to get on the tour bus today even though it was almost impossible to leave home this morning.

Carter made it clear this mini tour wasn't for him, which I understand even better now, and the tour was a must for me. Even so, when the time came to get out of the house, I felt a pull to remain right where I was, cooking for two and watching four-hour-long historical movies with him because he claimed they were too good to miss. The feeling made no sense; one of the reasons I accepted Carter's proposal at first was to have a real tour bus experience, and now that it was time to go, the need to experience it had disappeared. I had a strong feeling it was mostly due to the man who was reinstalling the freshly-painted cupboard doors back into place.

"Anything you need before I leave?" I asked an hour ago, duffel bag thrown over my shoulder as I stood next to the front door.

He looked up. "Already?"

I didn't know if it was disappointment or simply surprise I heard in his voice.

"It's only for three weeks. You won't even have the time to miss me," I teased even though I knew *I* would. Carter hasn't just become a presence I can tolerate. He's become a presence I crave, one that's made my days so much lighter. I don't know how I'll deal with the loss of him once our two years are done and he leaves. We might only be four months in, but I've already begun to anticipate it. If it's this hard to leave him now, what will it look like when I've had even more time to become attached? To become *addicted*? I have a feeling it won't be anything like when my ex left me after almost three years together. Then I'd felt a deep sense of relief, like I didn't have to pretend that relationship made me happy anymore. I was too scared to leave by myself, a small voice in my head telling me he might be the only person who could stay, baggage and all. I only realized once he was gone how much I had settled. Being alone all my life was a better alternative. It won't be the same with Carter, though. I might never *have* him, but once he'll leave, I know I'll miss being able to pretend, even for a minute, that he's mine.

"Let me get you to your car," Carter said this morning, wiping his hands on a rag before eating the space between us with his long legs and taking my bag from me. I didn't argue, knowing it'd be useless.

"You'll be careful?" he asked once the bag was thrown over the back seat and my seat belt was on.

"Yes, daddy." I threw him a wink, which made him look up at the sky, begging for patience. "I'll be fine," I added, serious this time.

"Good," he said, then remained there, squatting in front of my car so his head could pop through my window as if he wanted to say or do something else. Finally, he tapped the door twice, then pulled back. He didn't add anything else, but he remained in the driveway, watching me until my car was out of view.

"Lil!" Ethan shouts from the living room area of the bus when I step in. The others join in, Emmett from his spot on the couch facing Ethan and Joe from the dinner table's built-in bench, waving at me before returning to his card shuffling.

"Am I the last one here?" I ask as I drop my bag where the others have left their stuff, then join them on the couches. Even though I've spent a lot of time with them, without Carter here, it almost feels like I'm intruding in their space. I've lost my tether.

"We're waiting for Bong too," Ethan says. "He's never *not* been late, so might take a while."

I shrug, then look around the place I'll be calling home for almost a month. This bus is huge, with a modern design and brand-new appliances. As you enter the bus, you find a kitchen that's bigger than what I would've imagined and a living room. A set of doors separates what I assume is the bedroom with all the bunks and bathroom. I wasn't expecting much when they said we'd be traveling by bus, but this is nice.

"Want to play Spades before he gets there?" Joe asks. "Bong always cheats anyway."

"Facts," Emmett says.

We all join him for a game, and a quarter of an hour later, we spin toward the door when it creaks open.

"Bong, get your ass up here before we leave you here!" Ethan shouts.

Except it isn't Bong's head that appears at the top of the three steps leading into the bus.

"Carter? The fuck are you doing here, man?" Ethan says as he gets up to clap him on the back.

I'm too shocked to react one way or another, not sure I should even believe what it is I think is happening, until Carter's gaze falls on me and remains there as he says, "Got some new ideas. Thought we could do some recording between shows."

He's here. He's really here.

I can't control the smile I throw his way, and when the right side of his mouth curls up, I feel like I've just won the lottery.

"Someone was scared to miss all the fun?" I say when I finally find my voice, shifting my body to the left so he can have a place to sit.

"Sure," he says as he takes a seat next to me, the entirety of his right side pressing against me. His body is stiff, and as he looks around the bus like I did a few minutes ago, I recognize traces of panic in his breathing.

"Hey," I whisper. "It'll be okay." I can't begin to imagine how it feels for him to be on a tour bus after what happened on his last one, but this won't be the same. "I'm right here with you."

He nods tightly as he lets out a deep exhale. Meanwhile, I continue staring at him like he's something from another world. I'm not sure I believe his excuse for being here—maybe he realized it'd be weird if I was here without him and that's what made him change his mind—but honestly, I couldn't care less. *He's here.*

If I wasn't this euphoric at the thought, I'd probably think about how worrisome it is that I'm so relieved that we won't be apart for three weeks. He's not my real husband. Not even my real *partner*.

I'll worry about it another time.

I'm probably still smiling like a lunatic because Ethan gives me a look, brows high. I shrug, pretending I have no idea what he's thinking. With the way I'm acting, everyone's probably noticed the tiny, senseless crush I have on Carter, but so long as I don't acknowledge it, it doesn't *really* exist.

"Whadup, people!" Bong's voice says as he steps inside the bus, a beanie hanging from his head and kid floaties around his arms. "Who's ready to party!"

The band does some mix of eye rolling and grunting.

"I don't even wanna know," Emmett mutters with a shake of his head as he walks to the front of the bus. Then he shouts, "All right, Pete, let's roll," probably talking to the driver.

Meanwhile, Bong drops his stuff next to ours and takes a seat on the couch, then pulls a small plastic bag from his sweatpants pockets. "Anyone down for some Addys?" He proceeds to pop a pill in his mouth before passing the bag around.

Ethan takes one and so does Joe before it reaches Carter. He doesn't even peek inside, only swinging the bag toward Emmett, skipping me entirely. "We're good," he says.

I give him a look, then say in a low voice only he can hear, "What if I wanted to take some? Hallucinate some funky stuff later?" I wouldn't have, but I'll say anything to ease the tension off his body.

His lips twitch, and he fights it all of two seconds before his quiet, discreet smile he reserves for me appears. Bingo. "That's with shrooms, honey, not speed."

Right.

"Don't need to be taking any of that shit anyway."

"And why not?"

"Think you have enough energy sober," he teases, and honestly, I can't even contradict him. Then he nudges my thigh with his long fingers. "And I'm not messing with your health."

I don't know what sends the shiver down my back, the simple touch or the even simpler thought. The only thing I do know is that it might have been better for us to be apart these next three weeks after all.

Chapter 26

"We need to find you a new name."

"I'm sorry?" Carter says, faltering in his steps.

"Carter's just not personal enough," I say as we pass a beaver tails stand that smells so good it makes my stomach grumble, even after the amazing poutine dinner we just had. "And you don't seem to like Andrew." There was no missing how he winced every time his brother called him that. "Hence, you need a new name."

"Carter's fine," he says, not even bothering to turn my way. He's been on a mission since this morning to show me every part of the city, and while I'm tired from having walked a million miles, it's been fun to have him as a guide.

Today was the first time since we started this leg of the tour that we had a day off, either from shows or from recording sessions—apparently, Carter wasn't lying when he said inspiration had struck—and when he walked up to my bed this morning and asked if I wanted to have a tour of Montreal, I almost hit my head against the top bunk from how excited I was. We haven't had time to visit much in between stops, only a few hours here and there, so I wouldn't have given up on that opportunity.

He wasn't kidding when he said he'd show me around. In a single day, we've gone to almost all the big attractions the town has to offer, tasting delicious foods and seeing a city that's both modern and from another era.

I close an eye. "Drew?"

Carter doesn't answer, keeping his stride toward the hotel we're staying in tonight before tomorrow's show. Being able to have some privacy and take a shower in a real bathroom for the first time in days will be a treat.

"Andy?"

When he turns toward me at that, I'm already grinning. The sun is slowly starting to set, creating a halo of golden light around his frame.

"No."

"You're boring," I say, nudging him with my shoulder.

"Deal with it."

"I think I'll stick with Andy."

"Not a chance in hell."

Riling him up truly is my favorite sport.

"How far are we from the hotel?" My shoulders are burnt to a crisp and I can't wait to spend an hour under a cold jet and bathe in aloe. Who knew summer days in the city could be so brutal?

"Almost there."

The hotel isn't our next stop, though. Two minutes later, I grab Carter's arm, pausing in front of one of the most beautiful churches I've ever seen, an ancient monument smack dab between two skyscrapers. The way the end-of-day sunlight catches the stone walls and statues, drenching them in orange and marigold all the while ricocheting from the windowpanes of neighboring buildings, takes my breath away.

Even with the hand on his arm, Carter continues walking as he follows the traffic, hundreds of workers crossing the street as they walk back home, and I have to pull on his shirt to make him realize I've stopped.

"What are you doing?" he asks.

"Forcing you to enjoy the moment for a second."

I expect him to grumble, but somehow, he doesn't, simply standing next to me facing this scene that could be a painting.

"You're alive. Take it all in," I say, closing my eyes at the warmth caressing my cheeks, inhaling the scent of freshly cut grass while the sound of children playing and someone strumming their guitar in the park nearby fills my ears. I focus on the feel of Carter's shoulder brushing my skin, on the thrum of my heart in my chest, on the tickle of the blades of grass against my sandals. A moment like this, so perfect, so fragile, is worth a thousand bad ones. I want him to feel it too. To see how lucky we are, how our own lives can feel like movie scenes despite it all.

When I finally reopen my eyes, I don't know how much time has passed. What I do know is that light is lower in the sky than it was before, and Carter's gaze is hotter on me than the sun ever was.

"Okay, we can go now," I say, my voice steadier than how I'm feeling.

He doesn't move right away, his hazels studying me, and when they dip to my lips, even for only a second, I feel it *everywhere*. I remember the taste of his lips, the way he sounded when he kissed me, like he could never get enough. How heavenly the heat of his body felt under mine.

Focus. It was a mistake. We both said so.

I clear my throat, and when I resume our trek toward the hotel, I feel him following me.

At the next red light, I stretch one of my ankles that's been screaming at me to stop for a while.

Carter catches it. "Sorry I pushed you around all day." He scratches his cheek. "Wanted you to see it all."

"I loved it," I say, not even lying. Other than Boston and one time in Salt Lake City with Finn, I've never explored another city. It was worth all the cramps. "How did you know so much about the place?"

The pedestrian sign turns green, so we follow the mass of people across the intersection. "Montreal's a good music scene. My parents traveled here a few times for work, and we tagged along."

I hum. "Did you like it?"

"Nah." He turns to me, squinting against the fading light. "Today was all right, though."

I grin.

We're not far from the hotel, only a few more blocks until we reach the entrance of the chic-looking building. Carter opens the door for me, allowing me a whiff of his scent—I need to know whether it's his deodorant or his shampoo I have to blame for all those tingly feelings I get every time I get a hit—and once we're in, someone calls, "Cart! Lil!"

"Cart?" I whisper against Carter's arm as we turn to find Ethan hollering for us from the lobby bar.

"Forget it," Carter mutters.

"Hey," I tell Ethan once we join him. "Had a good day off?"

"Yeah, yeah... Look, there's been a fuckup."

"What kind of fuckup?" Carter says.

"Bill, the tour manager, he didn't know you'd be there when he booked the rooms, and anyway, you're supposed to be married, so..."

"So we only got one room," I finish for him.

"Right. And I checked, but the hotel's full. Some kind of music festival happening this weekend."

"Check again," Carter grunts.

I roll my eyes at his lovely mood, putting a hand on his arm as I tell Ethan, "It's fine." It's not like we have much of a choice anyway. I wish Carter didn't have to react like being in the same room as me is the equivalent of going on *Survivor* and sleeping naked in a tent made of branches, but I won't change him overnight.

"Sorry, guys," Ethan says as he gives me the keys, but his apologetic eyes are on Carter.

"It's okay, really." When I turn to my husband and find him with a tight jaw, I tell him, "It's only for one night. Calm your horses."

He doesn't say anything as he picks our bags up from where we'd left them this morning, and then we're in the elevator, a thick silence enveloping us. I don't know what's gotten into him. It's not the end of the world. In fact, even if the tour manager had known Carter would be there, we couldn't have asked for two rooms. It would've blown our cover.

I shouldn't be surprised to see the single king bed in the room once we open the door either, but surprised I am.

Carter must've expected it because he doesn't react to it. He walks in and drops his things on the small love seat in the corner of the room. "I'll sleep here."

"Come on," I say, taking a seat on the plush bed. "The bed's big enough for both of us."

His gaze is dark when he looks up.

"We're grown adults. We can share a bed," I tell him, but I almost sound like I'm trying to convince myself.

He glances at the bed for a long, long moment, then turns to his bag and grabs a few toiletries. "Wanna jump in the shower first?"

"Go ahead," I say.

I lay a hand on the bed, the covers silky smooth. This is going to be fine. I can control myself.

The mantra becomes a little harder to believe when Carter comes out of the shower ten minutes later, steam billowing behind him, his hair still wet, chest on almost full display as he steps through the room in black boxer briefs and a damp white shirt that hugs every single line of his body.

I stop breathing.

I try to look anywhere but at the delicate water droplets running down the tight column of his neck or at the shadow of hair on his stomach that reminds me of our time in my bedroom, where

I got to feel it, even briefly. My entire body becomes aflame as I fail to tear my eyes away, tracing the contour of his narrow hips with my gaze. Even when he catches me staring, I'm frozen in place. What's worse, he doesn't move away as if...as if he *wants* me to keep looking.

"All right, my turn," I say after clearing my throat and forcing myself to look at my toes. I'm careful not to brush him as I walk over to the bathroom, but it doesn't matter; the damage is done. As I turn the shower on and wash my hair, I can only think of Carter being naked here a few minutes ago, and I'm hot and bothered all over again. This was a bad idea. I should've let him be grumpy and ask for separate rooms, no matter what.

It's stupid. We've shared a bathroom before. We've shared a *house* for months. And yet this feels so much more intimate. Like there's no escaping each other.

Once I'm done and have dried myself, I put on the PJs I brought with me and immediately regret them. They're a set of tiny shorts and tank top, which was fine when I was alone in my bunk, but not so much when I'm sharing a room with the guy I'm supposed to pretend I feel nothing toward. It's even worse when I walk out of the bathroom and the AC hits me with the force of a blizzard, sending shivers down my arms as my nipples tighten under my tight top.

Fuck me.

I cross my arms to cover myself the best I can and make my way toward the bed, jumping under the covers. Carter's now wearing a hoodie, thank God, so for that, I'll forgive the fact that he's not wearing pants over his boxers—who knew calves could be so freaking erotic? All those lines of tight muscle... He's seated on the edge of the bed as if ready to jump at the first chance.

"You okay?" I ask.

"Mm-hmm."

I don't miss the double take he does when he sees me, and I've never regretted my choice of clothes this much before, especially with how freaking cold it is here.

Carter's gaze traces my bare arms for a second longer before he gets up and goes to mess with the things in his bag. I pull out my phone and start messing with some of the pictures I took today. Some will make for great content.

"Here."

I look up to find Carter holding out a sweater. It's one I've seen him wear to sleep a few times, black with an almost erased printed logo, and I always thought it looked comfortable.

I slowly take it, running my fingers over the overwashed material that's become soft from its thinness. Then I lift a brow at him.

"You're always cold," he says casually as if this is the most normal thing in the world. *The human body is made of 206 bones. The Declaration of Independence was signed in 1776. Lilianne DiLorenzo always gets cold.*

"What?" he says, probably wondering why I'm looking at him like he's grown another head, and it might be the shadows playing tricks on my eyes, but I'd swear pink colors his cheeks.

He needs to stop. If I want this stupid infatuation to disappear so I can make it out of this fake marriage alive, he can't continue being this thoughtful. I'm starting to fantasize about things I have no business wishing for.

But I must be a real dummy because I still put on his sweater, knowing damn well I'll never want to take it off. His smell envelops me like a crisp early spring morning, and yes, this is definitely mine now.

"Thank you."

"Sure," he says, then stands there, staring at me while I pull my hair out of the neck of the sweater and settle back in bed.

"What are you doing?" I ask.

"Nothing," he says, still not moving.

I open the covers on the other side of the bed. "Stop acting like a prudish seventeenth-century woman and just get into bed already." When he *still* doesn't budge, I add, "I won't jump you, don't worry."

He mutters something unintelligible as he finally gets into bed, keeping as much distance as physically possible.

I must stink. Or maybe he does think I'll get all over him if he gets too close. Am I that threatening?

I spend the next hour working while Carter pulls out his sudoku book like an eighty-five-year-old and finally seems to relax. Then, when 10:00 p.m. hits, my phone vibrates, a pill emoji appearing on the screen.

I get up and grab all the medication I need to take at night while attempting to make the least amount of noise possible, then I walk back to bed, where my water bottle is waiting.

"You ready for bed?" I ask.

"Yeah," Carter says, putting his book on the bedside table, and then I turn the lights off. I take advantage of the complete darkness before our eyes have gotten used to it to swallow all my pills in one go, then gulp a few sips of water and join Carter in bed.

"Why do you hide?" comes his gruff voice a few seconds later.

I turn to my side. "Huh?"

"Your pills. Why'd you hide them?"

Why do I always forget this man is more perceptive than anyone gives him credit for?

"I didn't hide," I lie. "I just don't boast about taking them."

Movement comes from my side, and the bed dips as if he's now facing me too. "Waiting until it's dark to take them feels a lot like hiding."

"What are you, the pill police?"

He doesn't answer, only shifts closer as if he knows his silence is even more poignant than a question, and damn him, it works.

"It's not something I like to talk about, that's all." With my followers, sure. It's what started my channel, after all. Talking about my journey through illness and interacting with people who have gone through similar hardships. But with the people close to me, I try to keep it as silent as possible, even when I wish I could share my concerns with someone else.

"Why?" Even with the loud AC, I hear the rustle of the sheets as he moves closer as if he wants to be close enough to see all it is I'm not saying.

"Because I learned it's not what people want to listen to." I hate the rasp in my voice at that small sentence that's such a feat of vulnerability.

There were times after my transplant when I felt ill and was worried I might be rejecting my new kidney, and I preferred absorbing this anxiety than sharing it with others, even those I trusted the most. I didn't want to be their sick friend, or their sick granddaughter, or their sick colleague. I only ever wanted to be Lilianne.

"Someone hurt you," he says, not a question but a statement.

"I... What..."

"You mentioned the other day how you wanted someone who could actually love you. Meaning someone hurt you before."

I swallow. It doesn't hurt anymore to think about Greg as a person, but it does hurt to think of all the years I wasted with him, watching everything I said, the way I breathed, everything not to make him notice another thing that might be wrong about me. I saw the way he looked at the bruises on my arms from being poked, saw how he tried his hardest to pretend that I wasn't sick. So I did too.

"Maybe," I say, to both his previous questions.

After a long time where I almost wonder if Carter fell asleep, he says, "It's not something to be ashamed of."

"I know." In theory, I *do* know this, but old habits die hard and all that.

"I don't want you to hide the next time." Again, not a question or a suggestion, but a statement. Straight through, just like him. "Okay?"

"Mm-hmm."

"I'm serious." Suddenly, a hand lands on my waist, so warm even through the sweatshirt. I don't think he even realizes where he's touching me, his expression so focused. "You're a survivor. Own it."

My nose tingles, and I breathe deeply to keep myself under control.

"What about you?" I ask, wanting to change the subject before I burst into tears or worse. "Anyone important in your past?"

Now that I've gotten used to the darkness, I can see the shake of his head.

"Not one?"

Another head shake. "Never been a relationship guy."

I'm not sure I want to explore whatever that means, so instead, I say, "So you decided to skip the girlfriends stage and go straight to being married."

"Wasn't such a bad idea," he answers, and before I have the time to react to the lack of humor in his answer, the little tease has the gall to nudge me with his feet under the covers. I startle.

"Jumpy, are we?"

"You keep those feet to yourself, Andy." The truth is, I *am* jumpy. Having him this close to me, barely covered, his scent targeting every single one of my olfactory nerves so I can't smell anything but him... It's temptation incarnate.

He groans. "I'll sleep with my feet all over you if you continue with these stupid nicknames." For good measure, he hooks his legs over mine.

I push him away, which only makes him press harder. I laugh, bringing the covers higher up to hide my grin behind. "I was wrong about us being able to share a bed, apparently," I say.

It's as if my words are a magnifying glass that makes both of us realize just how close we've gotten. He might've started off at the other end of the bed, but our legs are now tangled, the soft hairs of his calves—*don't think about his calves*—brushing against my shaven ones. His hand still rests on my waist, and when his fingers flex, even a little, I shiver. Our heads rest on neighboring pillows, turned to face the other, breaths mingling in the middle.

Carter's gaze travels across my face, and when it lands on my lips like it did earlier, I almost beg him to kiss me, consequences be damned. So what if I fall for someone who only wants my body? So what, when that man is him?

His hand glides down my body at a torturous pace as if the pads of his fingers need to memorize every inch of me. I don't think he even realizes he's doing it, his expression lost in another dimension. Goose bumps cover my waist, then my thighs, where his fingers caress my skin before stopping at the bottom edge of my pajama shorts.

On an inhale, my lips part, and just as I move to shatter this never-ending wait and kiss him, it's as if a light turns on in his head. First, his hand lets go of me like I'm a burning object, and then he scoots away and turns on his back so he's facing the ceiling. I follow the bob of his throat that looks almost painful. "Don't worry," he says after an eternity. "I'll behave."

I remain where I was, both hoping he'll come back and thanking him for being stronger than me.

"Good night, Lilianne."

After a breath, I flip to my back too, our bodies now separated by enough space that I can trust myself again. "Good night, Carter."

I don't fall asleep for a long, long time.

Chapter 27

It's rare that the living area of the tour bus is empty, and while I love hanging out with everyone, I cherish those precious moments of quiet. This morning, we stopped at a rest area to shower and shop around before our stop in Nashville tonight, and since I didn't feel like spending money I don't have, I decided to come back early and enjoy an empty bus. Carter came back with me, but he's been in his bunk for a while, maybe napping or reading.

My father's guitar sits in my lap as I strum it mindlessly, something I've gotten in the habit of doing, all the while reading on my computer. I didn't plan on landing on the AA website, but one thing led to the next, and my screen quickly went from my YouTube page to this article on the signs that someone close to you might be suffering from alcohol dependence.

Personality changes. High tolerance to alcohol. Drinking all day. Impulsive decisions.

Nothing about this sounds like him. Maybe I could recognize my father in tiny details here and there, but he's never been inappropriate at home or in public. I don't think I ever even saw him drunk.

"What are you doing?"

I jerk at the sound of Carter's voice, slamming my computer shut in a way that clearly makes me look guilty. I'm not sure why I'm hiding this. He saw what I saw in that bedroom. He knows the questions running through my head even if we don't talk about it.

"Nothing," I still lie.

"Find anything interesting?"

So he did see what I was scrolling through.

I shake my head.

Carter doesn't answer, but he also doesn't look away as if he thinks I'll crumble under his stare and spill everything that's been going through my head since we found those flyers, and I won't. It doesn't matter that I've started to have some doubts about whether there's a possibility that Carter's right and Dad might have had an alcohol problem without me knowing. I'm not acknowledging it.

After what must be a long thirty seconds of staring, he looks down at my hands on the guitar and says, "Lilianne, I need to—"

The front door of the bus bursting open interrupts him. We turn to find a panicked Bong step inside, Joe in tow.

"We're fucked," Bong yelps, breathless.

"What's wrong?" I ask, already on my feet, guitar discarded.

"Emmett's sick."

"Sick how?"

He must realize I just tensed up because he gives me an apologetic look. "Like throwing up everywhere. Food poisoning or something."

Something inside me loosens.

"So what's all the shouting about?" Carter grumbles.

Bong looks at him like he's stupid. "We're playing a sold-out show in five hours and our guitarist is currently shitting his guts out."

"That *is* a problem," I say.

"We can't cancel a show. Not during our first tour when our name is just starting to get out there," Joe says, only slightly calmer than Bong.

"Can't we get him to a hospital so he can get rehydrated before tonight?" I say.

Bong lifts a brow. "You haven't seen this, Lil. It's bad."

I don't think I *want* to see it either.

"So, again, we're fucked," he says, dropping onto the couch.

Carter moves my guitar away to take a seat next to Bong, then starts messing with the knobs and strings.

"I mean, there could be one solution." Everyone's ears perk at that, but my eyes are only on Carter.

It takes him a moment to realize what I mean, and when he does, he becomes stock-still. "Fuck no."

"You know all the songs already. No one else could replace Emmett."

"I'm not doing it."

I regret putting him on the spot. Now Bong and Joe's attention is on him, which is probably only making this worse. It's not that he doesn't like them, but Carter's a private person, and having others weigh in on his decisions is a bad idea.

I take his hand and force him to his feet, then tug him toward the bunk section of the bus. He grumbles the whole way. "Get it out of your head, Fireball."

Once I've closed the partition between us and the others, I say, "What's holding you back?"

"I told you. I don't play anymore."

"Yes, you do. You might not have picked up a guitar in years, but you're still a guitarist. It's in your head. In your body." He still reaches for the instrument when he needs something to do with his hands, even if most of the time, he doesn't even realize he does it.

He stretches the neck of his hoodie.

"I've seen the way you look at that guitar," I say, pointing toward the living room. "You miss it. It's obvious."

He doesn't deny it, which I know is a win.

"It fucked me up," he grunts out.

I hate the way it seems to hurt him just to think about that time in his life. Still, I don't think this is a bad idea. "Being in that band was bad for you, but that doesn't mean *playing* is." I take a step closer to him, then look up so I can meet his eyes. "Don't let the bad experience you had take away from your love for it."

In the end, no one can force him. If he doesn't want to play, he won't play, simple as that. It would be a shame, though, for him to let go of something that used to be so important to him. That still *is* important to him, even if he's pushed it aside.

He runs a hand over his head, and something coils in my gut, the way it does during every one of my follow-up appointments with my nephrologist, like this might be the moment everything changes. Except this time, it's not about me, and it's somehow worse to be nervous for someone else.

I see the moment his mind shifts. His eyes flit back to the living room, where Bong and Joe are probably on their toes waiting for his answer. Or maybe he's looking toward where my father's guitar lies on the couch behind the partition, waiting.

He doesn't need to say the words. I know him.

I smile, then tap his hard chest. "Come on, rock star. Let's get you ready."

~elle~

I might be more nervous than he is.

It feels as if I'm the one about to go on stage, my heart pulsing in my throat, nausea threatening to make my dinner come back up. I could faint at any moment, but I just swallowed a pack of table salt and drank a juice from the bar to make sure it wouldn't happen.

I could never do this. Talking to thousands of people behind a camera is one thing, but performing live is a true nightmare. I almost feel bad about pressuring him to do this. Almost.

He needed the push. If he doesn't like it, he never has to do it again, but this could be his opportunity to learn how to enjoy playing again, even if it's just for himself, and what a gift that would be.

The first act, a girl with pink hair and what must be ten-inch heels, announces her last song, sending my jitters into a tailspin.

He'll be fine. He's done this before. No reason for him to mess up. Unless he chokes and walks away, and then we'd be in real trouble.

I shake my head, then try to focus on the performance in front of me. I'm not filming anything tonight, too nervous about what's about to happen.

Way too quickly, the singer finishes and says her goodbyes, and the following fifteen minutes of break are pure torture. I should've gone backstage, made sure he felt okay before going on. What if he's having a panic attack? What if he feels like drinking and I'm the one who put him there?

My rambling thoughts are interrupted when, in one heartbeat, we're bathed in darkness.

Too late now. This is it.

The concert hall is packed, bodies surrounding me close enough that I barely have room to breathe, but I'm not sure I could anyway. Screams erupt, some fans chanting Ethan's name, and even through my nervous haze, I take the time to realize how insane it is that people have started recognizing the members of Crash & Burn by name. This is getting bigger than I ever could have hoped for them.

I know the show always starts with Emmett playing the first note of "Be My Guest," one of the most popular songs of their debut album, and I wait for it like a sprinter expecting the shot of the gun. My hands are clasped under my chin, and I whisper over and over again, "You got this, Carter."

The time in between the lights closing and the first strum of the guitar feels longer than usual. Another bout of faintness hits me, and I squeeze every muscle in my body to stay upright. What if something happened?

I mutter another prayer to whatever god is listening.

And then, the strum of the guitar shatters the room, the note so loud and electric it buzzes under my skin and stops time.

My screams blend with the other fans' as the spotlights open over the band, illuminating every single one of their beautiful faces as they enter into "Be My Guest" with the control and energy of a group that's been doing this for years.

The sound is so loud in the room, I can't even hear my own shouts, and it doesn't matter one bit. The music infiltrates my body, my blood, as if my heart beats to the rhythm of Bong's drums.

And when my eyes land on Carter, I almost pass out.

He's standing slightly in the shadows, way farther back than Emmett usually does, almost as if he wants to disappear from view, but I couldn't miss him even if I tried.

I was scared he would be uncomfortable on stage, but I've never seen someone so in his element. His eyes are closed, head thrown back so his face is tilted toward the top of the room as if he's playing for no one but himself. I'm close enough to notice the sheen of sweat on his forehead and neck. The black T-shirt exposing his tattoos and the muscles of his arms flexing as he hits note after note is the most beautiful sight I've ever seen. No one has ever looked this good. I know it for a fact.

The music seems to come to him as easily as breathing as if he'd never stepped away. I might be a crybaby, but it brings tears to my eyes to see him like this. With others and even at home, he always looks so reserved, so casual, but here, passion is dripping from his fingers, from the strands of hair falling over his fingers as he finishes the song and jumps straight into the next one. He looks almost orgasmic, with the way the tendons in his neck are stretched and his lips are parted, connecting to the music in a way only he can understand.

My hands move from under my chin to rest on my heart, where they remain for the rest of the show.

The moment the band walks off stage, I'm moving, apologizing left and right to the people I bump into as I try to make my way toward the front of the room, where I'll be able to climb backstage.

I can't believe I've just lived this moment. I don't think a lifetime could erase the memories of this night. How it felt to witness Carter transform from a simple man into a burning comet right in front of my eyes. I'd seen only a few clips of him performing in the past, but nothing could ever compare to seeing it live.

My hair is matted to my forehead, skin covered in sweat as I rush through the throng of bodies. I don't waste a moment to put myself back together. The second I reach the door where security stands guard, I show my badge, then walk backstage.

A lot of people have made their way to the small room, most of them industry professionals or fans who paid for a meet & greet, but even through the crowd, I find Carter in a nanosecond. Ethan is clapping his back, Bong shouting at him in excitement, but he doesn't give them any attention, gaze lost in the crowd, searching.

And then he lands on me and stops there.

I can't control myself, launching into a run before throwing myself at him, graceless. Thankfully, he catches me, strong arms forming bands at my lower back, solid enough that I know I couldn't move even if I wanted to.

"You were so goddamn magnificent out there," I say in his ear so he can hear through the cacophony.

When I pull back, Carter frowns, and I remember my face is probably still covered in tears that never stopped streaming. I can't even muster the embarrassment I should feel. "I'm so proud of you for doing it."

Finally, he seems to realize my tears are ones of happiness because he buries his head in my neck again, one of his hands moving from my back to my nape, holding me tight. Critics and fans are in the room, so he might be pretending for the sake of realism, but somehow, I have a feeling he isn't.

When Carter finally speaks, it's to say, "Thank you." The movement of his lips against the delicate skin of my neck activates every single one of my nerve endings.

"For what?" I ask.

He pulls back as he carefully lowers me down, although he never lets go of me, even when my feet hit the ground. The only thing he does is bring one of his hands to my face so he can wipe the tears from my cheeks. He's not smiling, and yet he looks so freaking happy, it does something to my heart.

He brushes my cheekbone another time, this time as if only for the sake of touching me, then says, "Everything."

Chapter 28

I'm drenched in sweat.

 I close the door of our rental home behind me, trying to catch my breath as Paramore blares through my earphones. I'd initially gone out for a walk while I called Nan, but as she started droning on about who was sleeping with who in her home, I started getting antsy and decided to go for a run instead.

 Bad idea. I'm terribly out of shape, hence my inability to catch my breath. Still, when Gran hung up because she had a poker game to attend and she "wouldn't miss that just to talk to me," I decided to put on music and push myself to run as long as I could. It wasn't very long, but it still shook some of the restlessness I'd been feeling for the past few days while being stuck in a bus with five other people. Even now that we're in an Airbnb for the next day, it's still stifling.

 As I walk to the kitchen to grab a glass of water, I pick up various items of clothing strewn across the floor, from lone socks to jeans and even boxers—how they all got there, I have no idea. I sure won't miss this when I get back.

 Tonight's my last night on this leg of the tour. I've gathered and produced enough content to last for weeks while I traveled with the band, and anyway, Finn and Lexie's wedding is in three days, so I have to return home.

I grab my water, then finish picking up all the stuff the guys left out, dancing to yet another song at the same time. We've only been here for one night, but the entire living area is a mess, just like it was on the bus. I clean the kitchen, then the living room, and only when I get to the dining room do I notice the box of grocery store chocolate chip cookies left on the table with my name written on it, in Emmett's calligraphy. I smile, thinking back to the moment a few days ago when I said I missed baking in my kitchen. He might have thought I meant I missed the products more than I missed the act of baking, but the intention means just as much.

Yeah, never mind, I'll miss being here.

I grab two cookies, then make my way to the second floor, where the bedrooms and the bathroom we all share are. Everyone left for sound checks right before I went on my run, so I'll be able to take as much time as I want in the shower before I have to return to my editing.

◻I hum the new song that's been shuffled from my playlist, throwing my stinky tank top and shorts in my bedroom before stepping into the bathroom.

And then I freeze.

The sounds die in my mouth as I take in the scene in front of me, blinking repeatedly.

Carter is standing in the shower, steam billowing around him as he leans one hand against the tiled wall, water dripping over his head and down his chiseled back and ass. He's facing the shower wall, so he doesn't see me, but even so, he looks too focused to notice anything.

Movement makes my eyes drag lower, and a volcano erupts inside of me as I notice the grip he has on his length, jerking up and down the thick girth.

Oh God. I can't be here. I need to carefully walk away and forget I ever saw anything.

And yet I don't move. I don't know how to. My mouth falls open as I take in the rapid rise and fall of his chest, the sharp way his hips thrust in his hand, those damn tendons in his neck tensing as he pleasures himself, shudders running through his body. My ears drown out the music still playing in my ears as if all my senses need to dull so I can give my entire attention to this.

Carter's jaw shifts as he bites into his full lower lip, and even though I can't hear him, imagining the sounds he makes is enough to build a throbbing ache between my legs.

I've never seen anything so hot. Scratch that, I never even thought something so hot could exist.

I really need to get the hell out of here. It's too late to erase the image from my eyes—I could never forget the way Carter looks like when gripping his cock—rough, decisive, entranced—but maybe if I leave, I'll get a slim chance of being able to move on and also make sure he never knows I was here.

But I must be a masochist because I stay, inhaling each of Carter's sharp exhales, dreaming of the taste of the droplets sliding between his tense shoulder blades, wishing it were my hand around him instead of his.

I'm going to hell, fantasizing about my fake husband I'm developing very real feelings for and watching him like this.

My heart races as I continue tracking his right hand that moves from his swollen tip all the way to the clean-shaven base and back. It's something I've seen some of my exes do plenty of times, yet this is a world away. I've never felt this crazed while watching a man touch himself, never felt like crawling out of my skin from how aroused I was. Wetness pools at my entrance, and when his movements get faster, I hold my breath, almost as if I'll get my release instead of him.

I thought Carter was hot before, but he looks god-like as his control loosens on his movements, muscles bunching in the arm holding him up against the wall. So much so that when he releases a groan loud enough for me to hear through the music, I gasp.

His head turns my way, and our eyes lock.

Oh God. No, no, no.

Neither one of us looks away, and while I know this is the moment I need to leave, I'm rooted in place. One of us should acknowledge what is happening here, how we're shattering the glass wall we've erected between us. I should be the one doing it, looking away, but I physically can't. He doesn't stop either, his hand only moving faster around himself, and something that looks almost like pain crosses his face before he shatters, spilling against the wall, his glowing eyes never leaving mine.

I follow every jerk of his body, every twitch of his back. His orgasm seems to last forever as his knuckles turn white where he's holding himself against the wall. When he's done, the veins in his neck pulse as he catches his breath, body looking weak. He blinks. Blinks again.

And that is the moment I realize the full extent of what just happened, and freaking finally, I get my body to move, running all the way back to my bedroom and locking the door behind me.

I pull my earbuds out as I lean my back against the door, heart thrashing against my ribcage. The sound of the running shower disappears a few seconds later.

Shit. Shit, shit, shit.

I messed up. There's no way I'll ever be able to look at him again without imagining him in all kinds of pornographic images, and that's not what we signed up for. At least not what *he* signed up for.

Footsteps come from the hallway, making me tense up.

I hate that I stayed and watched him. I hate that I wanted to stay and watch him.

More than that, I hate that I want to get my vibrator and come with his name on my lips.

The footsteps slow in front of my door, and I hold my breath and close my eyes as if I can get him to forget about me if I try hard enough. I can't have a mature conversation about this. Not now, at least, when I'm still amped up and need to control all the lust I feel for him.

A moment passes, then another, and finally, the footsteps resume.

My muscles loosen enough that my back slides along the door so I fall on my ass. The wood burns my skin, reminding me that not only did I stare at my fake husband jerk off, I also did so while only wearing panties and a sports bra.

Fantastic.

I pull at the roots of my hair, trying to get me to think about something other than the face Andrew Carter makes when he comes. It doesn't work.

I need to leave first thing tomorrow morning. Hopefully, the time away will do me good. It has to. The way I felt for Carter had already gotten bad, but this has made things so much worse. I can't be thinking of him like this. Not if I want to get out of this marriage in one piece. I know a part of him cares about me, that's obvious, but his small infatuation will never equal my deep feelings, and I'll only end up hurt.

And yet there's a tiny voice inside of me that says, *he let you stay*. He could've jumped and told me to get out. He could have yelled or hidden. Maybe he was too lost in his moment to react properly, or maybe, just maybe, he wanted me right where I was.

Chapter 29

"You are the prettiest bride to have ever existed."

I have to hold back my tears as Lexie fixes a curl that escaped her bun, glowing. Her white dress is simple, nothing but pristine silk that falls into a short train covered by the prettiest lace veil. I know my best friend will bawl his eyes out when he sees his bride, and I'll be right there with him. I've never seen two people so in love and so deserving of this moment.

"Do you think the makeup's too much? Maybe I should—"

I stop her, hands on her shoulders. "You're perfect."

She gives me a shaky smile. I've seen this girl perform at the Olympic games, yet she's never looked more nervous than she does right now. It's all good nerves, though. After a two-year engagement, I know she's so ready to marry Finn.

"I wish I'd convinced him to elope."

"I know, but selfishly, I'm really happy you failed," I say, squeezing her into a quick embrace. I seem to be overflowing with love today, crying left and right and wanting to hug everyone I pass. I might never have a real wedding, but at least I can live vicariously through this one.

I glance down at my ring, the gold band perfectly matching the necklace I found in Dad's bedroom. My own wedding was nothing like today's, and yet it's a very real longing I feel at this moment.

After the *incident*—what I've called whatever happened in that bathroom in Chicago—I left straight for the airport in the morning, leaving a note saying I'd see everyone when they were back in New England. I couldn't face Carter, especially not when there was a chance I'd ruined the friendship we'd spent months building. But now it's been five days, and I miss him like crazy. I didn't know how much I'd gotten used to having him around until I came back home and he wasn't there. I used to be fine eating alone and doing everything by myself, but now, my food tastes bland when I look at the empty seat next to mine on the couch. I should not be missing him like this, especially since I miss more than his friendship. I miss his warmth when his leg touches mine while we watch a movie, miss the way I feel when I succeed in making him laugh, like I've won the lottery.

The door opens behind me, making Lexie and me turn to find Wren there, wearing a tight dress in a similar shade of green as mine. "It's time," she says, eyes glinting.

"All right. Show time," I tell Lexie, who's got her game face on. She decided to walk down the aisle by herself, so I'll be joining the other bridesmaids to leave her alone. "You got this."

She nods, and I follow Wren out the door of the main house on the Evermore Christmas Tree Farm before we join Finn's and Lexie's sisters, who are hidden by large fir trees right next to the start of the aisle, decorated with large assemblies of colorful flowers and candles. Finn decided on having only a best man, so Aaron waits with the girls, grinning widely when he sees his wife approaching. As soon as the Canons in D begin, Aaron takes her arm and kisses her cheek with so much tenderness I nearly melt before they start making their way down. Then it's my turn.

The decor looks fabulous, but my gaze immediately travels to Finn, who looks as nervous as Lexie did, but who also seems happier than I've ever seen him. I can't stop smiling as I realize how lucky I am to be here today, witnessing the magic that exists between these two people I love so much.

There isn't a large crowd, only the people closest to Finn and Lexie. I meet a few faces I recognize as I take slow steps, hands wrapped around a smaller version of Lexie's wildflower bouquet, and just as I'm about to look back at Finn, I almost miss a step and regain my balance at the last second. Because right there is a face I never thought I'd see here. One I could never have missed even if I didn't know what I was looking for. Carter's seated in the third row, surrounded by smiling people, but my gaze is snagged on him like a magnet. Seeing him is a breath of fresh spring air after a long winter. And dressed like this, with what appears to be a black suit and crisp white shirt... I won't survive this.

I know I should be bringing my attention to the front as I approach the end of the aisle, but there's no way I can break the contact when he's looking at me like that. Like maybe he's feeling as out of control as I am.

When I reach his row of chairs, I finally get over my shock and smile at him because I'm so freaking happy he's made his way to me.

And when he gives me a subtle grin back, I know I'm done for.

"You clean up well, husband."

Carter turns from where he's grabbing a soda at the bar, and somehow, he looks even better from up close. I'm not sure where this suit comes from, but I know I want to see him in it again and again.

He doesn't answer, only walking my way with a second drink in his hands. When he hands it to me, his eyes rake over my body, and even if he doesn't say the words, I know he's returning the compliment.

The ceremony has just ended, and instead of leaving to take pictures, Lexie and Finn have already joined the party, music blaring under the white marquee. Finn's twirling Lexie around, the two of them laughing out loud like kids.

"What are you doing here?" I ask him, trying to sound casual. I want to jump on him, hug him like I haven't seen him in a year, but I also don't know how that would be received. He might be thinking about the last time we saw each other, when only a fogged-up room and heavy breaths separated us. I'd be okay if we never brought it up again, but he might have a different thought about this.

Carter's throat bobs, but before he can answer, the music switches to a Beyoncé song I adore. I gasp, then grab his hand. "Want to dance?"

His brows draw together at the sudden change of topic, the question, or both. Then he gives me a small shake of his head. "I'm good."

I shrug, then join the newlyweds and the rest of the guests who fill the dance floor, immediately starting to dance with a group of people I don't know. I'll get answers from Carter later.

I move my hips to the rhythm, eyes closed and head tossed back. The day smells like pine trees and freshly mowed grass, and the end-of-summer breeze is a delight against my skin. I continue dancing as we roll into the next song, and when someone takes my hand, I go with it. I laugh, hair loose as one of Finn's cousins, a short guy with a mop of brown hair, twirls me around, but my spin ends abruptly when two large hands catch my hips. The guy looks behind me and immediately lets go of my hand. I don't care, though, not when all my attention is now on the bergamot smell coming from behind me.

Carter squeezes my hips before he says, "The things you make me do, Fireball." And then he begins moving with me.

The fabric of his dress shirt brushes the bare skin at my back, making me gasp. There's no reason for this to feel so intimate, but the simple movement of his hips against mine, of the tips of his fingers so close to my panty lines, brings images back to me I've tried desperately to forget. Carter naked, touching himself, burning me with his stare as he comes undone. Sweat gathers at my nape as his breath caresses my shoulder, then my neck. He's so close, and I don't think I've ever wanted anyone more.

When the song ends, it switches to a slower one, forcing me to spin so I can wrap my arms around his neck. It's such a bad idea, but I can't help myself. He doesn't hesitate either, lifting his hands from my hips to my waist, never letting go of my body. Then he starts swaying to the soft music, bringing me with him.

"You didn't answer me earlier." I crane my neck so I can meet his eyes. "What are you doing here?"

His cheek twitches. "My job on the tour was done."

That's BS. His work isn't done as long as the band's second album isn't done, and even if it was, he wouldn't need to come here, to my friends' wedding. No one knows me here. It's not like we need to keep up with our marriage pretense.

My hands slip from his neck to his shoulders. "What are you really doing here?"

His gaze searches my face, from my brows to my lips to my nose, then back to my eyes. Then, as softly as a breath, he says, "I missed you."

Three simple words that mean an entire universe. He doesn't need to say anything else. It already means everything.

Applause breaks into the room, probably as Lexie and Finn kiss, but I don't move my gaze away from him. This man who followed me back home because he wanted to spend more time with me.

My lips curl up. "I'm really glad you're back, Andy."

Chapter 30

I've never danced this much in my life.

The relief I feel when I tug my shoes off as I walk inside my place is endless. It's barely 1:00 a.m., but after Lexie and Finn disappeared from the dance floor—her on his shoulder, him running across the field of trees toward the little cottage they'd kept for themselves for their wedding night—I grabbed Carter's hand and figured the party was over. I'd exerted myself enough anyway, dancing the night away with my friends and with the man who'd said he didn't want to dance.

"I need to burn these," I say as I let my shoes fall to the ground and stretch my feet against the carpeted floor.

"Should've removed them a long time ago if they hurt you," Carter says, taking his jacket off. I almost pout. He looked so good in it.

"But they make my legs look really good," I say over my shoulders with a wink.

He keeps a straight face. "They'd look good regardless."

My next breath is difficult against the tension enveloping the room—or is it just the tension between the two of us? Ever since I saw him sitting in those garden chairs, I haven't been able to keep my eyes off him, and I think the feeling's mutual. In fact, I've been attuned to him for far longer than that. Even before the shower, before the bed we shared, before the kiss. He feels right in a way I never thought I'd experience again, and as he loosens his tie and unbuttons the top of his shirt, I find myself wishing he were *actually* mine, that I had a right to walk over to him and help him undress. It's unhealthy, but I can't help it.

"Tired?" I ask. I know I am, even though being this close to him has my body on high alert.

He hums, not taking his eyes away from me.

"Time for bed, then," I answer. "Thanks for tonight."

"For what?" he asks.

"Dancing with me? Just coming down and being there?" I would've loved Finn and Lexie's wedding regardless, but Carter made the night flawless.

"Course," he says in that deep voice of his that sends a wave of heat down my spine.

I nod, then turn toward my room but stop midway when I remember how hard it was to get in that dress, however good it looks.

I walk back to Carter, offering him my back while I bring my hair over my shoulder. "Unzip me?"

An abnormally long pause ensues as if he's hesitating or wondering how to do it. I feel exposed, my skin in full display to him with that back décolleté.

Finally, the shift of fabric rustles as he leans closer, then his fingertips graze against the skin of my shoulder blades as he slowly pulls the zipper down. Only when it's just above my panty line does he let go and step back.

"Thanks." I turn to him, stomach hollowing at the fire burning in his eyes as they continue roaming my body. I should take a step back, protect my fragile heart, but I remain in place, letting my gaze drop to the fine bristles of hair at the top of his chest, then to the tight fists at his sides, and finally to the strong muscles in his clenched jaw.

"Lilianne," he says, voice tight as a drawstring.

"What?"

"You gotta stop looking at me like that."

Even with the heat scalding my cheeks, I ask, "Like what?"

"Like you want me." His tongue darts out to wet his lips. "You think I haven't noticed the way you've been checking me out?" A deep breath puffs out of his chest. "My self-restraint's at its end."

I need to replay his words a few times to make sure I've actually understood what he meant. I knew a part of him wanted this, but this is more than casual wanting. This is pure craving.

He meant it as a threat, a reason to walk away, but I only take a step closer. His nostrils flare as he looks down, where the straps of my gown are dangerously close to falling down my arms.

"I don't think this is a good idea," he says, but his body tells me the opposite. It looks as if he's trying his hardest to hold himself back, and I want him unleashed. I want him to tell me what I do to him, to do what was playing out in his head while he jerked off. I don't care that he's right and this is a terrible idea that could make the next year and a half of our lives a living hell, or that I'll probably only end up hurt. I can't handle this anymore. Not when I know he feels the same. A part of me also tells me this isn't just physical to him. He wouldn't have come here from tour because he missed me if he just wanted sex. He could get that anywhere.

This is more.

I take another step closer, my chest now brushing his, breasts sensitive against the silk fabric of my dress.

"Lilianne—"

"Goddammit, will you just kiss me?"

And kiss me, he does.

My words seem to be his undoing because one moment we're standing in the middle of the living room, and the next my back is forced against the wall, Carter's hand wrapped lightly around my throat in a possessive embrace as he kisses me breathless. His head bent, mine extended back, we're perfectly crooked to allow the most contact.

My hands immediately climb to his hair, pulling as he nips at my lips in teasing bites, then tangles my tongue with his in a way that makes my toes curl against the carpet.

He kisses me like a starved man, like someone who's waited years to finally get to this moment. And I eat it all up, meeting him blow for blow, bite for bite. He smells like pine trees and the musky scent of what I now know is his aftershave, the combination making me want to scream. I want him more than I've ever wanted anything in my life, more than I need my next breath.

The way his fingers caress my neck sends chills all over my skin, and when I jump to wrap my legs around his hips, he catches me with his other hand before rolling his hips against mine, pushing me harder against the wall while also showing me how hard he is already.

"You look so goddamn gorgeous like this," he whispers against my lips before kissing me once more, his lips soft but claiming. "With my hands on you and my ring on your finger."

I'm panting against him, my core clenching when he rubs his cock against me once more.

"Did you enjoy watching me touch myself?" he breathes, so low I barely catch it.

"You have no idea," I say, riding his hips for any hint of friction I can get, then suck at the spot where his jaw meets his neck. "Now get my dress off."

His hands never stop roaming my body. "We don't have to."

"I said take my dress off," I repeat before kissing him, this time biting his lip.

He winces, but the hurt only seems to excite him more. His lips even curl against mine, eyes dark. "As you wish."

He steps back just enough so there's space for him to push the straps of my dress down my arms, exposing my naked breasts to him. My nipples harden against the cool air, but the sensation is immediately forgotten when Carter pushes me back against the wall and wraps his warm lips against one nipple, licking and sucking until I'm gasping out loud.

"You make me crazy, you know that?" he says before lightly biting the edge of my left breast. The back of my head rests against the wall as I push my chest against his mouth, feeling like my mind has left my body and I'm only chasing sensations. "With that tight dress showing that perfect ass, barely covering your tits." He rubs a thumb over my nipple, looking at it like he's mesmerized. "Fuck. I wanted to kill every single man who stared at you." He punctuates his sentence by moving to my other breast and licking it from top to bottom, dragging a moan out of my throat.

"I didn't care about any other man," I say, rolling my pelvis against his hardness so I can get some friction where I need him the most.

"Better not." He trails kisses down my sternum as his hands move up from my thighs higher, caressing all the sensitive skin there. "I don't give back what's mine." Another long kiss. "I'll give you everything you want." His gaze looks lost as he stares at the wet spot he left on my skin. "Everything."

His hands continue to climb my thighs, up until his thumbs brush my panties. Against my neck, he whispers, "Are you wet for me?"

I nod, mouth dry. There's not enough air in this room, on this planet.

"Show me," he says, rubbing his finger back and forth at the edge of my panties, so close to where I want him but never getting there.

Not wanting to waste another second, I push my panties to the side and grab his hand, bringing it to my drenched middle.

Carter hums, dragging one finger up from my entrance all the way to my clit, giving it one rub that has me shaking before he pulls it away. I almost cry as I watch him bring the finger to my lips, making me suck on it, taste myself. The groan he lets out reverberates all through my strung-out body.

"Not what I meant," he says, then picks me up and brings me to the couch. He lays me down on my back. "Showed you mine, now show me yours."

I stare at him, breaths erratic.

He runs a hand over my belly, once again looking lost, like he's in a haze. He traces my transplant scar with a sort of reverence. Then he brings his gaze back to mine, glazed. "Touch yourself, honey."

I have the reflex to be embarrassed and hide, but he's right. He *did* show me his, planned or not. It's only fair I return the favor.

It takes all the courage in my body to bring my trembling hand down to my core and spread my legs under Carter's carnal stare. Then I start stroking myself gently, so gently, but even those light touches make me shudder. It feels so different from when I do it by myself, and I attribute it all to the way Carter watches me, like I'm all his daydreams turned into reality. His cock strains against his zipper, outlined in his trousers, the sight giving me another boost of bravery. He's enjoying this as much as I am.

I roll my hips against my fingers, rubbing my clit faster and faster, feeling warmer than I've been all night. Carter's eyes have gone completely dark as they're fixed on my drenched middle, following each movement of my fingers with bated breath.

It's too much. I've imagined him so many times while touching myself, but watching him as I do so, the part of his lips and the way he has to adjust himself in his pants as he continues watching, it's too overwhelming. I push my head back against the cushions, closing my eyes as I circle faster, legs starting to quake.

He tsks, pulling my chin so my face is tilted back toward him. "Eyes open. I want to see you when you come."

I gasp a breath, hips undulating to get more friction, more movement, more, more, more.

"You're doing such a good job," he says, then crawls closer onto the couch so he's on his knees between my legs. "Want a finger inside?"

I nod, unable to speak.

He doesn't waste time inserting a knuckle, then another, the feeling so delicious I almost come right there.

"Jesus fuck," he mutters before he finally leans over me and kisses me once more. His finger never stops pumping inside me as his tongue plunges into my mouth once more, curling against mine, stealing the breath right out of my lungs. I'm not sure I'm even kissing him back, too focused on the way his finger curls inside me at just the right spot while I continue rubbing my clit, pressure building and building in my body until finally, I explode.

"Carter," I moan as I pulse around his finger, gripping him between my legs while I pull his face closer to mine, his hair clenched between my fingers. It feels like my orgasm lasts forever, my lips parted against his like he's inhaling every sound I make, looking at me with a hunger I've never seen on anyone before.

"That's it, honey," he coos, pumping until I can't take it anymore. I push myself away, catching my breath as his hands knead my thighs.

"Jesus." I sigh. "You really are the whole package, aren't you?"

He grins, a minuscule lift of his lips, making my heart go *whoosh* like it does whenever he smiles at me, except this time, it's filled with anticipation and lust. I don't think I could ever get enough of this man. He could touch me a million times and I'd ask him for just one more. And maybe this will end one day and I'll have to grieve what it feels like to be handled by Andrew Carter, but I'll cross that bridge when I get there. For now, I want to enjoy every beautiful inch of him for as long as I can.

I lift myself on my elbows so I can catch his lips between mine, then lift a hand to wrap it around his cock outside of his pants. He hisses in my mouth but doesn't pull away, instead grinding himself against my hand.

"You need to stop touching me if you want to stop here."

"I don't."

I continue rubbing him up and down as he says, "I could just touch you all night and I'd be fine with it."

I know he means it, which makes me even more eager to take him into me and give him the same ecstasy he did.

"I think it's time I take care of you." I unzip him, keeping my eyes on his when I lower his trousers and boxers and grip his hard length, rubbing it up and down twice. Then I look down at it, all smooth skin and raised veins, and bend so I can tease the crown with my tongue.

"Fuck," he grunts as I continue running my tongue around him, tasting the salty tanginess on his tip. Then I take him in as deep as I can, relaxing around his length. The muscles of his thighs bunch under my hands as he fights to keep control over himself. I don't want him to remain in control, though. I want all of him, rough and rugged. I peer up, maintaining the eye contact as I suck him deeper.

"I don't want to think about how you got this good at blow jobs," he grunts, hips shifting lightly. "But I'm really fucking thankful for it."

I grin, then twirl my tongue around him.

"Gotta stop, honey." He pulls out of my mouth in one swift move, then shifts me so I'm on my hands and knees, his length prodding against me. "Are you okay?"

"Yes," I moan, pushing myself against him. It's embarrassing how much I want him, need him still.

"Fuck. I don't have a condom."

I glance over my shoulder, his disheveled hair and wrinkled shirt making him look as desperate as I feel. "I'm on birth control, and I'm clear."

"Got tested a year ago and haven't been with anyone else since," he says. I try not to show my surprise at that, only nodding before I push myself closer to him, this time letting a bit of his tip enter me.

Carter wraps my loose ponytail around his fist once, twice and pulls me back. "That hair. That fucking hair." And then, he plunges into me.

My back arches at the sudden intrusion, my body suddenly lit with high voltage. Carter stills inside me as I try to relax and adjust to his size. He's breathing hard but giving me the time I need, and eventually, I rotate my hips so he can hit the spot I need and clench around him.

Carter runs his other hand over my backside, rubbing soothing circles. "Do you know how long I've been dreaming of this?"

"Since we shared a bed?" I guess as I move so his cock pulls back.

"Way before then, honey. Since I saw you across the bar that first time."

I shudder, then I sit back on him, making us both groan.

With this go ahead, Carter starts moving in and out, setting his pace to the sounds I make, to the way I shiver and falter under him. The way he pulls at my hair creates the perfect mixture of pleasure and pain, and when he brings his free hand to my clit and starts rubbing, I almost lose it.

"Do you know how beautiful you look around me?" he says against my ear once he pulls my hair enough that I'm standing on my knees, my ass stuck to his hips as he rolls them, hitting me inside at an angle that's almost too much. "You've done something to me. I can't get you out of my fucking head." He continues rubbing me at the perfect speed and pressure, having learned from the way I did it before.

"I don't think I can take it much longer," I whisper, moving against him so I'm as much in control as he is. I'm not sure what gets me off the most between his words and the way he touches me.

"Good." He pulls my head to one side so he can nip at my neck on the other. "Me neither." Then he keeps the same speed but somehow finds a way to go even harder and deeper. "You're gonna come for me again, aren't you?"

I nod, reaching back so I can grip his hair, his back, anything as my orgasm builds and builds, and when he turns my head and kisses me with a tenderness he hasn't shown before, I explode.

My nails scratch at the skin of his neck as I come again, this time contracting against his cock as his pace quickens, movements ragged and jerky until he lets out a groan and collapses against my back, emptying himself inside me.

It takes me a moment to come back to myself, both of us catching our breaths, our lower bodies tangled together. Once I do, I still don't move, unsure where this evening is going to go. Carter could just as well get up and go to bed.

No, he wouldn't, a small voice tells me.

And he proves it right when he wraps his arm around my waist, keeping me as close to him as physically possible, still inside me. We might have just had sex, but *this* is the most intimate moment I've ever experienced. A promise he's not going anywhere.

Which makes me feel safe enough to turn my head and tease, "Who knew the stranger I married was so well endowed?"

Carter snickers, his lips twisting in a smile that feels like it could only be for me before he nips my collarbone, making me giggle. "You're the most annoying, you know that?"

"I think you actually like me," I say, pushing my ass back against him.

"Yeah. I think maybe I do."

Chapter 31

The moment I unlock the front door to the house, soft chords escape from inside and wrap around me.

I barely make a sound as I step inside, then lean against the wall to watch Carter play from his spot on the couch. It's the first time I've seen him pick up the guitar since the show he played in Detroit, but looking at him, you would never guess he stopped playing for years. The notes come out of his fingers like it's second nature. He's not playing on my father's old acoustic guitar but on the electric one I'd seen in his apartment when I'd visited. My hand clutches my chest as I watch him, all tall and strong but looking so very vulnerable at this moment.

When he strums the last chord, I applaud him loudly, making him jump and turn my way.

In a second, he's on his feet, guitar forgotten. "You're done already? Why didn't you call me?"

"Because I could walk just fine." I agreed to pick up a few shifts here and there to help out at the bar—something that's much less of a burden now that Jayson leaves me alone—and since the bar was pretty much empty all day, he sent me home at 9:00 p.m. "Barely dark out." My car somehow found a way to the garage once more. At this point, I should probably get rid of it since it spends the majority of its time broken, but I can't part from it. Every time I sit inside, I'm brought back to short summer drives with Dad to go grab ice cream in town. Even though he had his deadly accident in this same car, it brings me more comfort than pain to keep it, like he's still here with me, in this small way.

"I would've come to get you anyway," he says, then tucks a piece of hair behind my ear, sending tingles down my neck. The past few days have been a whirlwind, between my shifts and Carter's newfound success. After he went on stage with the band, some people recognized him from his time with Fickle, and some even made the connection between the guitar player/producer who's also married to me, and suddenly there were mentions of him online and edits with old pictures I know he hates. However, that recognition brought forth interviews and magazine articles—*who is Andrew Carter, guitarist and now producer?*—so his label is more than pleased with him, already planning on involving him in more projects. With all of that, we've barely had time to see each other. Even so, our cohabitation is nothing like it was before we left on tour. Sure, the most time we've spent together has been our few hours of shared sleep in my bed, but the differences are in the details. The way I can feel him looking at me when I pack up my lunch, the mindless brush of his hand against my waist when he passes me in the hallway, the short texts he sends me to know when I'll be back home and what I'd like to eat for dinner. What we did after the wedding should've complicated everything, and yet life has felt so natural since. We haven't clarified anything, but I don't feel the need to. Not when I can enjoy him in this simplicity for now.

"I know you would've." I take a seat on the opposite side of him on the couch. "But I didn't need you to."

He grunts. "What are you doing all the way over there?"

I lift a brow, then yelp as he grabs me under the legs and arms and pulls me closer to him so there's no space between our bodies.

"Better, caveman?" I ask, laughing.

He nods once, ever so serious, which makes me laugh once more. Then I let my head fall to his shoulder as he resumes his playing. It feels surreal to be doing this next to Carter. Even after sleeping together, after waking up tangled up in him, his breaths warm on my neck, I'm still not sure I'm not dreaming right now.

Carter has clearly cleaned around the house today, and with every blanket and pillow cleared up, my attention is dragged toward the box sitting at the edge of the living room and foyer. One I placed there yesterday.

"Maybe not tonight, okay?"

Carter continues playing soft, mindless notes, but his eyes find mine.

"Just...not yet," I add in a small voice.

I've lost track of how many times I've put the box in this exact spot, expecting Carter to bring it with the trash on his way out. The first time, I woke up in a panic at five in the morning, running to the door to make sure it was still there and bringing it back with me to my room. Since then, I've tried again and again to get rid of it, to no avail.

"You know you don't have to throw it away, right?" Carter says.

"Hm."

"What are you thinking?" he asks, voice feather soft.

I nudge myself closer in his embrace, cold seeping through my bones. "I'm thinking that I don't want to keep the reminder of all I might have missed in my home, but it also feels wrong to get rid of it." My gaze stays blank on the box. "You were right, weren't you? He did have a problem."

Carter's hand lands on my scalp, rubbing once. "I'm sorry, honey."

There's no lying to myself anymore. As much as I wish it wasn't true, the facts speak for themselves. He wouldn't have had all those documents hidden in his room for no reason.

"I don't understand why he didn't just *tell* me."

Carter's hands move from the guitar to rest against my nape, playing with my hair.

"He was suffering, and he never let me help." My voice is steady like all the tears and sleepless nights I've spent over this have finally settled into quiet acceptance.

"I'm sure he had his reasons."

The smell of Carter's detergent is a balm against my bruised heart. I pull back, enough that I can look him in the eye. "I need you to promise something."

He swallows, then nods.

"Promise me you'll tell me if you're ever struggling again. Don't leave me in the dark."

"I promise." He then presses a gentle kiss to my lips, one that feels like a seal to the deal.

Music resumes once more, like this conversation doesn't trouble him. He's not scared of broaching the harder topics, of seeing the parts of me I never let out of this house. He trudges on.

Now that the box doesn't loom above me so much, I tuck my legs to me and snuggle while I pull my phone out of my pocket. I need to answer messages from potential collaborators I didn't have time to respond to before.

The song he decides to play is one I love, an old rock classic, making me move my feet to the beat, but my body stills as a rock when I open my phone and see missed texts from Finn and Lexie, among others.

> Lexie: Are you okay? I'm here if you need to talk. x

> Finn: Need me to go beat up his ass?

> Finn: That fuckface.

> Finn: I'm sorry. But I also wish you'd let me beat up his ass.

I frown, entering my password before opening my social media platforms, knowing somehow that I'll find my answer there. I'm right. The first thing I see is a picture that's been shared by so many people I follow, one of a beautiful brown-haired girl showing off her massive ring while the man I used to call mine sits next to her, smiling as he presses a kiss to her temple.

I recognize her after a few seconds. She's also big on social media, a beauty influencer I've crossed paths with at a few events over the years. To be honest, I didn't even know he had a girlfriend. I don't follow him, and except for reshared posts here and there, I have no idea what he's doing with his life. At the end of our relationship, with the cheesy excuses he gave me for dumping me—*I need some time to figure out what I want with my life, it's not you, I swear*—I'd guessed another girl had caught his eye, but I never thought it would become something serious.

And here he is. Engaged.

"What's wrong?"

"Hm? Nothing."

"Lili."

My heart stutters at the nickname as if he fought using one for so long but finally lost. Still, he didn't use the same one as everyone, like he wanted something that was solely his. Solely ours. It fills me with warmth, enough that I feel okay saying, "My ex just got engaged."

Even though I'm not looking at him, I feel the physical way he takes this in, the muscles I'm leaning on contracting.

"Are you okay?" he eventually asks.

"I don't know."

Another pause, then, "Do you still love him?"

"No! God no." I pull back so I can look at him. I hate that the thought even crossed his mind. "I don't even miss him." In fact,

I haven't missed him for a long while, and once Carter came into my life, he flew right out the window of my thoughts.

Carter doesn't need to speak his next question. It's written all in the careful, confused way he's studying me. *Then why are you reacting like this?*

I look at the photo once more. They both look so happy, so in love. Did he ever look at me like that? Or was I blind?

"He kept telling me he didn't want to get married, ever." I let out a short huff of air, but there's no humor in it. "I guess he just didn't want to get married to *me*."

"Then he's even dumber than I thought he was."

I smile, squeezing his tense thigh. "You're sweet."

"I'm not. I'm being honest."

I can't with this man. He is everything.

"I was with him for three whole years. Gave him all I had, tried everything to make him see me as someone worthy of him, and he never even considered a future with me. And I was dumb enough to stay." It doesn't matter that he gave me so many mixed signals and led me on. I should've seen that he'd never truly love me, that he'd stayed with me out of pity. I should've been smarter. I shake my head, turning my phone off. "This is embarrassing. I'm sorry. Please go on." I try to put his hand back on the guitar so we can pretend this moment never happened, but he doesn't cooperate.

"It's embarrassing for him, honey, not for you."

"Sure," I say, wanting to get it over with. In fact, I'd very much like to go to bed and move on from this crappy moment. That Greg decides to get married to another girl is one thing, but that everyone treats me with kid gloves, thinking I'm about to break down, makes it so much worse. I hate when people see me like some fragile thing that needs to be handled with care. It's probably how Greg saw me too. I was too frail for him to leave when he wanted to but too delicate to imagine a real future with.

I get up, but he stops me with a soft hand around my wrist. "I'm not done. He's the dumbass for having someone like you and letting you go."

I smile at him. He truly is the best.

"I'm being serious. I don't even think you realize how fucking out of this world you are."

"Being the messy girl with no health insurance and stable job that I am?" I say with a laugh that isn't returned.

Carter shakes his head, grabbing my other wrist so he can pull me in front of him. "You're killing me with this. Every step of the way, people tried to knock you down, but you're still here. Don't you see?" His eyes burn, speckles of yellow blending with the dark green. "There's nothing more impressive than this. Life worked against you and you *still* made it."

I don't want to cry. I really don't, but he's making this damn near impossible. I don't know how long I've waited to hear those words, fighting day in and day out, crawling myself out of dark holes and sinuous roads that felt endless and always trying to do it with a smile because things could be worse. I'm so thankful for everything I have, but there are days when I'm so exhausted, I don't know how to pull myself out of bed.

And he's seen it all. Past the walls, past the barbed wire smiles, right to my core. And I can't even be mad at it because it feels so good to be seen entirely, the good, the bad, and the ugly all revealed. Nowhere to hide.

When a treacherous tear slips from my eye, Carter gets to his feet and wipes my cheekbone with a delicate thumb before he wraps me in a hug that feels like I'm finally where I'm supposed to be.

Against his chest, I whisper, "I don't think I've ever heard you utter so many words in a row."

He huffs a laugh, then pulls my head even closer to him. "Shut up and hug me."

That I can do. Forever if I need to.

Chapter 32

"I swear I'm almost ready!"

I'm not sure Carter believes me as he leans against the bathroom doorway with his arms crossed, watching me brush my hair frantically as I try to put socks on.

"You're going to hurt yourself," he says, voice dripping with humor.

"I don't want to be late." I have the nasty habit of getting lost in my tasks and forgetting to get ready until the last minute, which means the eggplant lasagna I decided to make from scratch at 5:00 p.m. left me in a rush to get dressed and tame my hair.

"I think your friends will understand if you get there five minutes late instead of coming on time but concussed."

I give him the stink eye as I grab my toothbrush and brush my teeth. Maybe I'm also jittery because I'm excited for tonight. Since Lexie and Finn aren't going on their honeymoon in Italy for a few months, they invited Aaron, Wren, Carter, and me for a game night to celebrate once more. I was afraid to ask Carter at first since this seemed like the last thing on earth he'd want to attend, but he surprised me by saying yes. Maybe he did because it was so obvious

I was desperate for him to accept the invitation, but I'm happy all the same.

Carter doesn't move from his spot in the doorway, looking hot as sin in his usual dark jeans and short-sleeved T-shirt showing off all those beautiful tattoos. Now that I've gotten to see them from up close, I'm even more awestruck. He explained each of their meanings to me one evening over dinner, from references to movies that shaped him—the pickaxe was a callback to Shawshank Redemption—to doodles he'd seen the tattoo artist make and liked. Ropes and vine are intertwined between the pieces, making them all appear to be part of one big masterpiece. I try to look away from him, but I can't find the strength to do so, and the smirk he gives me tells me he knows it too well.

I finally get myself to turn back toward the sink to spit, and I jump when I realize the toothbrush I'm holding is blue, not purple.

"Oh my God," I say, dropping it to the counter like it's a ticking bomb.

"What? What's wrong?" Carter says, now by my side.

"I used your toothbrush by accident. I'm so sorry."

I lean down to grab a new one from the cupboard while Carter rinses the old one, but when I straighten up, I find him with the blue toothbrush in his mouth.

"What are you doing?" I gasp, going to grab it from him.

He moves away, then spits his toothpaste in the sink before he says, "Honey, I think we've done way worse than share a toothbrush already."

Heat immediately rushes to my face, recalling the way he woke me up this morning with his head between my thighs before he had to leave for work. We still haven't had much time together, only stealing moments here and there, getting each other off in quick exchanges before one of us has to leave, but it's only made me want him more. I want time with him when I'm not in a rush, when I can explore him at leisure and discover all the ways to make him tick. I want a real repeat of the wedding night.

The look he gives me then, as if he, too, is remembering this morning, the way I tugged at his hair as I came with his name on my tongue, makes me want to say fuck it and make this moment now.

But we don't have time.

I pull my hair back into a ponytail and decide this will have to do. "All right, let's go." I pass Carter as I make my way out toward the foyer, and when I get a whiff of the cologne he's spritzed over his clothes, I use the self-control of a saint and don't stop to kiss him.

He doesn't grant me the same courtesy, though.

With a hand on my waist, he stops me in my tracks and tugs me to his chest before bringing his lips to my ears, sending tingles all throughout my body. "Maybe I don't mind being a little late."

Damn you, Finn, and your stupid game night.

I twist in Carter's arms so I can face him, and just as I've pressed the softest kiss to his lips, I pull back and whisper, "Tough luck."

The stunned look on his face is worth all the money in the world.

I walk out of his embrace, tugging at his hand. "Come on, Romeo. Monopoly awaits."

"You're a fucking cheater!"

Aaron cackles in Finn's face as he waits for his payment with an extended hand.

"You're literally too much," Lexie chastises her new husband, even though she also seems to be finding it funny. She wouldn't be alone. I've been wiping tears under my eyes ever since the game got spicy and everyone started being sneaky and making low-blows to others, especially Aaron, who loves to rile Finn up.

"I swear to God, this game is rigged," my baby of a best friend says as he counts his fake dollar bills to make his loser's payment.

"Who would've expected Monopoly to be so violent," Wren says, making Lexie snicker.

"I would've," she answers. "Those two are uncontrollable."

"Your turn, new guy," Finn says, handing Carter the dice, which he juggles before throwing them. Then he advances the required number of squares, which leads him to have to draw a card. He picks one up, then reads it in his head before a slow grin travels to his lips.

"What?" I ask.

It's not at me he looks when he answers, but at Finn as he finally reads aloud, "Have the player of your choice pay five thousand dollars in taxes."

"No fucking way," Finn says, and we all burst out laughing.

"Pay up, Finnigan," Lexie coos, her nose tickling his neck.

"You're the worst. All of you." He throws Carter a sizzling stare. "You'll pay for this."

Aaron's laughter is boisterous as he begins tormenting Finn, the way I've seen them do ever since we met.

"Gotta stop goading him," Wren tells Aaron, her feet snuggled in his lap on the couch as she sips on a glass of red wine. "They'll never want to do game nights with us again."

"Oh, I'm down to do this anytime." Lexie pokes her grumbling partner in the stomach. "Seeing him this fired up makes my day," she teases.

"You're a pain in my ass, Crabby," he tells her.

"Look who's talking."

He grins and kisses her.

"Get yourself a room," Aaron shouts.

"Oh, shut up," Wren tells him, chuckling, while Finn gives him the finger, never breaking away from the kiss with his wife.

I steal a piece of the *yaniqueques* Aaron brought over, smiling as I eat and look around at all those people I love so, so much. And when my eyes land on Carter, my smile finds a way to grow even bigger. That man, who I used to beg for even a hint of emotion, is now chuckling softly as he counts the money Finn gave him, all the while Finn starts bickering with him and Aaron again. That smile I'd started to believe would only ever make an appearance when we're the two of us alone makes me so happy I could cry. He feels comfortable here, for some reason. Maybe this is another place, or another set of people, with whom he could let his guard down.

I shift over the pillow I dropped on the floor and sat on so I can put a hand on Carter's thigh and squeeze it. I don't know how much PDA he'll be okay with since we ourselves don't know what we are exactly, but as soon as I touch him, he clutches my hand and lifts it with his to rest on top of the coffee table as if we've done this a thousand times before. I notice everyone's eyes darting toward our hands, but no one says a word, and the rest of the night goes like this, with Carter and me moving closer and closer until I'm almost in his lap. And as we finish the game of Monopoly—Aaron winning and Finn almost crying about it—and we move on to another game, then another, everyone eating and laughing, I realize Carter and I are acting like an actual married couple. With his arm around my waist, my long-time friends teasing him, the two of us exchanging knowing glances when Aaron says something about the city of Montreal or when Lexie mentions how strong alcohols aren't for her, it doesn't feel fake. Not one bit.

I now watch him moving his character on the LIFE board, and when he crosses the married line and throws me a private wink, I want it. I want it so freaking bad. This life, this marriage. I want us to keep coming here for game nights, not as friends or living partners but as an us. I want him to always look at me when he hears something funny and wants to share it with me. I want to be the person he teases when we play just like Lexie did with Finn. I want it all.

Those tingles I feel every time we touch, every time I even *think* of him, aren't just lust.

I'm pretty sure they're from being hopelessly in love with him.

We leave their place way past midnight, my cheeks hurting from smiling so much. Carter and I walk the few streets toward where we parked earlier, his arm around my shoulders, warming me. When we reach the car, he opens the door for me, and as soon as he sits in the driver's seat and closes his door, I can't hold back any longer. I take his jaw between my hands and kiss him.

I know with my realization from earlier, I should probably keep my distance and protect my heart, but I think it's too late for that.

"What was that for?" Carter asks when I pull back.

"I'm happy." Simple as that.

The five o'clock shadow on his cheeks tickles my fingers as his eyes alternate between mine. And then his lips are on mine again, hungrier this time.

His hands come to my hips as we deepen the kiss, his tongue sliding into my mouth and earning a moan out of me as he lifts me from my seat and drops me so I'm straddling him. The steering wheel jabs me in the back, but I could not care less as Carter's mouth travels down my neck, to my collarbone, and then to the top of my breasts, where he presses wet kisses before dragging my face back to his.

He tastes like cola and like the chocolate we shared earlier, each stroke of his tongue more delicious than the last. I feel dizzy, an ache building between my thighs, and when I shift forward, Carter is hard and ready in his jeans under me.

I can't get enough of him. The tight grip he has on my hair, like he's afraid I'll get away, the sounds he lets out when I lick a path from those annoyingly attractive neck tendons to his earlobe, the way his hips grind in rhythm with mine to create the perfect friction where I want him.

Still, it's not enough.

"I want you," I whisper against his lips, both our rapid breaths filling the silence of the car.

"Now?" he asks, not like a complaint but like he wants to make sure we're both on the same wavelength.

"Yes." I unbutton his jeans, then drag his zip down. "Now."

The next moments are a blur of limbs as we pull Carter's pants low enough to release his cock, firm and glistening with lust, and then to lift my skirt up to my waist.

The street we're parked on is in a secluded part of town, and not a soul seems to be out at this hour. I don't think I could stop even if I wanted to anyway. This need is too intense, too profound for me to think about possible consequences.

Carter tugs my panties to the side, not even taking the time to pull them off, then slides one finger up my wet slit, hissing. "Fucking hell. You're killing me, Fireball."

I gasp at the contact, then squeeze his shoulders tighter as he inserts his finger inside me, his slowness pure torture. I pick up the pace myself, riding his finger, head thrown back when he adds another.

"Greedy little thing," he whispers before pulling down my top with his free hand, then takes a nipple in his mouth.

"Carter," I moan, moving even faster. "I want more."

"More?" He brings his thumb to my clit and starts to circle.

"Shit," I mutter, then reach between us to grip him. "I need you."

"Good, 'cause I need you too." He pulls his fingers out, and I only have a second to mourn the loss before his tip is at my entrance, sliding in an inch. We both gasp, our faces aligned, mouths parted against the other's, his upper lip leaned against my bottom one.

"Take what you need, honey," he says, and our eyes remain locked as I sink down, taking him to the hilt.

His groan fills the car, but I don't give either of us any time to adjust, already moving against him. This is nothing like our last time, exploratory and slow. This is taking for the sake of taking, connecting because there's no other option, because I need him and he needs me and nothing else will tame this hunger.

The way he looks at me as I ride him, with his eyes glinting and his lips parted, makes me feel like a goddess, like this is just as good to him as it is to me. It gives me confidence I never knew I needed, enough that I fully take control, finding a pace that makes tension rise in my belly.

☐My nails dig in his upper back as he hits a spot that makes me gasp, again and again.

"That's it. You take me so good."

His praises only make me coil tighter, and when he brings a finger to my clit and resumes his circles, I know I won't last long. It's as if he knows what I need before even I do. As if he's letting me be in control, but he'll still make sure to bring me right where I need to be.

"I can't get enough of you," he says on an exhale, gazing at where his finger is wreaking havoc on my body. I move faster against him, that tension building even more. "You've got me wrapped around your pretty little finger." Then he takes my mouth in a breath-stealing kiss, and an orgasm stronger than I've ever experienced shatters me, wave after wave of pleasure cresting over me. I part long enough to call his name, then kiss him once more, feeling halfway out of my body as I continue spasming around him.

"Come inside of me," I beg, and a second later, his thrusts quicken until his warmth fills me, grunts escaping his throat as he holds me even closer than before.

We remain this way for a long time, and even though I know we should move away and drive home, I stay right where I am. He doesn't push me off either, instead running a hand through my hair with his nose against my cheek, his breaths a lullaby as our heartbeats slow.

This was more than sex. It felt like making love.

And while I know I'm down bad, there's a chance he's not that far behind me.

Chapter 33

"Happy birthday."

Carter groans at my excited voice, then tugs me from where I'm kneeling so I fall into his embrace.

"Come on," I say against his scratchy cheek.

"Since when do you get up early?" he says in that deep, sleep-laden voice of his that is enough to make my insides tingle.

"Since it's your birthday." I press kisses to his jaw, his neck, making him groan. "The earlier we wake, the longer we get to celebrate." I poke him in the chest, then try to pull away to make him follow me up.

It doesn't work. Instead, he pulls me even closer to him, then rolls us so his naked leg is propped on top of me, pinning me in place. The feel of his skin against mine makes me wish for a repeat of yesterday. And the night before. And the one before that. Since coming back from Lexie and Finn's, there hasn't been a single night we haven't spent tangled up together, every piece of him finding a way to connect with one of mine.

"I don't celebrate my birthday," he says, lightly biting my collarbone, just enough to get me writhing under him. He's hardening against my hip, too.

I flip us again so I'm straddling him, his eyes going right to my exposed breasts. "Well, with me, you do." In truth, I woke up with a throbbing headache and aching muscles and would want nothing more than to stay in bed all day, but I'd guessed Carter had never had someone celebrate his birthday in proper form, and he deserved it. "Happy thirtieth, Andy."

Something glimmers in his eyes as he looks at me, not at my body or my face but me, and then he tugs me down to give me one long but tame kiss. "Thank you." Then he begins trailing kisses down from my neck, to my breasts, to my sternum, then to my belly.

"Wait," I say, neck extended, not moving away just yet. "I need to give you your gift."

"I already have a gift all right," he says, never looking up, pushing me away from his lap so he can drag his lips to my stomach, my navel, my pubis. A shiver racks my body, one that makes me feel a little lightheaded.

"Later," I say, then pull away and leave the bed before he keeps me in there forever. His slow footsteps follow me from the bedroom to the living room, where I have a pink Barbie gift bag waiting for him.

His brow quirks up in question, grinning as he watches the present.

"Overestimated my gifting supplies. Sorry." Then I grab the bag and extend it to him. "It's nothing big, though, so don't be disappointed."

He rolls his eyes, then pulls at the tissue paper and looks inside.

He doesn't react right away—or even at all—when he sees the bird house I went to get at the hardware store yesterday. When I thought about what this man who lives so simply could want, it was the one thing that came to mind.

"It's also a little thank you for all you've been doing around the house." I'll never be able to show him just how grateful I am for all the pressure he's taken off me by doing those repairs I'd been putting off for years. "And I thought you might like this, to replace your old one." I cross my arms in front of me, his silence starting to feel thick as honey. "I want you to feel like this place is your home too."

His throat works as he pulls it out of the bag and starts examining the simple bird house from every angle. Still no reaction.

"It's stupid, isn't it?" God, maybe I should've kept that impulsive idea to myself. "I'm sorry, I—"

"Thank you," he says, finally looking up from the little wooden house, and the way he says it sounds genuine. It's in the thickness of his voice, in the way he holds the gift close to him, looking so fragile in his large hands.

I smile. "You're welcome."

His gaze doesn't stray, so full of emotions as he continues watching me, that the three words I've been thinking for days every time he moved inside me or brushed my hair out of my face or kissed me good night threaten to slip out.

But before I can decide whether I'm ready to make that move, a wave of fatigue swarms me, and as I reach for Carter, the world starts to spin. I have to brace myself against the wall to regain my balance, eyes closed tight against the jackhammer in my head.

"What's wrong?" he asks, his gift forgotten on the floor, arms around me.

"Nothing." I force a smile. I'm not ruining his day. "Just a little lightheaded." I hate the worried look he's sporting, so I push myself off the wall to reach the box, but this time, the tide of dizziness hits me so hard, I can't even stay upright.

"Lili." Carter falls to his knees beside me, then presses a clammy hand against my forehead. "Jesus, you're burning up. Why didn't you say anything?"

I shake my head. Already, my mind is veering down a dangerous path, one that wonders whether this could be anything serious. It's not, though. I have bouts of low BP all the time. I try to lift myself but can barely do so. Nausea suddenly hits my gut, and I have to breathe in slowly to make sure I don't throw up all over the floor.

"We're going to the hospital."

"God, no," I grit out. "I'm fine. Just give me a second." I try to straighten once again, but I gag and fall back.

My heart rate picks up, maybe because of whatever's happening or maybe because I'm starting to freak out. This feels different than the other times I felt like I was going to pass out. My thoughts are a sudden hurricane, hurtling nightmarish scenarios my way.

This can't be a rejection. It can't. We're two years post-transplant. The risks have drastically decreased.

If it is... I can't even allow my thoughts to go there. Getting through my transplant was one of the hardest things I've ever done. I couldn't do it again. Couldn't go back on dialysis either. Not after tasting freedom for two years.

I need to gasp for my next breath as the possibility anchors itself. This might be the time I wake up from my dream.

"Not up for discussion," Carter says, picking me up from the ground. I want to protest some more, but I don't think it'll be worth it, and even if it was, the safety of his arms feels too good for me to push him away.

"How are you feeling?"

"Exactly like I did five minutes ago," I tease Carter with a grin. He doesn't return it. "Better." The medication I was given to get my temperature down while the doctors ran some tests did wonders.

Carter still doesn't let go of the hand he's been holding for the past hour, his thumb rubbing the spot that usually holds the ring I had to take off to do some imaging.

"What a birthday, huh?" I feel terrible for ruining it.

He ignores me, only grumbles, "You scared the shit out of me."

Not going to lie, I scared the shit out of me too. I won't say that aloud, though. Not when he's already strung up this tight.

I'm not in the clear just yet, but the fact that I'm feeling better makes me hopeful.

"Lilianne? What are you doing here?"

We both turn toward the petite woman who just walked into the room. Carter's grip tightens around my hand, but I let him go as I sit up in bed, arms extended. "Zineb!"

She immediately comes to hug me. It might have been against the rules for us to be this close when I was still her patient, but with how close we are in age, I always saw her as some sort of friend.

"Just feeling a little under the weather," I say in her dark hair. "Nothing bad."

"Good. I'm glad I never heard from you again after your surgery," she says, smiling.

My social worker was a pillar during my time on the transplant waitlist and then when I was recovering post-op. There are so many confusing and sometimes contradicting feelings that come with going through dialysis and receiving a transplant, and she helped me as I went through them all.

"Me too," I say.

She holds me by the shoulders and takes me in like a proud mother would, then looks to my left. "And who is—" Her expression falters, words hanging from her lips as she squints at Carter.

"This is my husband. Carter." It feels almost natural to say this now, like every day we spend together, our marriage becomes less of a sham and more of a true engagement.

She tries to hide it, but I don't miss the rounding of her eyes. "Oh."

My brows furrow as I turn to Carter, but his expression is glacial and fixed on Zineb. His head moves slightly as if he's shaking it at her.

"I don't understand," I say, still grinning. "Do you guys know each other?"

She opens her mouth, then closes it, making my heart rate skyrocket. Another wave of dizziness hits me, but I ignore it, looking between Zineb and Carter. I can't tell what's happening, but my stomach twists in a knot like my body knows something my mind doesn't. I push myself so I'm sitting straighter.

"Can someone tell me what's going on?" My smile fades. The air suddenly feels wrong in the room, syrupy and foul.

Finally, Zineb breaks the strange contact she had with Carter and clears her throat. "It, um, it was great seeing you again, Lilianne. I hope you feel better." She doesn't hug or even so much as glance at me as she leaves, looking like she's come face to face with a ghost.

I spin to Carter, ignoring the throbbing in my head. "I don't understand. Did you, like, date or something?" Zineb talked about her husband a few times and told me they'd been married for years, but I guess it could've happened at some point.

A muscle ticks in his jaw as he shakes his head once.

"Then what? Why was she being so weird?"

He doesn't answer. His gaze doesn't meet mine either.

"You're starting to scare me," I say, voice cracking as if I know that the other shoe I was waiting on to drop is finally there. "What's going on?"

"Let this go, Lili. Please."

My hands are shaking in my lap. My entire body, actually. Even my teeth chatter. "Tell me."

He lets out one terribly long, terribly loaded breath, then his shoulders drop as if he's been carrying a weight he's finally laying down. When he meets my eyes, they're shining. "I never meant for you to find out this way."

I can't move, can't speak.

He goes to grab my hand, but I move it away, needing space to hear whatever he has to say. He swallows forcefully. "I knew your father, honey."

The world turns silent except for the faint ringing in my ears.

I must have misheard him. Must have because there's no way I've been lied to for the past six months.

Carter tries to touch me again, but when I move my entire body away from him, scurrying away like a hurt animal, he gives up. His hands crossed on the bed, eyes downturned, he says, "He was my AA sponsor."

"No," I whisper, only realizing once I hear it that I said it aloud.

"He was a good man. A *great* fucking man. He gave me my life back. I owe him *everything*." His voice becomes thicker as he rubs a hand over his stubbled jaw. "And... Fuck." Clearly, whatever he's trying to get out is even worse than all he's just said, but still, nothing makes sense.

Until everything clicks into place.

Zineb. Carter. Dad.

I owe him everything.

He must see in my face the moment I realize the truth because his eyes fill as he watches me.

I push through the thickness in my throat to say, "Why does the transplant unit social worker know you, Carter?"

He doesn't answer, which means even more than words could.

I shake my head, again and again, but I still can't make myself believe it. This is not happening to me. The man I've fallen for hasn't been lying to me this entire time. He hasn't...

"Lilianne, I—"

"Your shirt."

"What?"

"Lift up your shirt." For all the times we've been intimate, I just realized I've always been the only one completely naked. Even when I saw him in the shower, he never faced me.

Please, lift up your shirt and prove to me that this is all just a misunderstanding.

Carter's eyes fill, but I don't budge. His head drops between his shoulders. "I can explain everything,"

"Lift. Up. Your. Shirt."

He gives me a look that will forever haunt my nights before he stands and lifts his shirt just enough that I can see the eight-inch-long scar that's a mirror image to mine.

I bring a hand to my lips, twin tears falling down my cheeks. I couldn't have been this naive. This blind.

I want to puke, throw my phone against the wall, and rip out my hair.

"When did you know?" I blurt, my pulse thrumming in my ears. "When we met? Before?" My voice is shrill, like a fire alarm during the quiet night.

"God, no," he says, pleading with his stare.

"When then?" My teeth are clenched so tight it worsens the ache in my body, but it's the only thing I can do not to break down entirely. "Tell me." I can't have fallen for another man who only ever saw me as a pity case.

He runs a violent hand through his hair. "I only connected the dots when I heard your full name at the wedding."

My entire being shuts down.

"All this time?" I breathe. I can barely hear the words coming out, so full of shock, of self-disgust. They're the cry of a dying man.

"Lilianne, I—"

"Get out."

"Please, I can explain."

"It was all fake." I'm talking to myself now. All those moments of found connection, of sacred touches and whispered truths. All a lie.

"No, baby, it wasn't—"

"I said get out." I can't even look at him. It feels as if he's just stolen my heart right out of my chest and thrown it in a lit pyre. Nothing makes sense. Nothing ever will.

He knew the truth about my father all along. He left me rotting in my doubt and never planned on letting me know. And above all, he knew about *that*.

I look down at my belly, at the pink scar I know is hidden under the green hospital gown.

The room once again starts to spin. Acid climbs my throat, and a wave of heat stuns my body.

"Lili?"

The world turns black.

Chapter 34
Carter

Three years ago

I've been sober for almost a year by the time I step foot inside a bar again.

Eighteen more days, and I could've said I'd done it. I'd pushed through every single day and made it on the other side.

Who knew all it'd take for me to crack was a stupid birthday.

It's not like I've always been a big family man. I spent my tenth birthday alone, babysat by our neighbor Francine who smelled like mothballs and cat food and who entertained me by playing Scrabble, all because Brandon had a meeting with a casting company. Apparently, he was going to be the next big thing in cinema, or was it musical theater? I spent my twenty-first birthday, just like this, alone in a bar, not because I wanted to but because it felt like the only option. I could've stayed home and had dinner with my parents, but at that age, we'd realized that apart from our careers, we didn't have much in common. I don't think they even could've named my favorite movie or the name of my best friend (Lee, a guy who'd played the drums in my high school band and who I lost contact with after he moved on from music to work in tech in Silicon Valley). We didn't really know each other, and by that point, we'd kind of stopped pretending we did.

Which is why I'm so surprised at how badly I reacted to my mother's call today.

"Andrew," she said when I picked up. Not *hey* or *oh my God, it's been so long*, just my name, said in that tone of hers that isn't cold but isn't warm either. I could almost picture her, sitting in the parlor at home, a gin martini in her hand, tapping her foot on the ground as she waited for me to pick up.

"Hi," I said tentatively. We hadn't spoken face to face or even by phone in more than a year, and even though I received the occasional polite text asking me for updates, I couldn't say we'd *actually* been in touch since I'd left the band.

"Happy birthday, hon."

My shoulders tensed at the pet name. How dumb. Her *hon*, who she'd never offered to visit in Boston or even invited home for the holidays. Maybe that's because she knew I would've refused, but it wouldn't have hurt to ask.

"Thanks."

"How are you? How are things?"

"Good," I said, voice tight. It was mostly true, but telling that to her felt like a lie. She'd never see what I was doing as *good*.

"Glad to hear it," she said, not expanding further on what I meant. "Heard about our old friend Vernon a few days ago. You must remember him, right? Since he said you'd contacted him."

"Right." I'd figured my contacting old family "friends" would come back to bite me in the ass, but in the end, I did what I had to do. Starting to work as a music producer with no contact in the industry was like deciding to become a track Olympian at thirty-five. It didn't happen. So I'd stepped over my ego and called some people I knew from way back, or who my parents knew and I recognized by name. Not everyone called me back, but some did. Enough that I got to meet with people who knew people who knew people, and finally, I found a job at a record label in Boston. They don't necessarily release the exact music I want to work on, but for a first job as a producer, it'd do just fine. As much as I loved to play, messing with other people's music to bring it a step further tickles a part of my brain I never knew I had, and it brings me a sense of fulfillment I never knew I wanted.

"So you're sticking with this thing, aren't you?" Mom said, this time sounding bitter.

"What thing?"

"That quitting the guitar thing." She tsked. "After everything we've put into this. Such a shame."

My jaw clenched. "If this is what you called about, we can hang up now." A year of no talking, only to lead to that. No question about *why* I'd reached out to Vernon, or what I was doing now. I don't know why I expected things to change, but the realization that this time was no different hurt like a bitch.

"Oh, don't be like that."

"Like what?"

"Angry. You've always been so angry, Andrew." She tuts like I'm a petulant child. "You know where we're coming from on this."

Right. Because I'm sure my father was of the same point of view. He was probably sitting on the other side of the room, his earphones in as he read an article or worked on some new project. He hadn't deigned to call me today, so maybe he had an even worse opinion of me than she did.

I stood straighter. "Why did you call, Mom?"

"It's your birthday." As if that was a good explanation. Not because she wanted to or she missed me, but because she had to.

"Yeah. You know what? I think we're done here."

"Andrew, come on."

"Have a great year. Talk to you September of next year, yeah?"

And then I hung up.

It should've felt good to have the upper hand, to shut her down just like she'd shut me down ever since she and my father had started managing Fickle and decided the band came before all else.

It didn't.

I'd walked away from them because of the drinking but also because I'd hated the way I felt back then. Like I was never enough, like even when I was "living the dream," I'd feel so fucking empty. No one *actually* cared. I'd done everything right, followed all the steps, got the career and the money and the girls, and yet I'd never felt anything close to happy. Just...blank. That's what had gotten me to drink in the first place. The feeling that the only time I could actually feel good about myself was when I wasn't really there.

Eyes fixed on my phone, I watched the screen light up again with another incoming call from my mother, only to realize I'd never walked away from that feeling. I *couldn't* walk away from it. That emptiness was still there. That feeling of only floating from one thing to the next, never actually enjoying life but simply going through it, was still smack dab in the middle of my chest, and if running away hadn't made it stop, then nothing ever would.

Suddenly, the last thing I wanted to be doing was standing in the grocery store, buying food to meal prep for the week. The carefully balanced eggs and the hand-picked sweet potatoes seemed to be taunting me. *Thought you could have a healthy lifestyle, be happy? How pathetic.* And so, I walked away. I left my half-full cart right there in the middle of the aisle, walked out the automatic doors, and went straight to the bar across the street.

I wasn't thinking, really. Muscle memory took over, or maybe it was more of a self-destructing instinct that decided which way my footsteps should lead me.

And here I am now.

The Anchor, or whatever crass name the place has, smells like sweat, mildewed fabric—probably from the carpet being drenched year after year with melted snow dragged in by dirty winter boots—and cheap beer. Perfect.

The seat I pick at the bar squeals under my weight as I let my body slump over the sticky bar. I don't want to be here, but I also don't want to be anywhere else.

Frankly, I don't even want to *be*.

A gruff guy with a thick gray beard and wiry nose hairs comes my way and stands, not speaking but asking his question all the same.

"Double Hendricks, no ice."

He goes to prepare my order, not even nodding an agreement. He must be used to seeing all kinds of broken, desperate people here. One mid-twenties man with a depressed face and not enough energy to keep his spine up at 9:00 p.m. doesn't faze him. I should probably be embarrassed, but at this point, I don't think I can disappoint myself any more.

The ice he put inside the drink—either because he didn't hear me or because he didn't give a fuck one way or another—clinks against the glass he drops in front of me. Not like I have the luxury to be picky.

I grab it, the cold bite against the palm of my hand feeling so beautifully, horrifyingly familiar. I bring the glass to my nose, taking a big inhale of the alcohol I got sick on so many times before. This is it. All of the past year, in the drain. Or was it already there, and I only fooled myself into thinking I'd gotten out? Guess I'll never know.

I take another sniff, and then, just as I lift the rim to my lips, my eyes drift to the television above me, the sound low but still loud enough that I can hear the commentator over the basketball game. I don't follow the sport, but seeing it now sends a jolt down my back, making me lower the glass back to the bar.

What the hell would Frank think if he saw me like this? After giving me so much of his precious time, his patience, his trust, his empathy, to find me at a bar would probably make him give up faith in me entirely. He'd realize he should've known from the beginning I wasn't going to make it. He'd see what a waste I've been to him.

I haven't cried in years. Not when I got into my accident and realized how much of a problem I actually had. Not when I spent my first Christmas on my own. Not when I realized I'd probably never speak to my brother again.

But this, right here, realizing how far I've fallen and how disappointed Frank would be if only he knew, makes my eyes mist.

Before I know it, I'm grabbing my phone and dialing him. He answers fast as if he has nothing better to do than deal with my bullshit.

"Carter, how's it going?"

"I…" And then, the words freeze, right there inside my throat.

"Carter?"

I swallow. I was never going to escape him knowing, was I? I knew when I called, yet I did it all the same, like when you press on a sore muscle hoping for some of that aching relief.

I push against the shame and say, "I'm at a bar."

He doesn't skip a beat, foregoing the disappointed sigh I was waiting for. "Have you drunk yet?"

"No."

"Good boy. Now send me your address. I'll be there as soon as I can."

I should probably fight him off on this. I've needed him so much already. Asking this of him sounds like the cherry on top, like being yet another responsibility for him, but I'm selfish enough to take it.

I give him the name of the bar.

"All right. I'll be right there, but you get out of there in the meantime, you hear me?"

I hum my agreement, already getting to my feet. The task sounded like hiking Mount Everest five minutes ago, but now, it's surprisingly doable.

"I'm on my way."

"Thank you," I say, so relieved I could fall to my knees. I don't think I would've survived this night if he hadn't picked up.

"And, Carter?"

"Yeah?"

"I'm proud of you, kid."

He hangs up, and before I can think of whether I deserve his pride or not, I pay my tab, leave my untouched drink, and go wait outside for him.

But Frank never does show up.

An hour and a half later, when I've texted him five times and he hasn't answered, I figure he's fallen asleep and forgot about me, so I call for a cab. I'm not disappointed, only tired by then. I just want to be home and forget about this whole day. Maybe tomorrow, I can convince myself I never flinched, that I imagined that dank smell and the feeling of the glass in my hand.

The taxi driver who picks me up must be in his sixties and is blaring tech music through his speakers. As soon as I sit, he's speeding through the streets like he's playing GTA, all the while his loud bass worsens my headache. I lean back and close my eyes, only reopening them when I feel the car slowing down.

I don't realize right away what is happening. It's as if from the moment I look out the window and see the scene happening on the main boulevard, everything happens in slow motion. Sirens mix with the aggressive music in the car, muffled like they're ringing from underwater. Blue and red flashes in the distance, and the lights get brighter and brighter the closer we get.

"We'll need to take a detour," the driver says.

I don't answer, entranced by the lights. It's as if a part of me already knows what they mean.

But only when I see the flipped-over brown car with its cheerful stickers in the rear windshield and a stretcher pulling a sheet-covered body toward an ambulance do I realize what actually happened, although I'm not sure I could call it realizing. More like noticing.

Oh, look, a boot—he must've lost it when they dragged him out of the wreck.

The radio is still on. Was he listening to folk or rock when he died?

The keychain is hanging from the ignition, swinging. It probably still holds the pendant his daughter made him in art class a decade ago.

His phone must've fallen from the cupholder and shattered. Did it break before or after I called him back?

I'm not sure how I get home next. I was at the accident, watching it all with a painful numbness as if out of my body, and the next thing I knew, I was curled up in my bed, staring at the wall, spending God knows how many days like this. Not sleeping. Not crying. Just being there, forcing myself to take breath after painful breath.

Eventually, I get myself out of bed, draining a gallon of water while finally starting to think about what happened, and now that I do, I see it doesn't make sense. I must've imagined it. Maybe I did drink at that bar, and I got so drunk I invented some crazy scenario in my head. So I decide to drive up to Frank's house. I went once to hand him a document I needed him to sign, so I still have his address in my texts. I'll get there, and he'll be raking his lawn or washing his awful car, wearing some pompom-riddled hat and waving at me with a huge grin on his face.

But that fantasy doesn't happen. When I stop in front of his place, dozens of cars fill up the driveway, including a catering truck and some van where two people are pulling out vases of extravagant flowers.

I don't even stop in front of the house, only slowing long enough to see it all, then slam on the gas and drive back home.

I spend the next day doing the same thing. And the next. And the next.

I'm not sure what I expect to see there. I just know that passing in front of that house makes me feel like I'm doing something. Like I still have a piece of him with me.

I call in sick to work for two entire weeks, faking appendicitis, but really, I'd take an unanesthetized surgery over this kind of pain.

The realization that his death is on me comes slowly at first, and then it drowns me, pulling me down every time I try to gasp for breath. If I hadn't been stupid enough to call him at night, if I hadn't been so weak that I needed him to come pick me up, he'd still be there, spreading his annoying cheer everywhere.

Eventually, I return to work, and it's probably the only thing that keeps me standing. For the hours I'm in there, I can forget just enough that I don't crumble. But the moment I leave the studio, it all comes back to me, and the routine continues.

Driving in front of his house becomes some sick obsession. I imagine his clothes lying untouched, his gutters overflowing and never being drained, his roof cracking and needing to be replaced. The house remains the same, but I see it all in tragic fast-speed.

And then, one day, something new appears in the driveway.

His car looks just like it did that night next to the basketball court, scratched and rusted over, but other than that, it's perfect. As if it didn't go through some hellish accident mere weeks ago.

This time, I stop in front of the house, long enough for me to stare at that damn car. I don't know whether I love it because it's so *him* or I hate it because of what it represents. Me failing him. Me dragging him out. Me killing him.

I'm not sure how long I spend looking at those like-new windows and bumper, but when my gaze drifts to the back window, it's as if time stutters.

My daughter needs your help! Have an extra kidney? Get tested to see if you're a match and save her life!

His daughter. I'd almost forgotten about her. The one person Frank loved and wanted to protect more than anything in the world. I don't even know how old she is. She could be thirteen or twenty. Either way, I've taken her father away from her. Her father, who would've given everything he owned to help her.

I'll never be able to repay her. I'll never be able to repay Frank either, but she's probably the person I've wronged the most, and I didn't even spare her one thought.

I read over the line again, then look at the phone number below.

I don't consciously make the decision to call. I just know the longer I stare at those twenty-one words, the more obvious it becomes. The chances of us being a match are slim to none. I'd probably start believing in fate if we were.

But just for the infinitesimal chance it might work?

I dial the number.

Chapter 35

I sleep through most of the following twenty-four hours.

My nephrologist isn't certain of what is going on with me, so they're running some more tests. According to them, it could be something benign, or it could also be a sign of organ rejection. The worst part of it is I'm not even that worried. After everything that happened yesterday, it feels as if I'm numb and nothing else can shock me. Too many betrayals will do that to a person. I wouldn't be surprised if my body was turning on me again, too.

The moments I'm not asleep, I stare at the wall, mind reeling. It's a gift every time a nurse comes in to poke or prod me. The physical pain distracts me, if only for a few minutes. And then they leave, and I'm back to being alone with my thoughts in this cold hospital room I've spent way too much of my life in.

I never tried to put a face on my donor. When I got the call that I'd had a match a few months after Dad died, I felt infinitely grateful to the person who was giving me an organ, alive or dead, but it never occurred to me to try to find out who I'd received the kidney from, first because I literally couldn't, but also because it didn't matter. Sure, I asked myself some questions here and there, but I always thought the least I could do after they gave me the greatest gift was to leave them in their well-deserved anonymity. I didn't want to know if it was a living donor, and even if I had known, I would've assumed it was a random match. Never would I have guessed that someone would've voluntarily gotten tested to see if they were a match, save for my father and my best friends, who'd all done it already.

The irony that Carter of all people was a match isn't lost on me. The person who I thought saved me by marrying me had actually already saved my life once, for reasons I'm still not clear on, and then decided to keep me in the dark, also for reasons I cannot understand. I can't think of a single good one.

"What the fuck are you doing here?"

I twist in the direction of the door at the sound of Finn's voice from the hallway, heart launching. I ended up texting him earlier today to let him know I was in the hospital, and when he asked if Carter was with me, I simply said that he wasn't, and that he wouldn't be in the future either.

I need to see Finn. He's probably the only person who could make me feel better right now. I didn't want to worry him with this initially, but then I thought that my kidney might be failing, and I couldn't handle that news alone. I just couldn't.

"I need to know she's okay."

My chest hollows at that rough voice, tears immediately springing to my eyes. Is it crazy that I miss him already, despite everything? That even after all I've learned, he's the one I want beside me?

Get a grip.

What is he even doing here? Hours have passed since I kicked him out of my room.

"You need to go," Finn says, the door separating us dimming his voice.

"I'm not leaving until I know she's okay."

I bring my knees to my chest, wishing I wasn't hearing this but also straining my ears so I don't miss a word.

Finn's voice gets lower as he says, "I told you what would happen if you hurt her." I can almost imagine the scene, Finn in Carter's face, the two men breathing hard.

"You can hit me. I deserve it. But I'm not leaving." A couple of strained words ensue, but as hard as I try, I can't hear them.

"She doesn't want to fucking see you." I didn't tell Finn that, but I'm thankful he assumed so. I can't see Carter. Not now.

"I know. I won't force myself in. But I'm also not leaving my wife until I know she's all right."

I bite the inside of my cheek hard enough to draw blood.

"Your wife." He snickers, then mutters a string of expletives I don't all catch. Finally, he says, "Whatever." A second later, the door to my room opens, and I only get a flash of the pain twisting Carter's rugged features before Finn closes the door behind him.

"Lil. Shit. What happened?"

I don't have the strength to say it out loud. It's one thing to hear it, but another to explain the way I've been lied to. The way I don't even know how to feel about this donation that both saved my life and in some way ruined the best thing I ever had.

Finn seems to understand this because he steps closer, and the second he takes me into his arms, I break down.

"Ms. DiLorenzo, I have good news."

I jump in bed, straightening my scratchy hospital gown as Dr. Khan walks in a few hours later, his pristine white coat matching his perfect smile. The resident surgeon who operated on me two years ago obviously knows how good-looking he is, but everyone forgives him because he's damn good at his job.

"Everything looks great," he says.

"W-what?"

"All your labs look good." He takes a seat at the edge of my bed. "We looked, but there's no sign of rejection. That kidney isn't going anywhere."

The breath that fills my lungs feels like the first one I've taken in days.

"Your blood pressure was all over the place from your medication, so we adjusted that, and you were probably fighting some kind of viral infection that worsened everything, but I'm not worried about you."

I should probably be crying right now, but I think I've used up all my tears for the next year. Instead of being ecstatic or overwhelmed with relief, the only thing I find to say is, "Can I go?"

"Go? Now?"

I nod. "Thank you, Doctor, for everything, but if I just have a virus, I want to go home." I sound depleted, even to my ears.

He looks down at his watch. "But it's almost midnight."

"Please?"

He must sense that I need this because he says, "All right. Let me go sign your discharge papers and get those IVs out, and then you'll be all set."

I thank him again, then dress back into the clothes I walked in with, although I'd almost rather stay in my hospital gown. The last time I wore those jeans, I was snuggled against Carter, feeling like he was my fortress in a hurricane. All those moments are tainted now. Which were real, and which were lies? Were they *all* lies? I almost can't believe that, but my judgment clearly isn't something I can rely on.

The moment a nurse comes in and removes my IV, I grab my things and leave the room.

And stop in my tracks the second I see Carter's long body bent in an awkward seating position on the hallway floor, facing my door.

Immediately, he jumps to his feet, and I barely recognize him from how tired he looks. His hair is a mess, tangled locks falling over his forehead. Deep blue circles underline his eyes, and his hoodie is wrinkled and twisted around his body.

He opens his mouth, but no words come out, and he only stares at me as if wanting to make sure I'm truly there.

I swallow, hugging my bag closer to me. "I'm going home. Everything's fine." He looks distraught enough that I know some part of him *does* care, and I can give him that small mercy, at least.

It's as if Carter's entire being crumbles under my very eyes. His head drops between his shoulders, and he rakes his fingers through his hair as he lets out the longest, deepest sigh.

"You should go home too," I say, fighting with everything in me to keep myself collected.

A muscle ticks in his cheek. "Which home?"

I want to have him come back with me. I want it so bad it physically hurts. But I'm also not a complete idiot. Asking him to come home would be burying my head in the sand.

"Yours."

The back of his hand moves roughly against his mouth as he gazes left and right, looking like a lost man hoping to find answers somewhere.

I can't stand here any longer. I hold my breath as I pass him.

"Can we at least talk before? Please?" His footsteps behind me are loud through the calm hospital hallway. "You need to know the full of it. You need to know I—"

"A little late for that, isn't it?" I keep walking.

"I fucked up. I really did. But if you just let me—"

I jolt the second his fingers touch my hand, pulling away with a spin so I'm facing him. Nurses look up from where they're writing notes in their station. We're starting to make a scene, but it's the least of my concerns. The only real problem in my life right now is the man standing three feet away, looking devastated and shredding my heart into a thousand pieces.

"I need space." My hands have started trembling, so I tighten them at my sides, then squeeze my eyes shut. "Just looking at you hurts."

He curses, then releases a shaky breath. "All right. I'll give you space." His shoes squeak against the linoleum floors as he takes one step back, then another. "But the second you feel ready to talk about this, I'm right here."

I keep my eyes closed. It feels silly, but it's the only protection I have against him right now. The only thing that keeps me from unraveling. My emotions are a boiling tin can threatening to explode. Anger and pain swallow me from all sides, toward Carter who betrayed me, and toward my father's lies, and toward my mother who left, and toward the life that just can't give me a *fucking* break.

I don't move, and eventually, he starts moving. His scent fills me before his body heat, like an aura, beckons me to come closer. His breath is warm against my cheek as he says, "But just so you know, it was real. *All* of it."

When I open my eyes, he's gone, and I don't feel even slightly better.

Chapter 36

I've always loved this house. The shaggy carpet I used to play with my dolls on when I was a kid, the salmon-colored paint on the bathroom walls Dad let me choose at ten years old, the cozy wood stove in the basement, the chipped kitchen countertop from all our afternoons spent baking... It's part of the reason why I got married, after all. I couldn't find it in me to get rid of it.

But for the first time in my life, I think I might despise this place.

It's been a week since I told Carter to give me some space; since I learned the entire fantasy I'd created in my head was built on lies. And ever since I came home from the hospital, I've felt lonelier than I have before. It's as if the house is taunting me, making me notice everything I've lost at every corner. It's one thing to know you could possibly, in an alternate universe, have a partner by your side, but it's an entirely different one to have lived it and then to lose it. I look at the basement door and see Carter walking out of it, with bed-mussed hair and his scowl that lessens when he notices me. I look at the couch and focus on the two indents in it from the last time we sat there, watching the 2005 version of *Pride & Prejudice*, which Carter had picked because it apparently had one of the best soundtracks of all time. I even open the cupboard door to get the flour for my stress-baking session and see Carter replacing the doors so I could have a modernized kitchen. He's everywhere, and it feels suffocating to just exist in here.

I stop mixing the dry ingredients for my banana bread as a wave of exhaustion crests over me. Even this isn't helping. Nothing is helping. I've been avoiding my online job because every time I log in, I see all the messages and questions about my husband, and even though it's always been fake, now it feels more real than ever.

I let my head hang between my shoulders as I catch my breath. My body feels so freaking heavy. Even when Ethan texted me earlier today to let me know that Crash & Burn had been nominated for some big award for their first album and would be celebrating by hosting a show at The Sparrow in a few weeks, I couldn't get myself to be excited. It was all for this, and yet I feel like I've lost more than I've won.

I push the mixing bowl away. I won't even eat the bread anyway, and I've got no one to share it with.

Pressure builds in my chest once more, and I fight it off like I've been doing all week. I can't keep feeling sorry for myself. It won't lead me anywhere.

It's the middle of the day right now, so all my friends are probably working, but I know someone who's always free to see me.

I pick my phone up from the counter and dial her number. "Hey, Nan. Would you mind if I came over?"

"My darling girl," Nan says as she answers the door, her voice bringing me the comfort I've been craving since leaving the hospital. She pulls me in for a hug, and even though I'm short, I have to bend in order to rest my arms around her back. "I was so happy you called. Come in. I made that soup you like."

I follow her inside, the smell of Italian wedding soup wafting around me. I'm not actually a fan, but it makes her happy thinking I love her food, so I'll bring that secret to my grave.

With her stilted walk, she makes her way toward the kitchen area of her condo. "I was just coming back from playing shuffleboard—people there were dull as bricks." She pours me a bowl, and when I go to take it from her, she pulls it away and gives me a face like *no way am I not serving my granddaughter*. I let her bring the bowl to the table, her arm shaking as she lowers it.

I thank her, then pick up my spoon. My stomach grumbles, loud enough that Nan chuckles. I don't remember when I ate last.

"Where's that handsome man of yours? There's enough for him too."

And just like that, my newfound appetite is gone.

I didn't want to talk about Carter today, but then again, I should've expected it by coming here. Nan's a hound dog. She would've found it regardless.

I put my spoon down, and as much as I try, this time, I fail to keep a blank face.

"Oh, darling," she says, her pained expression probably mirroring mine. She lowers herself to the chair next to mine, then takes my hand in her warm, dry palms and squeezes. "Tell me everything."

When Finn came to the hospital last week, I was barely able to string two words together. Even so, I never would've been able to tell the entire story. I kept it brief, only telling him Carter and I were probably over before we'd even had the time to figure out what it was between us, but I couldn't go into details. The pain was too much.

But today, it pours out of me like a perforated water balloon.

I tell Nan everything, from my fake marriage to my real feelings and to the betrayal that Carter was actually my donor. I skip over the part where Dad was his AA sponsor, only mentioning that Carter knew Dad and felt like he owed him after Dad helped him through a rough patch. Anyway, I still don't know the whole story, and I'm not sure I ever will. I want to know the full truth, like Carter offered, but I don't know if I can stomach it. I want to bury myself away from those feelings, not dive into them.

"I don't know what to do, Nan," I say once I'm done, voice raw, the bowl of soup now cold and forgotten.

My grandmother gives me a pitying look before scooching her chair closer to me. "And why do you think he lied to you about it?"

I shrug. A question I've been asking myself for days.

"Do you think..." Nan's lip twitches, and then she looks away as if searching for her next words. I've never seen her looking for something to say. "Do you think he might have known things about Francesco he didn't want you to know?"

I narrow my eyes, and only after a long moment does it click. "You know? You *knew*?"

"It's been a long time," she simply answers.

"But...how? He told you?"

She smiles, but it's nowhere near her honest, warm one. "He may have been your daddy, but he was my son first. He didn't need to tell me."

I stare at her, dumbfounded.

"You were so young when it began. It was hard for him after your mama left. He struggled, fell into some bad habits. I'd babysit you more often, and I knew he didn't look well. He might've thought I was some old bat, but I could see it all." She coughs in a tissue she's pulled out of God knows where. "I got worried. Talked to him about it. At first, he denied it all, but eventually, I got to him. It took years, but I finally had him realize he had a problem. And then I went with him to get the help he needed."

My nana, so strong, so level-headed, releases a shaky breath. "It was hard, but he got better for you. So you wouldn't see him this way growing up. So he could be the daddy you deserved."

And he was. God, he was. I wipe a tear with the meat of my palm as I continue listening with bated breath, finally getting the answers I craved, as difficult as they are to hear.

"There were relapses, and there were moments I worried he wouldn't make it through, but if there's one thing Francesco was, it was a man of his word. And when he promised me he'd succeed in quitting, I believed in him."

My poor father, who struggled for so long in silence.

"I wish he'd told me," I say, voice sounding like broken glass. "I could've helped too."

"Darling, that's the last thing he would've wanted. I'm sure if he were here, he'd be crying tears of joy that you never noticed his struggle." She smiles. "That'd mean he did right by you."

That sounds like the kind of thought process he'd have had. Even when we were struggling financially, he never let me know, never let me share the burden of worrying with him. He allowed me to have a childhood that was as carefree as possible.

More tears fall, and this time, I don't bother wiping them away.

"I'm not surprised he helped others after he recovered," Nan says with a sniffle. "That was all Francesco."

"You're right." Now that I know, it makes so much sense that he used his own troubles to help others get through theirs. I can't fault him for the times he left me alone in order to get to his meetings. And as angry and heartbroken as I am at Carter and his lies, I'm so freaking glad Dad was there to help him with his recovery.

Nan gets to her feet and grabs the untouched bowl from the table. I stand too and swipe it from her hands. "I got it." This time, she lets me.

"You two are so similar," she says. Nostalgia is drawn all across her features.

I hum, and once I've poured the soup down the drain, I turn to her, hip leaned against the counter. "It's hard for me to reconcile the man I knew with these new parts of his story."

"Then don't. It doesn't matter in the end." Nan shuffles my way. "Your daddy might have had his struggles, but he was so much more than that, just like you've always been more than your struggles." She pats my cheek. "The only thing that ever really mattered is how much he loved you. His precious girl."

I feel her words to my core, like a stab wound she's tried to heal but that's only started bleeding harder. A sob escapes my throat, and I wrap myself around Nan so we can share some of our pain.

"I miss him so much," I say against her hair that smells like the drugstore perfume she's worn all her life, lilacs and peaches. It's a small beacon in this flood of newness and revelations.

"Oh, darling, I miss him too. Every single day." One of her own tears touches my shoulder, gliding down my arm.

She pulls back, her grip firm on my arms. Her plump cheeks are glistening under the weight of her grief. "But that just speaks to how lucky we are to have had our time with him. It was worth it, you see?"

I'm not sure when the ache of not having him around anymore will lessen. Maybe the answer to that is never. Even so, I wouldn't exchange my memories to have it go away.

"Yes." I blink the wetness away from my eyes as I grab her hand in mine. "Yes, it was all worth it."

Chapter 37

I don't know if I'm making a mistake.

My body sure feels like it. As I stand in front of Carter's apartment, I can't help the nausea threatening to make me barf at even the thought of what I'm about to do. But I have to push through it. I'm tired of hurting.

Another week has passed, and even though Nana told me to call him and give him a chance to explain himself, I haven't been able to. He texted, offered to talk, to come to me, but I couldn't agree. Every time, it felt like a kick to the face, mostly because I wanted to sweep everything under the rug and just forget. Go back to the way things were. But that would mean returning to a time when I was blind to all that had been hidden from me, and I can't do that, even if I wanted to. However, I also can't stay in this limbo, where every glimpse of the life I had a few weeks ago almost brings me to my knees. I just can't.

So this morning, I used all the courage I had left in me and texted him, asking if I could come by this afternoon. He answered not a minute later.

> Carter: Yes, please.

And so here I am, shaking like a leaf as I stare at the door, wondering yet again how we've come to this.

I lift a hand to knock, but before I can, the door opens, showing me a flustered Carter that sends my heart spiraling out of my chest. The scent of his cologne, of his skin, of him, hits me at the same time I notice his long-sleeved checkered shirt and combed hair, and mist clouds my eyes.

Those damn tears need to stop.

"Hi," he says, voice breathy. His hyper-aware gaze scans me from head to toe, then shifts back to my face, where we collide in a silent exchange that, in a second, makes me rethink my decision. I look away first.

"Come in," he says, almost tripping over his own feet as he moves to give me space to step inside. I don't look around. I don't want to see pieces of him that'll make this even harder. I'm too weak for this, and I know it won't take much for me to break and run into his arms, just so I can feel his warmth once more.

He lied to you for the entirety of your relationship. I need to repeat that sentence again and again in my head as Carter leads me to the living room, where he points at the seat next to his on the couch. I sit on the coffee table facing him instead and pretend not to notice the homemade cookies that have been set on the table.

"Thanks for agreeing to this," I say, hands in my lap.

"Don't," he says, scooting closer so his knees almost bump with mine. "This isn't some formal thing. It's just me."

◻Which is precisely the problem here. I need to be formal because if I'm not, emotions will tangle my thoughts, and I won't go through with my plan.

I don't even acknowledge his request. My voice is shaky as I say, "I've thought long about it, and I think this is the best decision for us moving forward." I zip my parka down and reach for the inner pocket.

"Lili, what..."

His words die in his mouth when I hand him the folded stack of papers. Even his body freezes as he stares at the documents, not opening them. "W-what is this?"

I swallow one time. Another. "Divorce papers."

His gaze lifts from the documents to me, and for all the uncertainty about him and his intentions, I know the pain in his expression can't be faked.

I'm not faring that much better myself. The feeling in my chest makes me feel like I won't survive this, but I know I have to push through. If I remain married to this man I fell for, I'll only keep missing him, and the agony will be prolonged, endless. I'll never stop thinking of the way he makes me feel, still now, like there isn't enough room in this world to hold all the feelings I have for him. And then I'll never get over him, and I *need* to get over him.

"No." He shakes his head, dropping the papers beside him. "No, baby, don't do this." His hands reach for mine, and even though I move them away, he still grazes my skin, lighting me on fire. I clutch my hands into fists, wishing I could turn all my senses off so

I wouldn't smell him, wouldn't feel him or hear the sound of his voice that made me feel safe so many times before.

"We both fulfilled our parts of the deal," I trudge on, eyes closed. "It doesn't matter if the end comes earlier than planned."

"Yes, it fucking does!"

I flinch. He's making this even harder than it already is. I've given him everything, and I'm emptied out. "The album got the recognition it deserved. The band's now much bigger than I am." My voice is level, but it cracks as I say, "What more do you want from me?"

He stands. "You! Goddammit, I want you."

Apparently, I wasn't all dried out because another tear succeeds in slipping away. I turn so I can wipe it away without him seeing.

When I turn back, he's right there, on his knees, eyes level with mine. "Lilianne, honey, look at me. I know I should've been honest from the start. I *know*. But it didn't feel like it was my truth to share when Frank had spent his entire life keeping it a secret, and—"

At the sound of my father's name, I get up. "What about once we found the pamphlets?" The venom in my words is dried out by my bone-deep fatigue. "You couldn't tell me then?"

"I tried." He releases a heavy breath. "I swear I did, but you'd just learned this huge truth, and it felt cruel to drop another bomb on you." He goes to reach for me but stops himself when he catches my flinch. I hate that I worry about the hurt in his eyes. "You were in shock, and even when I tried to explain, you wouldn't hear it. And then the longer we went, the harder it got to get the truth out, and I didn't know what I should say, and—"

"You gave me a fucking *organ*, Carter."

"I know! I know I did. And I'm sorry for not telling you. It wasn't right. But…" He drags a heavy hand through his mussed hair, breathing deeply. "But I knew telling you the truth would be the end, and I couldn't handle losing you." His eyes brim under the dim lights. "Not when I'd fallen for you."

"Don't say that." I take a step back.

"Why? Didn't you say you wanted the truth?"

I pull away, more and more, until my back is against the front door.

"Well, here it is. I never planned to fall for you. In fact, I tried my goddamn hardest not to the *second* I learned who you were. I hid, and I isolated, and I forced myself not to look at you or listen to your laugh. But, honey, you're impossible not to love."

I shake my head, another tear spilling as he walks closer, slowly, carefully. He's ending me with each step, with each inhale.

"I can't, Carter." I'm not even sure what I'm saying no to at this point. I just know this has hurt too much, and I've borne too much pain in my life to voluntarily risk myself once more.

He pauses in his tracks, staring at me like I'm a wild animal, and I take the opportunity to do just what he fears.

I run.

Chapter 38

The leaves begin to turn from their deep green to bright orange and burgundy, and still, I remain in a limbo.

Even if I don't see Carter, he's right there, every second of every day. I can't stop replaying the last words he said to me as if they've been branded onto each cell in my body. And I want to believe them, I do, but some part of me is holding back. The same part that told me our relationship could never survive if it became real.

Some local singer is performing on the scene of The Sparrow, strumming her guitar in a slow, sensuous rhythm while singing about loving someone for who they are, even the bad. I don't look at her, focused on cleaning glasses I've probably already washed. I can't bring myself to care about the music, or about the work, or even about my friends. Finn texted me a few times earlier, according to his name popping up on my screen, but I decided not to open my texts. I don't have it in me to fake being all right, and I don't want to worry him even more than he probably already is.

The public starts cheering as the song comes to an end, a moment I usually love, when the artists peek out into the crowd and you can see their pride, but I don't even look up today. I feel like a half version of myself, and I don't know when that storm hanging over my head will pass and I'll be able to breathe again.

And then, there's the part of me that doesn't want to go back to the way I was before Carter either. I hadn't realized how limited my life was until him. How I'd restrained myself to a version of life I thought had to be mine. Being with him made me want to do more, to experience more, and to be brave enough not only to wish, but to do. I'm not ready to let go of that person yet, even if she was built on an illusion of a relationship.

"Lil!"

I jump, almost dropping the glass I've been polishing all night, only to find Finn on the other side of the bar, looking at me with pinched lips.

"Where were you?"

"Huh?"

"I've called your name three times."

"Oh."

"And I've been texting you all day." Finn leans in closer, elbows on the bar. "You doing okay?"

Just lie. Just say yes.

With my friend scanning me, though, I can't. I also can't acknowledge how terrible I still feel about the ending of such a short relationship. In other people's eyes, it might sound like a fling, if that. But it was more. So much more. And even if I know he's a damn good liar, I can't help but feel like he was being truthful in some way the other day.

"Oh, Lil."

I clench my jaw so it doesn't start trembling yet again. *That* is why I didn't open his texts. I can't continue being this much of a mess all the time, and talking about Carter with Finn would lead to just that.

"What are you doing here?" I ask, praying this will lead to a change of mind. I'd be open to anything. Him wanting us to sign up for line dancing lessons. A talk on a newfound lactose intolerance. *Anything.*

"I have something for you." He gives me a pointed look. "Which you would know if you looked at my texts."

"What is it?" I ask, ignoring his prompt.

"You have a second?"

Finn's never come to my workplace just to chat. I look around and find no one waiting to order. The bar is quiet tonight and most of our customers are focused on the show, so I can take a bit of time off. Leaving my rag on the countertop, I gesture for him to follow me out back, where I pass an employee-only door that leads out the back of the building. The music muffles as the door slams shut, leaving us in the stillness of the early October evening. I don't have my coat with me, but the weather's still mild, only a mild breeze ruffling the hair from my ponytail.

"What's up?" I ask.

"Carter came by earlier." He doesn't sugarcoat it as if he knows that ripping the Band-Aid off is the easier option.

The simple mention of his name makes me feel lightheaded. I thought that was better with the new pills, but guess I was wrong.

Wobbly, I lean back against the wall, pretending I'm just making myself comfortable.

"What for?" I get myself to ask.

"He wanted me to give you this," he says, "and didn't want to make you uncomfortable by going to you directly."

I wait with my stomach in my throat as Finn hands me a tall envelope. It feels heavy in my hands, and even though I have an inkling of what it might be, it feels like time stops when I open it and see the divorce papers I handed him days before. I can't feel the wind on my face, can't smell the petrichor from the earlier rain, can't see Finn standing next to me, a hand on my shoulder.

I should not be shocked by this. I gave him those papers. I *wanted* him to sign them.

Or did I?

As I pull the documents out of their folder, something slips out. I bend to pick it up, the paper moist under my fingers from the wet cement.

An envelope with my name in his calligraphy. Neat, precise.

I clutch it tightly, forgetting about the documents I can see have been signed.

"I'm really sorry," Finn says.

I nod.

"You want me to stay with you for a while?"

"I'm good," I say. "But thanks for coming all the way for this."

"Of course." He hugs me, then begins walking in the direction of his truck. Meanwhile, I remain in place, gaze stuck on the eight letters of my name, never having looked as good as they do in his writing.

"Hey, Lil?"

I look up.

"If it makes you feel any better, he looked devastated handing those to me."

That doesn't make me feel better. Not at all.

When Finn has disappeared from view, I let myself slide against the wall to the ground, wetness seeping through my jeans, but I couldn't care less. Not when my mind feels like it's been doused in gasoline before stumbling into an inferno.

I only hesitate for a second before I tear the envelope and unfold the paper, breath catching when I see an entire page of his writing.

Lilianne,

First off, I want to start by saying that signing those papers damn near killed me. It makes me sick to think that this might be where it all ends, and I truly hope you'll never use them, at least until you've found another way to get insurance. However, after staring at these for days, I realized it wasn't my place to keep you from doing what you needed to. So if divorcing me is what you want, here. You can do so now.

But if this is really the end, I wanted to make sure you knew certain things. I'm not a man of many words, something you know already, but I'll try my best to show you what I'm thinking.

Those months we spent together were the best of my entire life.

Something breaks inside me at those words. The pain is physical, visceral, as if someone is carving those words into my skin.

☐

☐*None of the money and the fame, the shows and the parties, could've compared to how it felt to lie on the couch with you, watching you watch a movie, seeing all sorts of expressions move your beautiful face. Even if I never get more, those moments will remain with me forever.*

When I learned you were Frank's daughter, I couldn't believe it, at first, how fucking small of a world could we live in for you to be <u>her</u>? That girl I'd heard so much about but had never met? It made no sense. But then I got to know you, and I wondered how I could have missed it in the first place. You were just like him. You had his humor, his wit, his glass-half-full way of living. You didn't tolerate my shit, and as hard-headed as you could be, you were also the kindest, loveliest person I'd met since spending time with him. And just like I loved Frank, I couldn't help but love you, too.

I taste salt from my tears, and even though his words hurt, they also unscramble some of my thoughts. He did know him. At first, it almost felt like I'd imagined it, like Carter and Dad knowing each other was an impossible thing I could only have seen in a sleepy haze, but reading this... He *knew* him.

Marrying you was the best mistake I ever made. It ruined me for the rest of my life, but it also made me see I had a life to begin with. You made a man who hadn't laughed in years start to dream again.

And so I want you to know this last thing: Even if you never want to talk to me again, even if we'd never met in the first place, I could never regret what I did. Donating that kidney was the best thing I ever did. You light up the fucking world, Lilianne. Even if I was just a blip in your path, I'd be fine with it, so long as you never dimmed. So here. You have it all. You can take me out of your life forever. Even though my intentions were never to hurt you, I know I did, and for that, I'm so fucking sorry, and I deserve whatever decision you end up making. But I also want you to know that I'm not going anywhere. I know so many people walked away from you in your life, and I promise I won't be one of them. You're my one love. So I'll be there if you decide you need me.

You might not be mine, but I'll always be yours.

C

I read it a second time, and then a third, and each time, my heart only swells larger, eventually pushing against the restraints of my ribcage as if trying to break free.

I can try to continue hiding my own feelings from myself, but that'd be a waste of time.

I love this man.

It's useless to continue telling myself I can move on. My heart's decided Carter's the one it wants, and I don't think anything will ever change that. And this letter just proved why: despite it all, he's a good man. A man I decided deserved my trust after years of thinking no man could ever truly want me for me.

That doesn't mean I can just forget what happened, but I also can't continue playing dumb and pretend I can cut him out of my life like he was a simple hookup. Like he didn't hold my heart in the palm of his rough, calloused hands.

The edges of the papers ruffle with the breeze, and for a long time, I stare at them, wishing a powerful gust of wind could take them away from me. This way, I wouldn't have to make a decision.

Unless I don't need to make one yet. There's no real rush. I was the one who wanted it to be done and over with as soon as possible, but the truth is, it can't be. Even if I send over these papers, I'll still wish he were mine. Still wish for a different ending for us. No amount of time or legal separation will change that. The only thing that will allow me true clarity is the truth. What he's been begging to give me ever since the hospital.

Pushing myself off the damp pavement, I walk inside and ask Leah, my coworker, to cover for me. Then I grab my coat and keys and slip out of the bar.

It's almost midnight by the time I get to Carter's apartment, breathless as I knock.

It takes a long time for the door to open, and when it does, Carter looks half awake, rubbing sleep off his eyes. But the second he sees me, his entire body straightens as if someone poured a bucket of cold water down his shirt.

"I want to hear it. What you have to say, about your time with him." I swallow, trying not to notice the dark circles under his eyes or the way it looks like he hasn't shaved in days. "If you're still willing."

He blinks a few times as if not believing I'm actually here. Then he takes a step back, inviting me in. "Of course I am."

And so our nights of discovery begin.

Chapter 39

It becomes something of a tradition.

Every night I'm not working at the bar, I meet up with Carter, and we talk. Or rather, I listen as he tells me all about the things that were kept in the dark between us before, but also all kinds of things I didn't even think to ask. He tells me about the night he met my father for the first time and how he wanted nothing to do with him or his support. How his view of things started to change after a while, with Dad holding his ground until Carter had no choice but to relent. He laughs as he tells me all about the times Dad didn't take his shit. He also tells me about those days before they met, when he'd just quit his band and felt like nothing would ever be okay again. Slowly, our conversations widen in span, veering from only focusing on Carter's time with Dad to everything we've skimmed on before.

At first, I keep showing up at his apartment, but when he asks if he can make the journey to my place instead the next day, looking sheepish as he does, I find myself saying yes. I said once that I wanted this place to feel like home to him too, and I realize I still mean it. It feels right, to have him here, in this space he brought back to life. And whereas that first night I sat ramrod straight at his kitchen table, the more evenings we spend lost in dim lighting and hushed stories, the more comfortable I get.

The attraction I feel for him never dulls, only heightens with every visit, his honesty making me crave him more than ever before, but I pull at the emergency brake every time I feel myself falter. When he's right there, talking and looking so alive, I have to sit on my hands to stop myself from touching him, from tracing his lips as he grins while recounting a story or from grabbing his hands when they shake as he talks about the day he received the call that the two of us were a match.

"It didn't make sense at first. I never thought it'd actually work. But once I made sure it was real? I never hesitated." His throat bobs as his gaze slides to me, making me look away. That's what it all comes down to, isn't it? Not the fact that he lied, or even the fact that he kept Dad's story hidden. I can understand that he did it as a form of respect for him. It's clear in the reverence he uses when he talks about him. But the kidney... That's what's truly holding me back.

Yet still I come back, night after night.

Carter doesn't seem to mind my distance. He doesn't push me, only takes what I'm willing to offer. I, however, don't miss the corner smiles he gives me the first time I sit next to him on the couch, or the time I carefully let my head rest on his shoulder when he tells me a story about the time he and Dad got sick from eating raw chicken at a shabby joint. Dad apparently felt too bad sending his food back and ended up convincing Carter to man up and eat it, too. A wave of nostalgia hits me at the reminder of all that Dad was, and feeling closer to Carter is a small comfort I allow myself. His body tenses under my cheek, only to finally relax once more, his soft breath hitting my forehead as he resumes his storytelling.

One night, as we lie curled up on the carpet of his living room with our backs against the couch, his fingers resting a hair's breadth away from my thigh, he finally tells me about the night my father passed. It's a sore story to get out of him, and it looks just as painful to tell as it is for me to hear, but I think we both needed it to be out in the open. And as much as I want to bury my head under a pillow and never hear about Dad's last moments, I also smile through my tears at it because just like Nana said, it's so much like him to have died trying to help someone else.

Nana wasn't just right about that. The more I listen to Carter's stories about Dad, the more I realize how little they matter in the grand scheme of things. The person Carter is describing is the same one I grew up with. The same one who would wake up early on appointment days to make a batch of cookies I could use as a comfort in case I received bad news. And after all, I've begun to make my peace with the parts of him he hid from me. A person can have a thousand different facets to them, and maybe we don't need to know them all to know someone.

Because I knew my father. I knew he watched Christmas movies all year long and loved nothing more than a chilly October morning. I knew that his patience slipped every time he had to explain a problem to an appliance technician over the phone, and that his girlfriend abandoning him and the baby girl they'd just had was one of the worst pains of his life. And I knew he would've given away his life in a heartbeat if it meant being able to give a helping hand to someone.

"Thank you," I tell him once he's done, both of our voices raw. He dips his chin in understanding, not needing me to tell him why I'm grateful for these stories. Sometimes, it feels as if he knows me better than I know myself.

I haven't realized I've once again started crying until the pad of his thumb caresses my cheek, wiping a tear with such gentle care it makes my throat constrict. His hand remains there, and when I sniffle, Carter gets to his feet. "Let me get you something," he says.

"I'm good," I answer, reaching over for my bag where I always keep a pack of tissues.

I blow my nose, and once I'm back from throwing the tissue in his trash can, I catch Carter's attention stuck on my purse. I only realize why once I see the divorce papers peeking out.

I take a careful seat next to him.

"Why do you still have these?"

Hugging my knees to my chest, I say, "I haven't been able to get myself to send them." I don't shy away from the truth. It's too late for us to be anything but completely honest with each other.

"Then don't." His voice is no longer pleading or even convincing; it sounds tired. Hopeless.

My lips pinch together. "I don't know how to deal with this."

"With what?"

"Wondering whether you're with me out of duty toward my father." I shake my head. "I can't be with someone else who stays out of pity." From the start, that was what I was to him. A debt to be repaid.

Carter's face twists in what I can only describe as utter shock. "Is that what you think this is?"

I don't answer. It should be obvious to him.

His dumbfounded stare scopes out my face until he repositions himself on the ground. "Honey, what I feel for you has nothing to do with your dad. I can't believe you'd even think this." He blinks. "You might have been my saving grace when you were just a name on paper, but the second I met you, that was over." I tighten my fists as I brace for what's coming, my fingers trembling. The smile on his lips looks resigned. "I gave a kidney to Frank's daughter, but I fell in love with *you*, Lilianne."

Don't you dare cry again.

It's hard to hear the words, to absorb them and change my view on things, but a big part of me tells me that's his truth. Could he have been subconsciously influenced? Maybe. But that doesn't change that what he's telling me right now is real to him. That has to be worth something.

"Knowing my father, he never thought you had a debt to repay him."

The left side of his lips curves up, and even with the heavy bags under his eyes, his body looks lighter than it has in days. He doesn't even seem to care that I didn't answer his last statement. His arms mirror mine around his legs. "You're right. But it wasn't him I owed."

I frown.

"I took your dad away from you," he says as a way of explaining.

"No, you didn't."

Silence.

"Carter, you didn't."

When he tilts his head like *come on*, I realize for the first time just how contorted his vision of what happened with Dad is. What was an accident over a slippery road and a driver whose brakes failed turned into a burden of fault hanging over his head.

Moving to my knees, I scoot closer so I can clasp his cheeks between my hands. His breath hitches at the first touch, eyes flitting to mine. His irises look more brown than green in the 3:00 a.m. glow of the streetlamps, and the glimmer shadowing them looks lost between hope and fear.

It feels strange, to touch him after all this time as if dormant sparks have been lit up all along every nerve endings touching him. It's scary how good it feels. How addictive.

"I need you to listen to me when I say this." Unable to stop myself, I brush my thumb over his cheekbone. "You did nothing wrong that night. My father did not die because of you. He died in some dumb accident that was due to bad luck. It had nothing to do with you."

"If I hadn't—"

"I don't want to hear it." I don't even want to think about it, in fact. It shatters my heart to think that he felt responsible for his death all this time. I guess I wasn't the only one who needed clarity on some things. "You had nothing to do with it. Nothing."

His throat works as his eyes alternate between mine, our noses almost brushing from how close I got earlier.

"But I never thanked you," I say, my breath slipping away. "For giving me a new life."

"I told you." His jaw flexes as his gaze falls to my lips. "Best thing I ever did."

Getting lost in one's eyes has never made more sense than it does now. It feels as if I'm in a trance, like I couldn't move away even if the room were on fire. My hands are still on his face, the warmth of his cheeks reaching all the way through me, begging me to kiss him, just this once.

My lips part on his exhale, want clouding my thoughts. The clean smell of his soap makes me want to lean closer, to trace my nose against his neck, to taste his skin, his mouth.

I'm not sure how much time we spend like this, teetering on this tightrope, knowing we're one movement away from falling into something else.

In the end, Carter pulls back first, rubbing a hand down his face, but even with the distance, the hunger doesn't go anywhere.

For either of us.

Chapter 40

"I need you to tell me what to do."

Finn looks up from where he's piling some files on top of his desk in the small office he's made for himself at Evermore farm, decorated with memorabilia from all the years he spent traveling, but also with dozens of pictures, mostly of him and Lexie together.

"Well, hello to you too." He comes over to hug me, then smiles when he pulls back. "Looks like you've gained some color back."

"Right."

"Why do you make that face when you say that?" he asks, laughing.

I only answer with a groan.

Finn looks at me for a second, then as if realizing what I need, says, "Wanna go on a walk?"

"I have a party to go to." Crash & Burn is having their "return home" concert at The Sparrow tonight, and I need to be there for them. "I just needed quick advice."

"You can't give your best friend in the world a ten-minute walk?"

"You're a pain."

He smirks as he puts his arm over my shoulder and leads me outside. "So I've been told."

We start trudging through the forest that, in winter, resembles a true wonderland, but right now, as the farm is getting ready for its Halloween event, it looks more like something out of a scary movie. Scarecrows line the rows of trees and a haunted house is being set up in the barn next door.

We walk in silence, the chirps of crows and the crunch of pine needles under our boots filling the space. I love coming here, even when Finn isn't there. It's the most peaceful place on earth. Finn seems to be having the same train of thought as he looks around with a small smile. It's why he and Lexie decided to get married here, after all. The place that became a shelter for both of them.

"So," Finn says, interrupting our common reverie, "what's up with you?"

I cross my arms, finding the words hard to utter even though I came here for this precise reason.

"This about Carter?"

Instead of agreeing, I say, "I have no idea what I'm doing."

"Who does?"

I give him a pointed look. "You do." He might have found himself lost during his early twenties, but now, he has a job he loves, a wife he adores, and a clear path that is perfect for him.

"Well, I didn't use to." He nudges my shoulder. "The best's coming for you too."

I kick a pine nut. "I'm holding off on him. I want to go back to the way it was, but something's holding me back."

"You're scared to get hurt."

"Wouldn't you be?"

He laughs, raw and loud. "Oh, I was. I fucking was." His smile doesn't go away as his mind seems to slip to a place of memories. "But taking that risk was the best decision I ever made."

I know he's right, but it also seems easy for him. Lexie and Finn were perfect for each other, and the second I saw them together, I knew there was no way they wouldn't end up together. It's easy, with hindsight, to see how right they were to fall for each other.

"You love him," Finn says, not a question but a statement.

"I can't stop."

Finn sighs. "You know, he made some fucked-up mistakes, but I truly don't think he had bad intentions."

"I don't either." I tighten my coat around my middle. "I'm just afraid he's in this for the wrong reasons."

"That's bullshit."

I huff a laugh.

Finn takes one more step before turning to face me. "Can I ask you a question? And feel free to tell me to fuck off."

"That sounds ominous."

He doesn't return my smile, which makes mine dim. With his hands in his pockets, he asks, "Do you believe you're worthy of love? Like, truly worthy?"

I open my mouth, but no word comes out. It's strange. Before, I would've said yes in a heartbeat, but I would have also been lying. I could say all the positive, self-loving things I wanted about myself, but deep down, I couldn't imagine a world where I was loved fully, deeply. It started with friends who stopped inviting me to events or who would only speak to me as a patient and not as their peer when I got sick, and continued with Greg only wanting some of me while repressing aspects he wished didn't exist. I would always be loved in spite of certain parts of who I was.

But now I know what true love feels like. I know what it is to show every facet of who you are because you know it will be accepted. Embraced, even. Despite it all, Carter showed me how it could feel to be cherished in my entirety. I know how he felt wasn't a lie. He wasn't forthright about his past, but our present was real. I know it was.

"Yeah," I tell Finn, shoulders straightening under his gaze. "Yeah, I do."

His lips curl up, and he drapes his arm around my neck once more and resumes walking. "Really fucking happy to hear that because that man worships the ground you walk on."

I grin. "And how would you know that?"

"We talked, the two of us."

I halt in my steps. "What? When?"

"When he brought those papers for me to give you. We had a little chat."

"And you didn't tell me this because...?"

"Didn't want to influence you one way or another when you were so unsure of what you wanted to do about your relationship."

I swallow. "And why now?"

"Because now I think you've made up your mind."

A draft of cold wind wraps the scent of pine trees all around me. "I hate when you're right."

His lips quirk up. "You know I wouldn't even have mentioned it to you if I didn't think he deserved you, right?"

I inhale a deep breath. Somehow, this feels like the most encouraging thing he's said. I'm afraid I'm only seeing this situation through rose-colored glasses because of the way I feel about Carter, but to know my best friend believes this too makes me even more hopeful than I was before.

And in the end, I'll never know whether Carter's love can be differentiated from the guilt he felt for Dad's death, and that will never change. The only thing left to do is take a leap of faith, or risk spending the rest of my life wondering what might have been.

"What happened to 'If you even think of putting your hands on her, I'll make your life a living hell?'" I say in a deep voice.

He looks proud of himself. "Didn't you enjoy the theatrics of it all?"

A chirp sounds from Finn's pocket, and the second he opens his phone and reads his text, his face lights up like twenty high-voltage cables have boosted it.

"You two are unbearably sweet," I joke, not even having to ask him who just texted him. Not even Aaron could make him smile like this.

He texts something back, his cheeks warming, then he buries his phone back in his pocket. "You could have this too, I think."

My heart squeezes at that. Despite it all, I don't think I could ever have this with anyone other than Carter. He's my high-voltage plug, for better or for worse.

"You just have to decide if he's worth risking your heart for," Finn adds.

I turn to him, feeling lighter than I have in weeks as I finally admit the truth. "I really think he is."

"Then you have your answer."

Chapter 41

I show up late to the party.

 I wasn't planning on it, but after returning home from the farm, I started questioning everything, from what I should wear to how I should approach Carter, if he even decided to show up tonight. I'm hoping—praying—he's decided to make it, especially since the success of Crash & Burn's album is partly because of him. Still, it's not his scene, so I can't say for sure. And then I started spiraling, wondering whether I was too late and our story had been ruined.

 By the time I finally decided to push myself out of the house, with messy hair and asymmetrical winged liner, I had to say to hell with it and rush to the venue. Not like there was much I could do now anyway.

 In the end, Finn was right. You're never going to walk into a good situation without risk. And after a month separated from Carter, I can say it *was* a good situation. I'll never be as happy as I am when I'm with him, and if he's the key to my happiness, then I can't keep myself away from him out of fear. I've been a coward, and Dad would tell me it's not the way he raised me. Life's too short to play it safe, and despite everything, I believe in Carter. Believe in us.

The bar is jam-packed when I step inside, the first act bowing as the audience cheers for her. I missed the entire set. I clap anyway, looking left and right, trying to recognize familiar faces. I can barely walk over to the bar with the amount of people swarming the place, shouting and laughing, beers sloshing over cups onto the sticky floor.

There's no break between the two acts. The moment the singer walks off stage, the scene techs step on to arrange the set for the band, and not long after, the lights shut off. Screams erupt through the small room, and even with the nerves tightening my insides, I start cheering with the rest of the audience. I'm so proud of how far these guys have come, from that first night at the club, when they'd barely gotten their first taste of performing.

When the guys walk on stage, it's without a fuss, waving along to their fans. The decibels crank up, and I can't help but laugh at the way the guys who left their boxers lying around and got into burping contests are now being treated like stars.

"Let's hear it!" Ethan shouts in the mic.

The screams become almost unbearable, but even as I try to muffle the sounds with my hands over my ears, I can't stop smiling at the level of excitement they're receiving.

Once Ethan has motioned for the crowd to quiet down, he goes into a speech thanking everyone for their support of their first album and tour and for getting them nominated for the AMAs. I try to keep my focus on him—I'm here for the band, after all—but my body keeps twisting around, hoping to spot a familiar head of tousled hair, but with the way I'm being pushed in all directions, it's almost impossible to see.

"And there are also a few other people we need to thank." He begins by thanking their agent, their tour manager, the people from the label who believed in them in the first place. "Lil," he adds, "our promoter extraordinaire." Somehow, a spotlight finds me in the crowd, and I blow them kisses, those people who've gone from strangers to lifelong friends in a matter of months.

"And finally, we need to send a million thanks to the person who brought our music from good to great."

My breath somersaults, body stilling as I wait for Ethan's next words.

"Andrew Carter, we could never have done it without you."

The spotlight moves away from me, and I follow its tracks as it leads to a body leaning against a wall in the far corner of the room, arms crossed in front of his chest, a blush covering his face.

And his gaze is right on me.

It's as if I've put my hand in a power outlet, like my entire nervous system gets overpowered. As soon as the light returns to the stage and Emmett rips the first chord of "Be My Guest," I trudge a path to Carter. He never looks away from me, and I might be imagining it, but I'd swear his face softens the closer I get.

"Hi," I whisper once I reach him, the blaring music swallowing the sound.

"Hi," he answers, uncrossing his arms, then bunching his hands at his sides as if he was going to reach out at first.

"I was hoping you'd be here tonight."

His throat works on a swallow, eyes searching mine.

"I miss you."

His lashes flutter, and for a moment, he almost looks in physical pain. "Don't do this."

"Do what?"

"Give me false hope."

My breath catches, but just as I go to answer, the band moves into the next song of the set, which is a ballad they rarely play, one that always makes me emotional for some reason.

Hoping he'll see this as an answer, I hold out my hand. "Will you dance with me?"

There's still something like fear in his gaze, but after a moment of hesitation, he nods, then moves to take my hand, watching it like it's a treasure trove before slowly sliding his fingers between mine. His touch feels like a tentative caress, and the simple glide of the pads of his fingers against my palm makes my body tingle. He squeezes my hand once, then tightens his grip as he pulls my body flush to his. My free arm wraps around his shoulders and neck, making me arch my back so I can keep looking at him while his other hand falls against my side to land on my hips, a position that's safe but that still sends thrilling memories rushing past.

As we slowly sway back and forth to the music, I absorb the lyrics, my eyes closing at the feel of Carter's body against me after all these days of wanting from afar, Ethan's voice crooning about finding true love. I know we need to talk, but I want another minute of simply enjoying his presence.

"I love that song," I say against his collarbone. He's wearing a white dress shirt, unbuttoned at the collar to give a perfect view of his Adam's apple and the top of his chest. His skin smells so good it almost hurts.

"Yeah?"

"One of my favorites of theirs." If everything goes according to plan, it should be featured on Crash & Burn's second album, the one they're almost done recording. They first played it on tour last July, and I couldn't help my tears. The lyrics, the melody… It all spoke to me.

"It's mine, actually."

I look up. "What?"

"I, um, I wrote it. Play on it too, on the record."

I stammer something as I bring my attention to the music once more, even looking back at the scene to make sure I'm not imagining things.

I could fight it, but it's true

From the start, it had to be you

I turn back to Carter, blinking fast. "W-when did you write this?"

His thumb traces a pattern on my hip bone, a small movement that redirects all my nerve endings to that exact spot. "A long time ago."

My eyes well up, and I'm not sure why. Maybe it's the thought that time and time again, he's proven his love to me, and my self-doubt is what got the best of me, or maybe it's just the fact that, just like the song says, it always had to be him.

"I threw away the papers."

He misses a step. "What?"

"Burned them, actually. Before coming here."

"I don't..." He doesn't finish his sentence, studying me like I'm a complex theorem.

"I'm ready, Andy."

He blinks rapidly, love transforming his expression, his very features. How did I ever doubt this was real?

"I can't stay away anymore." I lick my lips. "Don't want to, actually."

His hands become firmer around me as if he needs to make sure I'm real, that I'm not going anywhere.

"Tell me again how you feel about me." I curl a hand over his cheek, the stubble rough under my palm. "Tell me again, and I promise I'll say it back this time."

He remains silent, but his face is alive with emotion, with questions and answers.

"Or actually, don't," I say. "Because the way I feel about you has nothing to do with how you feel about me."

Carter stops moving, keeping us still in a wave of swaying bodies, Ethan's melodic voice blanketing us.

"I love you not because you love me but because you're *you*, and that was the only thing I needed to fall in love." I shrug. "When I picture my future, it makes no sense without you in it. You're my one love, too." Even if at some point I wished I could've fallen for anyone else, there's no denying it. With his hands on my body and his presence near me, I feel like myself again. My lower lip trembles as I add, "For better or for worse, right?"

"Do you really mean that?" He breathes in deeply, his gaze so unlike the empty one I saw when we first met. "Because if you do, then I'm going to kiss you now."

I don't give him the time to make that decision. Instead, I climb on my toes and tug him down so his lips crash onto mine.

The taste of him feels like inhaling after being held underwater for a long time, like your body is refilling on something vital. *Whoosh*, my heart goes, again and again, overwhelmed to finally be home, to have gotten back the part of me that only exists when he's there. The part that's willing to move forward, to accept the things that happened, and to trust in the future. The part that wants to experience everything and that believes someone can love me just the way I am.

Carter's hands move from my hips to land on my back and behind my head, pulling me so close to him I'm crushed to his chest, lungs squeezed tight as his tongue traces the seam of my lips. I open for him, relishing the feel of him in my mouth, under my nails, against my stomach. He nips at my bottom lip and then at my chin, and I forget all about the people around us, my only concern being my need for him.

As I whisper his name, his nose brushing against mine, eyes glimmering under the spotlights, he says, "I missed you so goddamn much."

I hug him tight, relishing the way his heartbeat feels against my cheek. *I'm right here*, it says.

Carter pulls back slightly so he can stare at me for a long time, his thumbs brushing over my lips, my cheekbones, my nose, and then his face splits into the biggest, most precious smile I've ever seen. "This is real?"

"Yeah." I grin back, restraining myself from jumping in his arms. "It's real."

As if stealing the idea from my head, he picks me up and spins me around once, he too having forgotten about the people around. He kisses me again, allowing me to taste the smile on his lips. There are no secrets remaining, no faking our way around, no hesitation around our feelings. He is mine, and I am his.

And later that night, when we are back home in our own little world and he makes love to me, each one of his touches showing me how much he cherishes me, I find myself thinking: it doesn't get any more real than this.

Epilogue

A year later

Carter

I don't know whether this feeling will ever go away.

The tightening in my stomach at the idea of playing in front of a crowd. The thought of the adrenaline rush that's about to flow in the second the lights turn off and the ear-splitting screams begin.

"Nervous?" Ethan asks me with a nudge of his shoulder.

I don't bother answering, returning my attention to the sliver of the crowd I can see from the crack of the curtains in the backstage area. The opening act ended twenty minutes ago, so we're about to go on.

"You don't have to do it, you know," he says, the teasing tone gone from his voice.

"I know." I don't have to, but I actually want to.

It took me a while to realize I wanted to get back to playing, and that all stemmed from that first time Lili basically shoved me on stage. Since feeling that pure joy again, I knew I couldn't go back to never picking up the guitar in front of a crowd again.

I never signed up for playing full time—I still don't think tour life is the best place for me, even with my support system with me, but going on once in a while as a second guitarist for Crash & Burn when they're doing local shows is good enough for me. Scratches that itch I never thought I'd be able to soothe again in my life. I won't ever have a career as a professional guitarist again, and that's fine with me. I love my job as a producer, the one Frank encouraged me to reach out for and that changed my life, but what truly fulfills me isn't even close to work-related. That would be the girl with the blond hair who makes me get up every morning with a purpose. The one who's spent the past year and a half making me feel more alive than I have in my entire life. Who's taken the time to discover new passions and directions. Who's decided to attend college for the first time at the age of twenty-five because she wanted a degree in media and marketing and realized it wasn't too late to go get it. Who's taught me more about myself and about life than anyone else.

The band huddles over to the side of the stage a second before the room is plunged into darkness, and as expected, my heart rate jumps through the roof with the heightening of the cheers and shouts.

When the guys walk out onto the stage, I stay in place for a breath, but when Emmett's hand claps my back, I push through the nerves and follow. My vision blurs as I somehow find a way to my spot, half-hidden in the shadows like I want it. After the first show I played with the band, some old Fickle fans recognized me from videos that had made it online and started tracking the shows

I attended, and I'd rather get the least coverage I can. That's not why I'm here tonight.

I'll probably never be able to feel only peace and excitement when playing in front of a crowd—nothing that brings that kind of rush could be solely innocent—and that's something I've come to terms with. If Frank were here, he'd probably say that's a part of my recovery too, and I'd have to agree with him.

But when I finally steal a look at the audience and find the face of the woman I love standing in the first row with our friends at her sides, wearing a proud smile as she looks at no one but me, I know this is the real reason I want to play again. Not only for the joy of knowing I've aced a riff, but for the sight of the pride on my wife's face. It's the most precious thing I've ever earned.

"I love you," she mouths as if she knows that's exactly what I need to hear. But even if she hadn't said the words, love is written all over her. In the way she's filming the show on her phone, something she still does for old times' sake, making sure to catch moments she'll be able to show me later. In the way her eyes are rid of that ache she still sometimes carries with her, on the harder days when she needs an extra hug. In the way her body is angled toward me as if she's pulled to me in the same way I am to her. That love is the only thing I need to calm me before the show.

In the past year, I've made my peace with losing the relationships I had with my family members. They only made me feel worse about myself, and it was only when I met Lilianne that I realized love wasn't supposed to feel like that. I'm not saying I'll never talk to Mom or Brandon again, but for the moment, I'm staying away. I've built a new family with Lili, one that's made of trust, of encouragement and peace, and it's all I need.

My hands don't shake when the ticking sounds begin in my earpiece, giving me the counts until I start playing. I don't need to be nervous. Not when I know who's waiting for me at the end of the show.

―ele―

"You were so good out there!" Lili says just as she jumps in my arms and wraps her body around mine, tethering me back. I don't have to be scared to play because I know no matter what, she'll be there for me after the performance, my anchor who won't let me lose myself. "That song…"

I hide my smile in the crook of her neck. I knew she'd love the song I wrote for the band for the album we've only begun recording, but I should also have guessed she'd know right away it was mine.

"Glad you liked it."

I rub her ribs, where I know hides the tattoo I finally convinced her to get on her last birthday, one that depicts in delicate lines a small acoustic guitar. While we were there, I got an *L* tattooed on my ring finger to replace the wedding band I never did get myself.

"There isn't a single thing about you I don't like, Andrew Carter."

And when I pull back and look at her—*truly* look at her—I know she's telling the truth. As many things about myself and my life I'd like to change, she loves me for all of them. She's never made me feel inadequate, inferior, or unloved in any way. She's never seen my alcoholism as something I needed to hide from, but rather something I should be proud to be able to conquer every single day. She makes all the things I see as failures feel like part of what she loves about me, which in turn allows me to accept them, too. Now more than ever I see this.

With my arms still banded across her lower back and her legs wrapped around my hips, I say, "Marry me."

She smiles as her brows bunch. "Sorry to tell you, but we're already married."

"Marry me again." I tuck loose strands of blond hair behind her ear as she watches me with that chink in her forehead she gets when she's confused. "You can have the white dress and the flowers and the whole big thing, or it can be just the two of us. Whatever you want." I swallow. "I just want you to have a wedding day where you don't doubt for even a second how much I love you."

When I was young, I promised myself I'd never get married. I'd seen the way so many people's—including my parents'—marriages worked, and I wanted nothing like it. I didn't want a relationship that was transactional with someone. I never wanted to build a family, or get attached to someone who would then use me to their advantage. As much as my parents treated me and my brother like pawns in their lives, they did the same to each other.

And then, when I did get married, it was nothing like the thing I'd told myself I wanted to avoid. It was a business deal. A transaction without any real feeling involved.

And now, as I'm asking her for the real thing, I find myself thinking it was so fucking dumb of me to fear this. There's nothing scary about Lilianne's love. It's a gift. The only thing I could possibly be scared of would be not spending the rest of my life with her.

She's still smiling skeptically, but her turquoise eyes have become watery. "Are you serious?"

"I don't make jokes."

"I mean, you *can* be funny sometimes."

I pinch her thigh lightly, making her shriek. "Stop being annoying and give me an answer."

She jumps off my body and brings her burning hands to my jaw. "I... I don't need this, Carter. I have all I need already."

"Then do it for me." I've seen the way she looked at Lexie and Finn's wedding. I know she wants it, and if she's too proud to admit it, then I'll do it. Bringing her hands away from my face so I can clasp them in mine, I gently ease the golden band off her ring finger, then kneel.

"Lilianne DiLorenzo, marry me. For real, this time."

I don't care that I'm in the middle of the backstage area where the crew are pulling instruments off-stage and probably staring at me. Her reaction is the only thing that matters.

She falls to her knees right before me and kisses me before she even says a word. Then, with the tip of her nose brushing against mine, she says, "I feel like it's greedy to ask for more when you already make me so happy, but—"

"Is that a yes?"

She rolls her eyes. "Yes, you impatient man. It's a yes."

This time, I can't help the full grin that overtakes my face as I pick her up and spin her around. "You're everything," I say against her skin. Every morning when I wake up and see her sleeping next to me, her hair tangled on the pillow and her soft lips parted, I tell myself the same thing. It still doesn't make sense to me that this is real life. That so many coincidences have brought us together and have given me everything I could ever want.

"If I can get whatever I want, then can I ask that you wear that stupid hat we found in Dad's stuff?"

"Pain in my ass," I say.

She laughs, the sound so deep and beautiful, a song I'll never get tired of hearing, and then she kisses me once more, all the while the band and crew cheer for us. When I put her back down, the guys I now also see as family come to congratulate the two of us. Ethan claps my back while Bong lifts Lili in a bear hug, making her giggle. Even then, her eyes find mine over his head, crinkled at the corners and bright with joy and tears. And just like always, seeing her reminds me that I'll never have to fear feeling empty again.

She is where happiness begins.

Acknowledgements

Six books in, and I'm still so incredibly grateful to have such a great list of people to thank. A vast majority of you were there from the start, but some joined my side throughout the years I've been doing this, and I'll never stop being thankful for you all.

Melissa, Lil, Clara, Sarah. A quatuor of permanent supporters who I can always count on for encouragement or advice. You four girls have played a huge part in keeping me going in this career. Your belief in me encourages me to go on and to try new things because I know that no matter what, you'll be there to read it. I love you girls.

To my family, who have been so supportive of me and this career since the very beginning.

To my friends, who keep reminding me that quality is so, so much more important than quantity.

To my husband (I can say this now!!!!!), thank you for always indulging me with « one more chapter » to be read or written. I love you.

Mike, thank you for helping Melissa help me when she speaks sentences out loud, wondering which option sounds better.

Murphy, thank you for answering my thousand emails and always producing the most perfect cover.

Emily, thank you for humbling me with all your edits in order to make this book as perfect as it could be.

Tina, Isabella, Cassie, Jess, Sam, Lottie, Tori, Kristina, Anna, Melissa, Hannah, Lucca, Lauren, Amanda, Rea, Elsa, and all the other bookstagrammers/booktokers/bloggers who have shared my books with others. I could never have done it without you.

And to you, dear reader, who picked up one of my books, maybe for the first time or maybe for the sixth. Thank you for giving me some of your precious time and for allowing me to accomplish my childhood dream.

Want to learn more about Wren and Aaron? Read their story in WHERE TIME STANDS STILL!

Twenty-six-year-old Wren Lawson knows she will soon forget who she is. With early familial Alzheimer's disease written in her genes, it's a fact she's wrapped her whole life around; to indulge in friends or romance is a risk for everyone around her—one she's not keen on taking. Throwing herself into her work as a lawyer is the only thing she can do.

Aaron Scott-Perez was happy with his quiet life in Boston, but when a doctor's mistake leaves his father unable to run his Christmas tree farm, Aaron has no choice but to move back to the small Vermont town he used to call home. He never saw himself managing the business, but since it is so dear to his father, Aaron has given up everything to do it. To get his father the justice he deserves, he hires none other than Wren. She's emotionally blunted and secretive, but her kindness and competency provide something his family hasn't felt for a long time: hope. So much so that Aaron starts to think the life he didn't want might not be so bad when she's around.

Yet Wren cannot let him in, too haunted by her future.

As the two get closer and the lines become blurred, Wren and Aaron find themselves at a crossroads. But their attraction is unyielding, and together they must decide what risks are worth taking, and if love is better to lose than to never have at all.

Want to learn more about Lexie and Finn? Read their story in WHERE WE BELONG!

Lexie Tuffin has one goal in life: making it to the Olympics as a gymnast for Team USA. Her dream was almost crushed when she injured herself last year, but now she's back with a vengeance. Except her old coach fired her, and she's starting from scratch. The only gym that will have her is in Nowhere, Vermont.

Finn Olsen has spent his adult life traveling the world, never wanting to settle in one place until last year, when he had to come back to his dull hometown to take on a job managing a Christmas tree farm. And while he's slowly fallen in love with the job, he still feels like something is missing from his life. How could he ever feel fulfilled in a place that still sees him as his wild teenage self?

After a catastrophic introduction and an even worse second meeting, Lexie wants nothing to do with Finn. The fact that she rents a cabin on his farm makes their interactions unavoidable, to Lexie's great despair. However, the more they bump into each other, the clearer it becomes that the snarky flannel-wearing man might not be so bad after all. In fact, he might be the first person to really see her.

Her only focus should be on her training. He should not fall for anyone. But neither of them seems able to stop feelings from developing, and maybe in each other, they can find what they've been looking for all along: somewhere to belong.

Also by the authour

A RISK ON FOREVER
THE INFINITY BETWEEN US
OUR FINAL LOVE SONG
WHERE TIME STANDS STILL
WHERE WE BELONG

About the Author

N.S. Perkins lives the best of both worlds, being a resident doctor by day and a romance author by night. When she's not writing, reading, or studying, you can probably find her trying new restaurants, dreaming about the next beach she'll be visiting, or creeping the cutest dogs in the parks near her house. She lives in Montreal with her husband.

Find her on:
Threads: @nsperkinsauthor
Instagram: @nsperkinsauthor
TikTok: @nsperkinsauthor
Website: www.nsperkins.com

Printed in Great Britain
by Amazon